Born into a Jewish family in Dublin, **Sheelagh Coleman** was educated at Norfolk College, Dublin, before moving on to further study at Trinity College, Dublin, Trinity College, London, and The Leinster School, Dublin. She has contributed to the work of relief organisations for women and children both in Ireland and in Israel. Sheelagh is widowed and has four sons. She lives in Dublin.

Tessa Coleman was educated at Norfolk College, Dublin. After qualifying from Jill Fisher's School of Beauty, she moved to a training kibbutz in Reading, England, where she spent three years in preparation for living on a kibbutz in Israel in the fifties. She was married in Israel, but later moved back to Dublin with her husband. She has three children.

Sheelagh and Tessa are sisters. This is their first novel.

FULL CIRCLE

Sheelagh and Tessa Coleman

Town House, Dublin

Published in 1995 by
Town House and Country House
Trinity House
Charleston Road
Ranelagh, Dublin 6
Ireland

British Library Cataloguing in Publication Data. A catalogue record for this book is available from the British Library.

ISBN: 1-86059-009-8

Cover illustration: Liam O'Herlihy

Typeset by Typeform Repro Ltd
Printed in Ireland by ColourBooks, Dublin

In memory of our mother, Dora, who taught us and guided us, and of Neville, Sheelagh's husband, for his encouragement, patience and unfailing love

Acknowledgements

To Daphne Bell, without whose transcription of our spoken word we would not have had a first manuscript.

To everyone who has had faith in us, and to those who have given us information and devoted help.

BOOK I

Chapter One

The shimmering summer air was splintered by shrill cries of panic when Jessica Barker-Grey, sitting on an almost deserted Wicklow beach with her German cousins, looked up from her book and saw two young girls at the edge of the water waving their hands and screaming with great agitation. One ran towards two men who were strolling along the beach, calling as she staggered towards them, pointing back to the sea. The men dashed to the seafront without waiting to hear any details, and shouting instructions over his shoulder, one of them plunged into the water. Jessica remembered a lifebelt she had seen hanging on a wall not far away. Grabbing it, she rushed towards the second man and flung it into his hands. The man lost no time and had waded out into the water within seconds. Joined by her cousins, Jessica stood in silence beside the two young girls, frozen in an agony of suspense, watching the rescuers reach the thrashing swimmer, put the lifebelt on him, and then between them tow the limp figure back towards land.

'Get some towels and a rug!' Jessica called urgently to her cousin, Rudi von Zeit, who sped to do her bidding.

After hour-like minutes the two young men struggled onto the sand, carrying a limp bundle between them.

'He's alive,' the older one shouted. 'We reached him in time, thank God.'

Rudi spread the towels on the ground and the exhausted boy was laid down, gasping, his eyes closed.

'Help me to turn him onto his stomach,' the older man ordered, 'he must have swallowed buckets of water.'

They turned the youth over and covered him with the rug, for although the day was hot, the boy was shivering with shock and fatigue.

'Give him a moment, and then we'll get him up to the hotel and let a doctor have a look at him,' instructed the man, who was obviously in charge. He threw a grateful 'Thank you' to Jessica as he helped the rug-draped boy to his feet and, aided by the group, half carried him off the beach.

Jessica, Rudi and his sister Ava, feeling deflated after the excitement, gathered their belongings too and made their way back to Delahunt's Hotel, where they had arrived the previous evening from Wales. They and their parents were going to spend the first summer of the new century, 1900, in Ireland.

'Well, I certainly hope that all our stay in zis country is not zo eventful,' said Lady Matilde Barker-Grey as her daughter, niece and nephew recounted the morning's events at dinner that evening.

'I should not think that even my fellow Celts, with their love of theatre, would willingly stage such dramatic scenes on a regular basis,' replied Sir David Barker-Grey, his dark eyes twinkling and his voice, in which there was a hint of his Welsh origins, filled with laughter. 'Still, it all turned out well, and, after all, that is the main thing.'

Jessica looked around the crowded diningroom and, to her surprise, saw the participants of the bathing drama, accompanied by a middle-aged couple, seated at the far window table. She nudged Ava and pointed them out.

'I wonder who zey are,' said Ava, 'zey look as if zey could be fun. Maybe we will make zeir acquaintances properly quite soon. What an amazing colour hair ze older boy and girl have!' she said, alluding to their fiery red hair.

'I like it! And yes, they look very nice and friendly,' responded Jessica. 'I notice the boy they rescued is not with them. I wonder how he is.'

Later, as the Barker-Greys and the von Zeits sat in the hotel drawingroom, a gentleman approached them and addressed himself to Sir David, who stood to meet him.

'May I introduce myself? I am Henry Moore of Roundwood. A sitting Member of Parliament for the county of Wicklow. I believe some of your family were of great help in rescuing my young son, Christopher. I am glad to say that the doctor believes that after a good night's rest the scallywag will be none the worse for his adventure. His friend, Francis Thompson, pointed out this little lady to me,' he said, indicating Jessica. 'I have been told that it was this young lady's presence of mind in fetching the lifebelt so promptly that made the efforts of the rescuers easier. I thank you m'dear. I have left your rug with the porter, Sir David, to be returned to you. May I warn you that if any of your party intends to swim in our sea here, there is a strong current with a powerful undertow about half a mile offshore. That, and cramp, were the cause of Christopher's problem. The young divil should have known better, he has been swimming in these waters all his life. But I suppose that even the most cautious, and he's not one of them, is caught every now and then. In any case, my wife, Florence, and I would be delighted if you and your family would join us in the conservatory.'

After an enquiring look to his wife, Sir David said it would be a great pleasure. Henry Moore held Matilde's chair as she rose, and proffered his arm to her.

The younger members of the Moore party stood to greet their guests as they saw them approaching.

'M'dear,' Henry Moore addressed his wife, 'may I present Sir David and Lady Barker-Grey and their charming daughter Jessica, who was so helpful today, Baron and Baroness Otto von Zeit and their son and daughter, who, according to my informant, the porter, are all here for the summer.'

'How nice,' said Mrs Moore, as her guests were seated. 'Do you have any plans to travel in our country, or will you be spending all your vacation in Wicklow?'

'Oh, come day go day, we'll see what happens. The weather and so forth, you know,' replied Sir David in his bluff, hearty manner.

'On ze contrary,' interspersed Lady Matilde, 'we have very definite plans for the summer. We shall be travelling to Dublin for ze "Horse Show", and my sister-in-law and I shall go to the main shopping areas to make some purchases. Our children have just completed zeir schooling, and before my nephew goes to university, we all wish to spend some time togezer.'

Meanwhile, the younger people were getting to know each other. The two Moore girls, Margaret and Elizabeth, and the cousins Jessica and Ava, being of a similar age, had a great deal in common, as did Rudi and the Irish boys.

Jessica was drawn to the eldest son, Michael. He was very attractive, she thought, an opinion Ava thoroughly agreed with when the two girls discussed the evening later on, as they got ready for bed in the room they were sharing. 'I am glad we have made some friends,' Jessica enthused, 'The Thompson boy, you know, Christopher's friend, has promised to take us on some excursions. Apparently he spends one month each summer with the Moores, and Kit, as Christopher is called, spends another with his family. I am sorry they are only going to be here for this month, but I gather they don't live too far away from here, more inland.'

At first Jessica was very shy, and only answered Michael when he addressed her directly, but gradually she relaxed and joined in the general conversation with him, as well as with the others.

Nothing that was said or done during those halcyon days changed Jessica's first impressions of Michael Moore. On each occasion she looked into the most smiling blue eyes she had ever seen, she held a fan or book in front of her face to hide her blushes, and hoped no one could hear the thumping of her heart which, she felt, threatened to choke her. As the weeks passed, it became hopeless. She who had been impervious to all male advances, had fallen instantly, headlong in love with this fiery-haired, soft-spoken Irishman. It was evident to both families that Michael in turn was captivated by Jessica. He monopolised all of her time. The days and evenings were too short for all they had to say to each other, and when the time came to say goodbye, as the Moores were returning to their home, Glenavon, they both found the parting painful. They were delighted therefore when arrangements were made for the Welsh and German visitors to join the Moore family in August, at Ballsbridge in Dublin, where the Moores took a house each year for the 'Horse Show' week, as well as a box at the Royal Dublin Society show grounds. This was a very special year for the Moore family as Christopher, whom everyone called Kit, was a talented horseman and would be jumping in a senior event for the first time.

The courtship of Michael and Jessica continued with intensity during the months that followed. After asking her father for her hand in marriage, Michael proposed to, and was happily accepted by Jessica. In the course of correspondence between the families, the 22nd of June 1901 was set as the date for the nuptials, it being agreed that there should be no marriage celebrations until the period of public mourning for her gracious Majesty, Queen Victoria, had been observed. After the church ceremonies there would be a reception at the home of Sir David and Lady Matilde Barker-Grey, in Neath, South Wales. The Moores would arrive from Ireland a few days beforehand, *en famille*, and, of course, the von Zeits would come from Hamburg.

On the night before her wedding Jessica stood in front of her window, watching as the moon danced behind her beloved Welsh hills. 'Tomorrow', she thought, 'will be the most important day of my life, and I am so afraid. I love Michael with all my heart. I want more than anything in the world to be his wife. But I am so afraid that on our first night together, I will be a disappointment to him.' She lay down on her bed and looked around her. The familiar large wardrobe and chest of drawers stood empty. Her eyes fell on the trunks containing her personal belongings. It all seemed unreal. Soon they would accompany her on the journey to a hotel near Holyhead, where she and Michael were to spend the first night of their marriage on their way to honeymoon in Ireland. It still seemed strange, as if it were happening to someone else. But she only had to close her eyes, recall Michael's face and know that, not only was it all real, but it was all absolutely right.

Next morning Jessica was woken by the sounds of Nanny preparing a bath for her. The portable bath, placed in front of the fireplace, was being filled from copper jugs of hot water carried up from the kitchen by the servants. The sun poured in through the window as the curtains were pulled back.

'Happy is the bride the sun shines on,' said Nanny in her lilting Welsh voice, as she again left the room. Jessica, too impatient to wait for her return, jumped out of bed, and throwing a handful of sweetly smelling salts into the water, impetuously discarded her nightgown and stepped into the oval porcelain bath. She gathered her long hair in one hand, the front of which was curled around pipe cleaners. As she lowered her slim young body into the steaming water she relaxed. Resting her neck on the cool rim, she allowed her hair to cascade down the outside of the tub. She curiously ran her hands over her body, allowing them to linger on the nipples of her full breasts and wander to her hips and firm thighs. She imagined Michael's hands in place of her own and Michael's lips pressed hard against hers. She hoped he would find her body beautiful and fulfilling to his needs. Her lack of knowledge could carry her imagination no further.

'Miss Jessica!' admonished Nanny as she bustled back into the room carrying a large silk square. 'I only went to the washroom to collect this from the pulley,' she said pointing to the silk. 'I had taken it down to air after we finished using it to burnish your hair yesterday. I was going to wrap it round your head to protect it from the steam, and now, look you, you have got into the water, indeed to goodness, I hope you have not undone the hours of washing, the lemon rinse and the hours of brushing. Lord knows what her ladyship will have to say. Now be a good girl and let me try and undo some of the damage.'

Jessica, startled back to reality by Nanny's shocked tone, obediently sat up whilst the apple dumpling of a woman wrapped up her hair. 'And now, look you, your nightgown thrown down anywhere. Have I not taught you better? Who, I ask you, do you think is going to pick up after you when Nanny is not there?'

Jessica, hearing a hint of tearfulness in her darling Nanny's voice at their impending parting, patiently allowed her to continue with her monologue, submitting to her ministrations with soapy sponge and loofah.

As Jessica was finishing her breakfast, which on this special morning she was having in her room, there was a tap at the door. Jessica was more than a little surprised to see her mother enter, for she had never been known to ask permission to come in, and certainly had never been known to knock on her door before. Kissing Jessica on the brow, she took her hands and drew her to her feet. Jessica looked questioningly at her mother, but was forestalled from speaking by the older woman putting her finger to her lips and saying softly, '*Liebchen*. Come, Papa is waiting for us downstairs.'

Jessica had never seen her mother so excited and could hardly keep up with her as she was drawn down the long flight of stairs, and straight into the morning room where her father was standing, almost in silhouette, facing the tall window, humming a tune Jessica remembered from her childhood days when romping with him in the garden.

On hearing them enter, he turned and hurried towards them, his eyes filled with love and devotion for these two women who were his life. In his hands, he held a gold casket which he proffered to Jessica with the simple words, 'From Mama and me, with our deepest love and wishes for your happiness.'

Jessica took the beautiful heavy casket. She was so overcome that words failed her. David Barker-Grey spontaneously embraced his wife and daughter in a bearlike hug, which rendered all words superfluous. Matilde almost succumbed to the moment, but Sir David, sensing the need for control, dropped his arms.

'Open the casket, *mein kind*,' said Matilde.

Jessica placed it on a sofa table and opened the lid. She gasped with pleasure as she saw, nestling in the red velvet lining, a collar of three rows of most beautifully matched pearls, fastened by a turquoise and diamond clasp.

'They are to wear today,' said her father.

'I am overcome by your love and generosity. Thank you, O thank you. I'll never be able to express my gratitude for everything both of you have given me all my life,' said Jessica, and tears spilled from her eyes. When he saw his child cry, Sir David in turn began to sob. Knowing that this must not continue, Matilde interjected, 'Come, mine daughter, zis will never do, you must stop at once or you will go to your marriage with your eyes all red and puffy. Besides,' she said, with an attempt at levity, 'you do not want Nanny to scold us, do you?'

Jessica took one glance over her shoulder as she left the room, and saw her father, his arms leaning on the mantelshelf, his shoulders still heaving with sobs.

Matilde left Jessica with Nanny while she went to check once again that every detail on her list had been attended to. She glanced at the fob watch pinned to her morning dress and saw that it was already ten o'clock. In two hours they would leave for the church.

Whilst her maid struggled with a button hook on a row of tiny buttons down the back of her gown, Matilde allowed her thoughts to wander to the last family wedding she had attended, that of her brother, Otto von Zeit, to Hannah Mandelbaum, several years earlier in Hamburg. She remembered the opposition to the union of a Protestant aristocrat and a Jewess. Since then, she had felt shame at the narrowmindedness of such attitudes. How wrong, and ignorant, she and they had been. For time had made Matilde come to respect, admire, and even develop an affection for her sister-in-law, for the efficient way she ran her household, for the way she had brought up her children, and for her obvious devotion to Otto.

Returning to the present, and having finished her toilette, Matilde went to meet the dressmaker who had arrived to help

Jessica into her wedding gown and to make any last minute alterations that might be necessary.

After the service that united them as husband and wife, Jessica and Michael walked back down the aisle together. Jessica now felt calm enough to be aware of the congregation and the banks of creamy white flowers that decked the church. As she floated down the aisle on her husband's arm, she thought that her heart might burst with pride in her handsome escort. She remembered her own reflection in the mirror that morning, her heavy satin and lace gown nipped in at the waist, the long train, the sleeves encrusted with pearls, and the ruched headdress anchoring the flowing veil. She looked at the gift that her parents had given her, the pearl collar, sitting magnificently on the high Edwardian neckline of her wedding dress. The hour it had taken to pin her hair in coils on the top of her head, held in place with combs of seed pearls, had been well spent. She felt beautiful, her mirror said she was beautiful, as had her father when he came to escort her to the waiting carriage.

That same beribboned carriage was now whisking Jessica and Michael back to the house for the reception. The white-plumed horses seemed to sense the occasion and speeded the young couple along the country road. When they arrived at the Barker-Grey residence, Michael led Jessica out to the conservatory. He covered her with a profusion of kisses, and she felt his passion for her, a passion he had controlled in his embraces up to now. They stood, her arms entwined around his neck, his enfolding her and holding her close. 'At long last, my darling, you are my wife, and I will treasure you always,' he whispered. She heard her mother calling to her, and, blushing, she caught Michael's hands, and gently said, 'Be patient, my darling, we must go now and greet our guests.'

They joined the reception line under Matilde's disapproving gaze. 'Where have you been?' she demanded. 'Ze first guests, they have already arrived.'

Jessica and Michael were saved from replying by the appearance at that moment of Mr and Mrs Henry Moore. Florence Madeline Moore was a beautiful, delicate woman. Her hair, now faded in middle age, retained some of its original dark red. Henry was a large ruddy-faced man with a shock of white hair which contrasted strangely with his bushy black eyebrows. His heavy whiskers covered a generous mouth, ever ready to smile. From what he had seen of Jessica's father he felt they would get along famously. Their common love of good food, good wine and the hunting field would create a bond between them. He did not have the same faith as to his future relationship with Jessica's mother, as Lady Matilde appeared to him to be a formidable lady.

Matilde greeted them graciously. 'My husband and I thank you both for the delightful dinner party you hosted at your hotel last evening.'

Sir David's two spinster sisters, the Misses Olwyn and Bronwyn Barker-Grey, arrived back from the church, in the company of Otto and Hannah von Zeit, and their children, Rudi and Ava, who was Jessica's bridesmaid.

Jessica wafted through the afternoon, being greeted by relatives and friends, receiving good wishes and introducing Michael to family and friends. The white-gloved staff handed around silver salvers of appetising delicacies and glasses of champagne. When all the company had been served, Sir David called the attention of the assembly. 'My lords, ladies and gentlemen. The happiest and saddest part of the day has arrived for my wife and me. Happy because it is the time for me to thank all of you, my dear relatives and friends, for being here to join with us in our joy. My dear Matilde, I must first address you, and thank you for all the years of fulfilment you have brought to me, and for the splendid way you have prepared our beloved daughter for this day.' He stopped for a moment to kiss his wife's hand. 'Next I would like to say to Mr and Mrs Henry Moore, and their large and lovely family, how delighted we are to welcome them to our home on what, we are sure, will prove to be a memorable and happy day for them, and for us. And now I address the young couple. Michael, we know you are a fine man to have captured the heart of our Jessica, and we have no reservations about entrusting our only child into your safe keeping. It is with great pleasure we welcome you into our family.' At this point Sir David was finding it difficult to control the trembling of his lips, but he continued. 'Now, for my wife and me the sadness, for in the very nature of things, we must part with our daughter. My darling Jessica, you have been a source of pride and joy to your mother and myself, never giving us a moment's sorrow. Your goodness and beauty will be an asset to your husband, and your mother and I wish for you and Michael the same happiness we have shared over the years. You go to your new life with all our love and blessings.' And he gently kissed Jessica, to the sound of loud applause. He then asked those present to raise their glasses and drink the health of the bride and bridegroom, Jessica and Michael, which was done wholeheartedly, amidst cheers.

Then Michael's best man, his brother Christopher Moore, asked for silence for the groom to respond to the toast.

'My darling wife, reverend gentlemen, our dear parents, m'lords, ladies and gentlemen. Because Jessica and I are of one mind regarding the brevity of this part of the proceedings, I am going to challenge convention a little, and with his consent and permission, will speak on behalf of my father as well as myself. My parents wish me to say what a joyous day this is for us all, and to welcome Jessica into the Moore family as one of our own, and to reassure Lady Matilde and Sir David that she will be treated as their own daughter. They further charge me with extending their appreciation to our generous and gracious hosts for the manner in which they have been regaled since their arrival in Neath. For myself, words seem inadequate for the happiness I feel. The fates have been more than kind in sending this wonderful girl into my life. I reiterate my promise made in church most solemnly, and in front of all of you, to repay the fates by guarding and cherishing Jessica all the days of our lives. My eternal gratitude to you, Sir

David and Lady Barker-Grey, for giving me the hand of your only daughter, and for the wonderful celebrations you have arranged to make this a glorious occasion. Jessica has asked me to thank her bridesmaid, her cousin, Ava, for standing by her today and through their years of growing up. Also to thank her pretty flowergirls, who carried out their part in the proceedings with great charm. Finally, my own thanks to my brother Kit, for acting as my best man, and helping me through some rather difficult moments. My wife and I,' he stopped and smiled at Jessica, 'would like to add our own heartfelt thanks to Sir David's to all of you for your kind thoughts and good wishes, and to add that, if any of our good friends and relatives should find themselves on our side of the water, we would be delighted to see them at our home.'

Kit waited for the strains of 'For they are jolly good fellows' to subside before, his voice trembling slightly with nervousness, he added his own congratulations to the young couple.

When Jessica and Michael had changed into their travelling clothes, which had been laid out for them in separate rooms, the bridal couple prepared to leave. First they took their farewells of their guests and a tearful Nanny, and then of their parents.

As the carriage drew away from the house Jessica looked back. Even on this warm, sunlit and happy day she gave a little shudder, and felt a sense of loss. For she knew, with an awful certainty, that she would never again see the home in which she had grown up.

Chapter Two

Jessica and Michael travelled by train from Neath to Carmarthen, where they were to spend the first night of their honeymoon. They were met at the railway station by a carriage from the hotel, and on arrival there were escorted to the bridal suite, which had been lavishly decorated with flowers. Champagne and a cold collation, which was to be served in the sittingroom of their suite, awaited them.

When the maid, whom the housekeeper had sent up to help Jessica change out of her travelling clothes, had left, Michael found his wife sitting at her dressing table in a nightgown and peignoir. He had never seen her hair loose before, and crossing over to her, he ran his fingers through the shining mane. Pulling it to one side he bent his head and kissed her on the nape of her neck, as he whispered 'My love'. His suppressed desire almost overcame his concern for her innocence. Jessica wondered if this was to be the moment she would truly become Michael's wife, and suddenly all her fears resurfaced. She was relieved therefore when he led her into the sittingroom, and held her chair as she took her seat at the supper table. Neither of them paid much attention to what they ate. The champagne filled Jessica with a warm glow. They talked of the day that had been, and of the days that were to come when they landed in Ireland. As soon as they had finished their meal, Michael rose to his feet. Placing his napkin on the table, he went over to Jessica, and taking a pendant on a long chain set with diamonds from his pocket, he fastened it round her neck. 'A token of my undying love through all eternity,' he said. She stood, her hand on the locket, then ran into the bedroom to see her gift in the mirror. The lovely heart-shaped ornament nestled on her bosom. Turning to Michael, her eyes glistening with tears of happiness, she flung her arms around his neck, saying over and over 'I love you, I love you, I love you, I love you'. Michael could control himself no longer, and kissing her with a passion to which he felt her responding, he picked her up and carried her to the bed. Jessica had never felt like this before. As Michael caressed her, thrills swept over her body. Although the moment of penetration was painful and sharp, the sheer ecstasy of the hours that followed made her forget her discomfort. Michael was surprised but delighted at the way his bride, who had always kept him at a distance, so readily united her body with his. He took as much joy from her rapture as from his own fulfilment. Afterwards, they lay in each other's arms.

They made the sea crossing to Ireland the following day. As they travelled through the counties of Ireland they became more and more as one, their lovemaking at the end of each day growing in excitement, deepening their mutual fulfilment during the seven weeks since their marriage. Their minds, too, met on a myriad of subjects. Michael came to admire and, gradually, rely on Jessica's intellect.

It was a first visit for both of them to Connemara, in the west of Ireland. The splendour of the scenery filled them with awe. They swam in the ultramarine Atlantic, made love on deserted beaches of golden sand that stretched for miles and miles, and picnicked in the ruins of castles and monasteries. Lying in the shade of an old stone wall one morning, Jessica asked Michael to tell her again about their house in Dublin and of their new life together as he foresaw it, a conversation of which she never tired.

'As you know, my uncle, Michael Green, my mother's only brother, never married, and he left Priory House to me, his eldest nephew, when he died, along with a small trust. The house is in Blackrock, a small village south of Dublin, not too far from the "Horse Show" grounds – do you remember? O Jessica, he was a lovely man. We had some wonderful times in that house as children, and he and I were particularly close, perhaps because I was named after him. There are several fields around the property, in which we rotate the crops, a wooded area nearby, and I have recently planted an orchard of mixed fruit trees.'

'Michael, it all sounds heavenly, go on.'

'Well, soon you will be there to see everything for yourself, my dear one. Downstairs there is a morningroom, a diningroom and a drawingroom. Tucked away at the back of the house is my study, where I spend a lot of time running the farm and working on my inventions. Of course I also work on the farm itself. I am afraid we will not be very rich until one of my inventions is a huge success, but with my share of the income from the Green trust, and the family estate in Wicklow, and of course the interest from your dowry, we will never go hungry.'

Lying in bed after lovemaking one night, Jessica shyly murmured, 'Michael, I would like a large family. I do not want any little one of mine growing up lonely, as I did, waiting for some other children to be allowed to come and play.'

'I too want lots of children, my darling,' Michael replied. 'The joys, in spite of the irritations, of growing up in a large family, hold only the most wonderful memories for me. My two sisters, whom so far you have only met briefly, were pretty good sports as kids. Margaret has always been a very good horsewoman, often beating Kit and myself in races over our fields. She is reckoned to be the champion horsewoman in Wicklow, having won every prize available at the gymkhanas. Besides, she can drink a glass and dance for hours as well as any man. Beth, on the other hand, has never liked horses. She is much more at home on a tennis court, or a croquet lawn, but she too can dance the night away. They are both very proficient on the pianoforte. My father loves a sing-song, and when we are all together, especially at Christmas and New Year, we use any excuse to ask some of the neighbours to come in and join us. There should have been two more of us between Beth and Kit, but they died at birth. Kit is a lot younger than I am, but he is not a bad chap, there is hope for him yet,'

Michael laughed. 'He is mad about horses and dogs, and hopes that Father will, now that he has left school, allow him to have a say in the purchasing and breeding of the animals.'

Whilst still in Connemara, they heard of a local fair, and took the opportunity to go to see the famous Connemara ponies. Jessica could never have imagined such sights and sounds. The wind, which never seemed to drop along these shores, blew the tangy scent of salt and seaweed inland, and this helped somewhat to mask the more earthy smells of unwashed humans and of the animals. She and Michael wandered hand in hand among hawkers, selling anything from a brass bedstead to a basket of clothes pegs. Children ran barefoot through crowds of women in their homespun, home-dyed garments.

Jessica spotted a gaudy tent with a sign 'Fortune Teller – Palmist' over its opening. 'O Michael, please, please may I have my fortune told? I have often heard the maids at home tell about having theirs told, and I would love to know what it is all about.'

'Did I hear you right, Jessica? You want to do what?' asked Michael in astonishment.

'I want to have my fortune told, it would be so exciting. O please, Michael.'

'Certainly not,' he replied in a tone of voice that she soon learned to heed without further argument.

'O Michael, just this once,' she wheedled.

'You, my wife, want to go into that charlatan of a woman, so that she can tell you a pack of lies which could possibly destroy your whole life if you were foolish enough to believe such drivel. I'm surprised at you Jessica, being so silly. Come now! We will go and see the ponies,' and he firmly tucked her arm into his and drew her away.

At first Jessica was taken aback at Michael's attitude. She had never experienced this sternness in him before, and, feeling dejected and put out by the slight, she stumbled along at his side.

Soon, however, she was fascinated by the horse trading, some of which she could not follow, as it was conducted in Irish, or, if in English, so fast it was difficult to catch. But before long she understood that, after all the shouting had been done, each of the protagonists to the bargain spat on their hands, their ruddy faces wreathed in smiles at a good wrangle, and a good sale, which they then sealed with a handshake. Michael spoke to several of the men, while she stood back and looked on. When he rejoined her she asked if she might have something to drink. He led her to a busy tent. 'Wait there!' said Michael, disappearing inside. Soon he reappeared carrying two frothy glasses of black porter. 'Drink that, it is nectar, especially good when you are very thirsty. The foam on top is called milk, and the beer is like velvet running down your throat.' She sipped it tentatively, then wrinkled her nose in distaste. 'Ugh, it's awful, it is so bitter, how can anyone drink it!' Michael laughed at her expression, and, taking the glass from her, quaffed both his own and then hers, before he disappeared back into the tent, leaving her waiting for some time. He then reappeared, grinning, with another glass of porter in his hand. 'There is more of this stuff drunk in a day in Ireland than anyone can count, but come along my darling, I will get you a more civilised cup of tea and a piece of pie. Angry with him for leaving her for as long as he had, she walked in silence beside him.

She tried many of the traditional dishes on their travels, and liked most of them very much. But she was vaguely disturbed by the amount of wine, beer and spirits Michael drank with his meals, and throughout the day, and she made up her mind to keep a watchful eye to see if it was only now on holiday that he did so, or if it was a habit she had not previously noticed.

She listened to old people telling stories of Irish legendary heroes, Diarmuid and Gráinne, Queen Maeve, Cúchulain, the Fianna, but Michael told her that his mother was the best storyteller of all, weaving the mountains and mists of Ireland into stories of the fairies and leprechauns. Jessica wrote engaging letters to her parents, aunts and Ava, describing the utter bliss of her life. Michael had the newest model of camera, and he took many photographs to show the families, and to put into albums for the future.

The last week of their honeymoon was spent at the Moores' home, 'Glenavon', in County Wicklow. On the first night of their stay, Mr and Mrs Henry Moore held a ball in their honour, inviting half the county to meet them. Jessica was told that the orchestra would play traditional airs and waltzes with equal facility, that gaslight chandeliers would sparkle on the jewels worn by the women, and the whole house would be filled with laughter. Consequently, not since the day of her wedding had she felt as nervous about meeting people as she did at this moment. She wanted Michael and his family to be proud of her, and, with Maeve, the young parlourmaid whom her mother-in-law had sent to help her dress, she looked at and discarded every garment in her wardrobe, calling Michael a dozen times to approve of her choice of that moment. He laughed indulgently at her dithering and agreed with her each time, which only made her more uncertain and frustrated, almost to the point of tears. Finally she chose a lilac and ecru lace gown, with a *décolletage* that revealed her beautiful shoulders and the crests of her full breasts. Maeve piled her hair on the top of her head and secured it with pins attached to buds the same shade as her gown. She looked into her jewel box and tried to imagine what Mama would have chosen for her to wear on this important occasion. She wavered between the pearl collar and Michael's locket. The pearl collar would help her to feel her parents were with her and give her confidence. She had just decided to wear the pearls when the picture of Michael's face came to her, and she had no hesitation in choosing the locket, realising she had no need for the support of anyone else, now that she was Michael's wife.

'O Miss,' said Maeve, 'saints preserve us, you look a picture, you look gorgeous,' and she crossed herself, clasping her hands in joy as she looked at this darling lady Mr Michael had married and brought to Glenavon from across the water. The praise raised Jessica's spirits as she sprayed on her toilette water, pumping the bulb at the end of the stopper in the crystal bottle. When Michael came to escort her downstairs she met his look of unrestrained admiration with her head held high, whilst her heart fluttered, as it always did when she looked at this man she had won. They descended the staircase, the train of Jessica's gown sweeping the stairs. One hand rested on Michael's arm and she held her ostrich plume fan in the other. When they reached the drawingroom they stopped and waited, whilst Duffy, the Moores' butler, filled with importance, announced, 'Me lords, ladies an' gent'men. Please be upstandin' for Mr and Mrs Michael Moore.' Henry Moore rushed forward to meet them, and taking each one by the hand, as if they were small children, he walked with them to the end of the room, which had had its large rugs removed for dancing, to where the orchestra was set up. Holding up his arms as if about to conduct the musicians, he bellowed, 'Everyone quiet. M'new daughter-in-law, the former Miss Jessica Barker-Grey of Neath in Wales, and m'son, Michael, are about to commence the proceedings with a waltz, and when they have done a circle of the room, m'good woman, Florence, and m'self will join them, and then all of you please join in.' The music struck up and the young couple took to the floor and danced to the applause of the assembly as they floated around the ballroom.

The sedateness of the beginning of the night gradually lessened in direct proportion to the amount of spirits imbibed by young and old alike, and the music grew louder and wilder as the young people leapt and swirled to the pulsating beat. Jessica's eyes grew wider and wider as she watched the uninhibited joy expressed in the unselfconscious movements, and she found herself clapping and stamping her feet, laughing aloud with the sheer joy of it all.

When they finally retired for the night Jessica drowsily mumbled, 'My head is spinning with all the people I have met tonight.'

'The parents were very proud of you,' said Michael nuzzling into her, 'I could tell, and I was bursting with admiration myself, how beautiful you looked, how charming you were, and how you captivated everyone.'

'Thank you, Michael.' She gave a sleepy little giggle. 'Do you know, I never got a chance to taste any of the delicious-looking supper. Every time I was about to eat I got whisked off to dance or to meet someone else. I am starving, but too tired to do anything about it now. O Michael, I love everyone I met, and even if I did not adore you so much, I think I still would love them.' And she drifted into a happy and contented sleep.

Chapter Three

Jessica's first sighting of Priory House was in the late afternoon sunlight. Its imposing wrought-iron gates and short avenue of mature trees ended in a broad sweep of gravel in front of the house. The golden sun warmed the russet brick and made the granite facia sparkle. Smoke from the kitchen range curled gracefully from one of the tall serried chimney stacks that stood sentinel against the sky.

Michael jumped down from the carriage and helped Jessica to alight. She had to try very hard not to show how excited and nervous she felt, for she knew that Michael would expect her to appear dignified in front of the servants. She also had to curb an impulse to run up the shallow steps, fling open the hall door, and rush from room to room.

At the entrance, a man stood dressed in livery. He moved aside to allow his new mistress to enter the hallway. 'Darling,' said Michael, who had followed her, and who now put a hand under her elbow as if to support her, 'this is Eamonn, who doubles as butler, footman, valet and any other role that may be required of him, and without whom I could not have made the house ready for your arrival.' Eamonn acknowledged the praise with a pleased expression, and, conscious of his importance, introduced the three women who stood in front of a fireplace in the black-and-white flagged hallway, which was heaped high with fir cones.

'Mrs Moore,' said Eamonn, in a rich Irish brogue, 'may I present our cook, Mrs Mahony, Ita our house parlourmaid, and

Mary, who helps both Cook and Ita.' Mary dropped a wobbly curtsy, which she had been practising for days. Jessica smiled and said how pleased she was to be in her new home and that she felt sure they would all be happy together. Now, for the first time, she allowed her eyes to take in her surroundings.

Eamonn dismissed the three women, and enquired from Jessica, 'Would ye be requirin' some tea now, Mam?'

'That would be very nice, thank you,' said Jessica.

After tea, which was served in the drawingroom, Michael saw that Jessica could not wait any longer, her curiosity was at breaking point, and he took her on a tour of the house, which, whilst roomy, was not too large. The rooms were well proportioned and filled with light. 'As you see, my love, Mother and I have only put in the bare necessities, you can finish the furnishing of the house to your own taste.'

'You have both been very thoughtful, and I am so excited and happy about all the many tasks to be done. It will be thrilling finding where to place all our beautiful wedding presents.'

She sat back in contentment, her daydreams interrupted by Michael's voice.

'I have arranged with Mrs Mahony to serve a cold supper to us in front of a fire in our bedroom,' he said.

The rest of the evening passed in mutual enjoyment, planning their schedules for the next day. Soon, after gentle lovemaking, Michael fell asleep. As she lay in his arms Jessica thought over the events of the past few weeks. She relaxed, grateful for finding a man who was gentle and compassionate, and yet with a firmness which she admired and on which she knew she could always rely. She made a solemn promise to herself that she would uphold her vows to love, honour and obey her husband till death did them part. These were her last thoughts as she fell asleep.

Next morning, Jessica was in a half-waking sleep when her door burst open and Michael rushed in, shouting, 'It works! It works!'

‘What works?’ Jessica asked, still hazy with sleep.

‘My electric feeding machine,’ he shouted. ‘It works, it really, really works.’ He gathered her into his arms, rocking her backward and forward in his enthusiasm, crushing her against his rough jacket.

‘Michael! Michael!’ she gasped laughingly. ‘Do calm down. Where have you been? What are you talking about? It’s only a little after dawn.’

‘Darling, don’t you understand? Don’t you remember me explaining to you that I had invented an automatic feeding machine for the battery hens. Don’t you remember me telling you that I had been experimenting with it for months and months, and now it is working. Get dressed. Hurry! Hurry! You have already brought me luck.’

Amazed and excited that Michael would want her to see his invention, she jumped out from under the covers. It was a part of their lives that, as a woman, she had not expected to be included in, and against all her upbringing, she snatched a shawl from a chair, put on a pair of outdoor shoes, and ran, hand in hand with him, down the stairs and out through the kitchen door, sweeping down the hill to the outbuildings, stumbling in her haste to keep up with Michael’s unconscious tugging and pulling. Gasping for breath, she followed him through a low doorway, pulling up abruptly as the stench of dozens of clucking hens hit her. Her instinct was to turn and plunge back into the fresh air, but one look at the flushed excitement on Michael’s face fortified her to suppress the heaving she felt in her stomach. She followed him further along the straw-strewn path to the very end of this dim building, where he proudly pointed to his invention. She hardly heard his long explanation of the workings of his brainchild. The nausea became unbearable and, to her great distress, she was violently ill on the floor.

Michael reacted with speed and caught Jessica as she swooned. He carried his bride swiftly back to the house, through the hall, calling ‘Mrs Mahony, come and help me.’

The large woman came puffing up the stairs from the kitchen, where she had been preparing breakfast, wiping her hands on her spotless white apron. 'Lord, Sir, what ails the young missus?'

'I don't know, she just fainted,' Michael replied anxiously.

Between them they put Jessica into bed, all the while Mrs Mahony crooning comfortingly, 'My poor lamb. My sweet pet, you'll be all right now you are in your own bed, there now.'

Looking up, Cook saw the ashen colour of Michael's face and heard him mutter to himself, 'What is it? What can it be?'

'Lord,' said the Cook, 'young women often take the vapours. Would you mind tellin' me Sir, where was she?' Michael explained and Cook smiled knowingly. 'Sure, Sir, maybe a visit from Dr Ryan might be in order.'

Quickly agreeing with her, Michael dispatched Eamonn to fetch the doctor. When he returned to the bedroom, he found Jessica sitting up against her pillows, the colour returned to her cheeks. 'My dearest darling. What did I do to you?'

'Nothing, nothing,' she replied. 'It is I who am so ashamed to have behaved so badly and spoilt your wonderful moment.'

Cook, standing erect with her hands clasped in front of her, her chin wobbling with emotion, saw the concern, one for the other, on the faces of her young master and mistress, and mumbling something about getting a 'cup a tea', made a hasty retreat from the room, leaving the lovers together.

Eamonn did not even stop to saddle a horse, or hitch a carriage, but ran through the grounds of Priory House and crossed the main road through the village as fast as his legs would carry him, until he came to the crescent of houses on the seafront, where Dr Ryan lived. The doctor's door was quickly answered by a young housemaid, who, frightened by the wildness of his demand to see the doctor at once, left Eamonn on the doorstep while she summoned Darragh Ryan.

Dr Ryan, a tall angular man in his late twenties, appeared immediately, and, trying to make head or tail of what was by now an almost incoherent Eamonn, said 'Right, I'm coming back with you. We will leave at once.' He took up his bag, which was always ready by the hallstand, and asking no more questions, told Eamonn to get into the gig, which was harnessed and standing by the kerbside, and set off for Priory House.

Meanwhile, Jessica was protesting that she did not need a doctor, but when he was announced, she smiled resignedly and said, 'Very well, if the doctor is here now, I will see him to please you and to ease your mind. But as I have repeatedly told you, I am perfectly all right now, Michael.'

At that moment, Eamonn knocked at the door and ushered in Dr Ryan. Having introduced himself and hearing the full story from Michael, Dr Ryan asked to be left alone with his patient. Taken aback by this request, Michael said, 'My Mother has always been present when my sisters are being examined by a doctor. Perhaps I should call Mrs Mahony back.' His offer being kindly but firmly refused, he was left with no option but to go out of the room.

Michael paced up and down on the landing, glancing unseeingly out of the windows at either gable end of the house. After what seemed like an eternity, the bedroom door opened and Dr Ryan came out. Michael could read nothing from his expression.

'Would you like to go into Mrs Moore now?'

Without answering, Michael rushed past the other man and ran into the bedroom. He pulled up short when he saw Jessica lying back on her pillows, eyes closed, hands clasped over the bedclothes. Fear filled him. Walking more slowly to the bed, he gently enclosed Jessica's small hands in his larger ones. Her eyes opened. 'Something I did not think could happen for a long time Michael,' she spoke softly, 'There will be a child in the early spring!'

Michael dropped his head onto their clasped hands in relief. Then the awareness of what he had just been told reached his consciousness, and, raising his head, he looked tenderly at his young wife, too filled with elation, love and pride to speak. She gently released her hands and opened her arms to him. This was how Dr Ryan found them when, several minutes later, Michael stood and walked towards him, extending his hand, which was gripped by Darragh Ryan in a clasp that was the beginning of a lifelong friendship.

On April 9th, 1903, as soon as Darragh Ryan would allow him into the room after the birth of Henrietta Jane, having first warned him not to overexcite Jessica, Michael went to his wife. He kissed her on the brow and said, 'Thank God you are through the birth safely, you and our little daughter. But you must rest now.' Jessica was slightly put out by Michael's reticence about the miracle that had just occurred.

The following Friday, Nanny, who had come from Wales the moment Jessica had sent for her, bustled into the room, carrying a bundle of newly washed and ironed baby clothes. On seeing Michael sitting in the armchair, watching his wife and daughter in turn, she wagged her finger at him, and shooed him out of the room, saying, 'Mr Moore, Miss Jessica needs all the rest she can get. She has been through a great ordeal. I will have to ask you to leave the room so that you won't disturb my precious.' Michael left as he was bidden, the years of experiencing the authority of nannies ingrained in him. In a while Jessica woke to see Nanny's ample back bent over the baby. 'Where is Mr Moore?' she asked.

'I have sent him about his business, Miss Jessica. Indeed to goodness, you must have your rest.'

Jessica was still too tired to argue with this woman who had been with her all her life. It was now three days since the baby's birth, and her bindings were uncomfortably tight over her breasts and stomach and she could not fall back to sleep. 'Nanny, have Mama and Papa come back from town yet? If they have, may we all take tea up here, please?'

Nanny frowned and tutted, but knew she could never say no to this girl who had become as dear to her as if she were her very own child. 'Very well,' she said, 'but only for a short visit, mind you, and you let them do all the talking.'

Jessica brightened up at the prospect of some company, and the mild feeling of tearfulness that had come over her earlier began to ebb away. Just then, she heard the carriage draw up and her mother's Teutonic voice ordering Eamonn to carry her packages carefully into the house. Nanny immediately went to meet her and to organise the tea party.

The door was thrust open and Matilde Barker-Grey swept into the room. 'What is zis nonsense about having tea in your bedroom? I have never heard of such an occurrence.'

'Please, Mama, I am so lonely. I promised Nanny that I would be quiet, only listen to you, Papa and Michael talking together.'

At that moment, Nanny reappeared and added her pleas to those of Jessica. Lady Barker-Grey finally gave in and sent Nanny to request Sir David and Mr Moore to kindly present themselves for tea in ten minutes in Miss Jessica's room.

Ita and Cook came in carrying table linen, trays of sandwiches, cakes and a tea urn, which they placed on the table near the window. Nanny took up a stance in front of the bassinet, as if to ward off any interference with her charge.

As Jessica watched her mother moving around, she thought how much she admired the aristocratic woman, who, underneath her Germanic stiffness, could show tenderness and love to her only child. Knowing her so well, she hardly noticed the forbidding expression and commanding presence, which often unnerved those who were only on nodding terms with her. But on closer acquaintance her fine mind and vast knowledge of literature, music, art and current affairs made her an interesting and charming companion.

Matilde dismissed the servants, saying that she would pour tea, and seated herself at the table. 'Nanny,' she said, 'when Sir David and Mr Moore have seen ze baby Henrietta, you may take ze infant to ze nursery.'

When the two men appeared, Sir David bounded over to the sleeping child, sidestepped Nanny, setting her off guard, and bellowed into the crib, 'Gran'pa's darling cariad. Another girly for Gran'pa.'

The child woke up screaming, and Nanny, glaring at Sir David, gathered the mite into her arms and rushed from the room mumbling to herself. Sir David looked bewildered and asked, 'Now, what did I do? Have I done something wrong?' Seeing the look of fury on his wife's face, he sheepishly sat at the table and gave a mischievous smile to his daughter in bed, who covered her responding smile with her handkerchief.

Lady Matilde, beside herself with fury, enquired of her husband in icy tones, 'Do you consider zat such lack of decorum is ze correct example to ze younger generation, notwithstanding ze shock to ze child's nervous system.'

Michael quickly forestalled any reply from Sir David by observing, 'My Nanny always said it was good for babies to cry, it aired their lungs.'

'Is zat a philosophy zat is acquired from gatherings around your peat fires, Michael?' Matilde enquired in a syrupy tone.

Michael reddened with anger at her sarcasm, but, allowing it to pass, coldly asked if she was ready to pour tea.

After an uncomfortable half hour, the three guests left. Jessica sighed with relief. 'That was not such a good idea,' she said to Nanny, who had come back into the room to supervise the clearing of the tea trays.

'Never mind, cariad, there will be other days. You settle down now and have a little sleep before your dinner.'

Later, Nanny helped Jessica change and get comfortable for the night, and Michael joined her for a nightcap of hot chocolate and biscuits for the patient, and a whiskey and soda for himself. 'That was rather a disaster this afternoon. Your mother didn't approve of the idea from the word go.'

'Oh, I know, Michael, it was awful. I'm sorry you got the rough end of mother's tongue.'

'Don't think any more about it. Actually I must confess it was great fun. The look on your mother's face is something I would have gone a long way to see. Sleep well, my love.' And he kissed

Jessica and retired to his dressingroom where he was sleeping for the present.

Jessica dozed, but was woken by the aching pains in her legs. She tried to get more comfortable, but her bindings pulled and she was unable to settle again. To distract herself, she allowed her eyes to roam around the room. In the lamplight, she admired its proportions, furnishings and decor, the blending of colours and old and new furniture. Through a chink in the curtains she saw the pale April moon. For the remainder of the night it provided some comfort to her when she woke from fitful sleep.

One morning over the breakfast table, having just read his post, Sir David said to Matilde, 'Williams, my manager at our collieries, has written a very disturbing letter to me, my dear, and I don't like the implications in it at all. He feels that there is trouble brewing among the miners, and that my presence would have a calming effect, and therefore, that I should return at once. Anyway, three months is long enough for me to be away from Wales.'

'Very well, my dear, I sink Henrietta is now well enough established for me to leave. I will make a list for Nanny of all the sings she must observe in the child's rearing, and we will have ze christening immediately.'

A week later Sir David and Lady Barker-Grey left for Wales, and everyone breathed a sigh of relief that they could now get back to the normal routine of the household. Jessica felt very disloyal, but she also felt that now she could again be mistress in her own home. She began to regain her strength after her long confinement, but, as Nanny often observed to Cook, 'The roses have never returned to Mrs Moore's cheeks, her pregnancy took more out of her than she is letting on.'

'Get away with you, Nanny,' said Cook. 'The bloom of youth don't last for ever you know.'

'All very well for you to say so, Cook, but I have known her, child, girl and woman, and you mark my words.'

Chapter Four

Jessica had never felt as contented and needed as she did now. The passing months saw the love between herself and Michael blossom and ripen with a passion she never believed could be possible. Her heart and body responded to her husband's every need, and her own pleasure.

Michael spent part of each day either in his office, workshop or doing the necessary chores around the farm. New ideas for innovative farming techniques poured from his fertile brain. Some of his inventions worked and were immediately patented and put into production, although only in small quantities. The many disappointments of those that did not work were softened by the companionship, interest, love and encouragement given to him by Jessica.

Baby Henrietta thrived in the summer sun, and her little fat legs became brown from lying, kicking in her perambulator on the lawn.

Soon it was harvest time and the autumn turned to winter. The air was redolent with smoke from the many bonfires. The berries, glowing on the holly bushes, heralded that the Christmas season was near.

In the middle of December, a hamper filled with seasonal fare arrived from Jessica's aunts in Wales, Olwyn and Bronwyn Barker-Grey, in which was included a note saying that they had been invited by some old friends to spend Christmas and New Year in Scotland. 'As we have never participated in a traditional "Hogmanay", we have decided to accept, even though your mother and father think us a little foolish to go so far north at this time of the year. But we are not going as far north as they are, for as usual they are going to join the Baron and Baroness von Zeit at their schloss in the Bavarian mountains.'

Although they were going to spend Christmas day quietly on their own, Jessica and Michael received many invitations to friends and neighbours for the rest of the season. Jessica, with Nanny's help, tried on all of her beautiful trousseau gowns to see which would still fit her since the birth of the baby. They were all a little tight around her waist and her bosom, but this was soon put right by a dressmaker, recommended by Joan, Dr Ryan's wife, who was called in to do the alterations.

So that she would remember all the things that must be attended to, Jessica made several lists, as she had always seen her mother do. She wrote greetings to family and friends, both at home and abroad. She and Michael went up to town to do some shopping. They stayed overnight in the Shelbourne Hotel, on St Stephen's Green. While they were there they took the rare opportunity in the evening to visit the theatre.

The week before Christmas, Michael had a fir tree, holly and ivy cut and brought into the house. The previous year Jessica and Nanny had made some tree decorations, and after 'Twelfth night' they had put them away. Jessica now brought them out, and along with some others that had been sent to her by her cousin Ava from Germany, she enjoyed adorning the tree and fixing small wax candles to the tips of the branches. She and Eamonn draped the holly and ivy in great swags, tied with red and gold ribbon – which she had bought in Minskys in Dublin – all around the hall, and along the backs of the mantelshelves of the fireplaces, in which great fires, with huge logs, were kept burning brightly all the time to fend off the cold.

On Christmas eve, old Colonel William Fitzgerald, an elderly local landowner and former friend of Michael Moore's uncle, the late Michael Green, and last of his generation, had made it an annual event to gather some of the gentlemen of the district around him for a late afternoon carousel. Michael returned home from the colonel's in very high spirits, as the carol singers, carrying lanterns, came to sing traditional airs in front of the house. When finished, as was customary, they were called in to the hall to have a hot toddy and mince pies. Michael kept pace with them as he served the hot whiskey from a large silver punch bowl, and grew merrier and merrier, until it became obvious that he was quite drunk.

'Please, Michael, you have had enough,' whispered Jessica.

'Had enough! It's Christmas!' he sang in a loud voice, waving his arms about. 'Come along everyone, let's have some more carols. How about "Good King Wenceslas"?'

'Please, Michael!' Jessica said again quietly, ashamed of Michael's condition in front of the townspeople.

'O please bloody nothing. Let your hair down, woman dear, it's the festive season.' He staggered to a chair beside the fire and collapsed into it, his cup clattering to the floor as he passed out. Jessica dropped a sovereign into the carollers' box, and tipping their forelocks they wished all the household a merry Christmas and left.

Michael was very pale next morning, and looked sheepish as he prepared for church in his dressingroom, where he had spent the night. He was very remorseful about his behaviour. Jessica decided to say nothing more on the subject, and he seemed to remain on his best behaviour throughout the holiday.

Joan Ryan had introduced Jessica to some of the charitable committees on which she served. Visiting an orphanage for boys and girls from one of the organisations and taking some gifts for Christmas, filled Jessica with such pity at the emotionally and physically arid atmosphere in which the children lived. She asked the manager if she might have a dozen or so of the children to visit with her during the twelve days of Christmas, so that they might see the Moores' tree and have tea with the family, a request which was readily agreed to.

On the appointed day, ten girls and two boys were deposited at Priory House. They were obviously overawed at their surroundings, and at the magnificent tree which stood in a corner of the hall, and they could not believe their luck when each was handed a small gift from underneath it by Jessica, as well as a box full of presents to take back to the other children in the orphanage. Jessica and Ita took the girls into the kitchen, where Cook started to show them some simple recipes, while Eamonn took the two boys out to show them the farm and the machinery. After a while he left them playing in the haybarn while he went back to the house to see at what time they were being collected. When he returned the barn was empty, and though he called and hollered for them, there was no reply. He started searching everywhere, and finally, to his rage and extreme exasperation, he found them in Michael's workshop where they had pulled everything around in their curiosity to see what they could find. Eamonn took each one by the ear. 'Ye pair o' vagabonds, what d'ye mean by wanderin' into other people's places. I left ye be yerselves for one minute and ye pair of eejits, ye couldn't stay put. I don't know what de master will be sayin'. One ting is certain, ye'll never set foot here again, ye or yer likes.' And he marched them back to the house, from where they were all packed off back to the orphanage.

Jessica was in a state of anxiety as to what Michael would say when he came back from hunting and discovered what had happened. She had written a note to the orphanage asking them not to be too harsh on the children, they were not to realise what damage they might cause. She also said that perhaps on another occasion, if they were to come again, someone from the staff should accompany them in a supervisory capacity.

It fell to Eamonn to break the news to Michael when he came in, and, before going to see Jessica, he immediately went to his workshop. When he returned, he stomped into the morningroom, his face red with fury. Jessica knew it was worse than she had feared. 'Do you know, the little blighters have undone four months of hard work. My papers are all over the place, and a model of a well digger, that could revolutionise farming, has been destroyed. I know you only had the purest motives when you invited the children. But, Jessica, they were your responsibility, and you must think before you act. If you do not feel capable of carrying out your duties yourself, and not leaving them to others, then I suggest you refrain altogether. Your incompetence has ruined all chances of my going into production this year!' He turned on his heel and, without giving Jessica a chance to say anything, left the room, slamming the door behind him. Jessica knew in her heart that Michael was right. But even so, she was hurt and upset at his attitude, and running to her room, she threw herself on the bed and cried herself to sleep. Nanny had tried to pacify her, but she would not be comforted, and it was only days later that Michael relented, went to her, and harmony was restored.

Chapter Five

At the beginning of February, Jessica found she was again pregnant. As the weeks progressed and the morning sickness was not lessening, Michael was concerned about his wife, and pestered Nanny about the normality of it, as there had been no such symptoms during the first pregnancy. Jessica seemed to be losing weight and was listless. 'Mr Moore, now don't be fretting yourself, man,' Nanny reassured him, 'it often goes that way, and is probably due to a change of birth, maybe a boy this time. And, look you, it will soon pass!'

One slushy grey morning, towards the end of February, the postmistress arrived at the front door. She asked to see the master. Eamonn, surprised to see the postmistress herself on the step, asked her what business she would be having with the master. 'Don't be so impudent, Eamonn Farrell. I would not have dragged meself here in person if it was not critical for me to see Mr Moore, himself.' Eamonn hid the scowl on his face and asked her to step into the hall while he went to fetch the master from his workshop.

Mrs Murray stood primly in the hall where Eamonn had left her, and drawing her black shawl closely around her shoulders, looked curiously around her. She noted the cheerfulness of the place and admired the large sprays of evergreens, the potted plants, and the posies of snowdrops and wild violets on the mantelshelf and tables. She moved over to the blazing log fire and warmed herself after the rawness of the east wind on her walk from the village. She held out one muddy laced boot, which immediately began to steam.

Just then, Michael appeared from the back of the hall, a little breathless from running up the hill, and looked enquiringly at Mrs Murray.

'Good morning, Mrs Murray. I believe you wished to see me.'

'Good morning yourself, Mr Moore, and a bad one it is. I am afraid I don't bring good tidings.'

With that, she handed him a telegraph envelope. He quickly opened it, and on reading the contents, gave an involuntary gasp. 'Thank you for your kindness in bringing this telegraph to me in person. I am most grateful.' He turned to Eamonn, who had followed him into the hall, and said, 'See that Mrs Murray is given a hot cup of tea to warm her up, and something to have in it. Now, if you will excuse me.'

Michael walked slowly up the stairs. Not finding Jessica in their bedroom, he knocked on the bathroom door, but received no reply. He went in, and, sitting on the edge of the bath, dropped his head into his hands. His darling was going through so much at the moment. How was she going to withstand this terrible blow that was about to fall on her. Would she have the necessary stamina to bear it all. He went to look for her in the nursery, and felt his heart ache as he watched her playing happily with little Henrietta, enjoying a short respite from her malaise.

She looked up as she heard him come into the room. 'O Michael! I'm so delighted you've come just at this moment. See what our clever little daughter has just learnt. Henrietta, show Father what you have just done for Nanny and Mother.'

'Not now, Jessica,' said Michael kindly, 'I need to talk with you.'

Jessica followed him to their bedroom, puzzled by his manner. Taking her into his arms to support her he said quietly, 'You must be very strong. I am trying to find words to soften the impact of what I have to tell you, but there are none. There has been an accident in London, and your father has been knocked down by an automobile. He died instantly.' He felt Jessica stiffen, and he held her even closer, trying to will his own physical strength into her body. 'Sir David was a good man, and God has spared him anything horrendous by taking him so quickly. I believe everything happened very fast, so he could not have suffered.' Michael felt the need to keep talking, and in this way he could put off the moment when he would have to look into her eyes and see the agony she must be going through.

Jessica detached herself from Michael and slowly walked to the nearest chair, and sat upright. Gripping the arms of the chair, she said, almost inaudibly, 'We must leave at once, Mother will need us.' She rose and made for the door, reciting as a litany, 'Nanny must pack, Eamonn must order the carriage readied, Ita must help me dress for the journey, Eamonn must pack for you, Michael, Cook must stay with Henrietta while Nanny is packing, I must write to the Coyles and say we cannot be with them for dinner tomorrow, we must write and inform your mother, Michael, and we must be quick . . . quick . . .,' and she disappeared through the door before Michael realised what was happening.

He rushed after her, and once again found Jessica in the nursery. He arrived to hear her telling the news to Nanny, without the realisation, in her own state of shock, of what the news would mean to the woman who had been a part of David Barker-Grey's household for so many happy years.

'Nanny, you must pack my bags, I am going to Neath. There has been an accident. Papa was killed in London. Mama will need me.' Nanny let out a long wail, and throwing her apron over her mouth, sobbed and sobbed, as if she would never stop. 'O dear God, what a terrible thing to happen to Sir David. Poor Lady Matilde, what will become of her? What will we all do? He was such a good man, loved by so many. O God, O God. The dear man has gone to his rest, and Heaven will be a better place with him in it, but O dear God, what will we all do?'

Jessica put her arm across Nanny's broad back. 'Come now, Nanny, this will never do. Mother would not approve at all. There are things to be done, and done now, so pull yourself together and let us get on with it. My tweed for travelling, Nanny. Mother will see to my black when I arrive. Tell Eamonn to fetch the trunks from the attic.'

Nanny looked at her in astonishment. 'Miss Jessica, you are going nowhere in your condition. Your poor mother has enough to contend with without you taking on the risk of such a journey at this time of the year, putting your unborn child in jeopardy.'

'What are you talking about, Nanny? Mother needs me, I must go, I will go!'

Jessica's voice had an unnatural calm, which frightened Michael much more than the outburst of grief and hysteria he had expected. 'I'm afraid, my dear, Nanny is quite right,' he said. 'You are quite right, Nanny. There can be no thought of you travelling, Jessica, I will attend to everything. I will be there for your mother and your aunts. All the necessary arrangements will be made by me, and I will stay for as long as I am needed. I will hear no more of your plans to travel. Do you understand? I am quite adamant about this.'

Next morning, Michael left Jessica rocking in a chair in the nursery, silent and blank-eyed. She had said nothing since the evening before, only hugging Henrietta so tightly that the child had cried and held her arms out to Nanny to take her. He had expected any reaction but this, and was afraid, and worried, knowing how attached Jessica had been to her father. 'Nanny, I want you to send for Dr Ryan immediately if you are at all anxious about Mrs Moore. Do you understand? Immediately.'

'Indeed you need not worry, Sir. We will take good care of Mrs Moore,' answered Nanny.

On his return to Ireland, some days following the funeral, Michael was shocked to see how ill and gaunt Jessica had become in the two short weeks he had been in Wales. He gathered her gently into his arms, and held her, as if afraid that if he let her go, she would slip away from him. She beat at his chest with clenched fists, highly hysterical, the calmness of previous days having completely vanished. 'I should have gone with you. I should, Michael. I should have gone with you. Mama and Aunt Olwyn and Aunt Bronwyn needed me and I let them down. Oh, how will they manage without darling Papa. There is so much for them to attend to. Who is going to see to everything? And the mines! What about the mines?'

Michael could not bear her self-recrimination any longer, and, gripping her shoulders and looking into her eyes, willing her to respond to him, he said firmly, in a very determined voice, 'Now look here, Jessica! Stop it at once, I won't hear any more of this nonsense. No, don't interrupt me, sit down!'

Jessica sat in an armchair, still agitated, and looked at Michael, bewildered at his outburst. He knelt beside her and continued in the same tone, but more quietly, to draw her out of the self-pitying and highly emotional state she was in. 'My own girl. Don't you see there was nothing you could do in your condition to help them? You would have only been an added anxiety. Your Mama expressly asked me to tell you how sensible it was that you stayed with Nanny and Henrietta at home.'

Jessica sat like a statue, and then the dam of her remaining control broke and the tears coursed down her cheeks, one after the other. Her shoulders started to shake, and as Michael put his arms around her once more, she cried, at long last the healthy tears of grief.

Chapter Six

Neath
Wales
April 1904

My dear Michael,

I am writing to you as you are now the head of the family. Imagine my anguish when I received a communication from my solicitors informing me that the new encumbant, Sir Jasper Barker-Grey, intends to live here, in this house, which he has inherited along with the titles and lands. My thoughts are in a turmoil. I have known no other home since my marriage to my dear heart, David. The house where my darling child grew from happy girlhood into a beautiful young woman and bride. The house that holds so many cherished memories. How can I bear to think of some other family here in my stead, some other woman looking after what I have looked after for so many years? How can I remove my person to another place, that will be empty of memories for me?

I am heartbroken and despondent, and do not know which way or which direction to face. My dear sisters-in-law have kindly offered me a home with them, but to be in Wales without my beloved husband, does not even bear thinking about. I have written to my brother in Germany to suggest perhaps I will live in one of the family houses there, for the rest of my years.

I would like to know your thoughts about this, as it would put a great distance between me and Jessica, and you Michael, and your family, all of whom are precious jewels in my life. You will know best how to impart this desolate news to Jessica.

Write to me post-haste!

Matilde Barker-Grey

Neath
Wales
May 1904

My dear son-in-law,

I say 'thank you' to you for your compassion and your words of true understanding.

I agree with the view you express about not telling Jessica of my position at this juncture – she has had enough heartbreak for the present. I leave it to your good judgement when the time is appropriate to tell her.

Her letters to me are so full of concern and sadness, I thank God in Heaven that you were sent to be her soulmate and protector. I, in turn, try not to reveal my true state of mind when I write to her. It goes against my nature not to be open and truthful with my child, but I am guided by your good sense in this matter.

My brother, Otto, will have received my letter by now, and I must listen also to what he will say when he will write to me.

My days pass so slowly. I must make the effort to gather my possessions together, so that when I decide where to go, I will be able to have them transported. I would like, if you would permit, to send to Ireland some pieces that will hold special memories for dear Jessica.

I cannot write more at present, my heart is too full,

Matilde

Neath
Wales
July 1904

My dear son-in-law, Michael,

The news that you have at long last been able to tell Jessica of my circumstances gives me the greatest relief, not least because it means that she is now much stronger and quite well.

I have received further communication from Otto. He has been so good in seeing that all estate matters have been settled and my future income secured. Apart from having no house, I am, I believe, a woman of substantial means. I did not appreciate how clever my David had been in his investments.

How typical of you and Jessica to suggest I live with you, and how wise Otto was to suggest I visit Germany before deciding to live there. I could not believe I would feel like a stranger in my homeland and in once familiar surroundings. I realise now that a return to Germany would hold no permanent enticement for my future, as I find the new political ideas not to my liking.

I must now think about accepting your generous offer. I have become so autocratic that I do not know how I may adjust to living in someone else's home – even that of my dearly loved daughter.

Whatever the outcome, your loving kindness will never be forgotten by me,

Your devoted mother-in-law,
Matilde

Neath
Wales
July 1904

My dearest children,

I have had very little sleep in this last week, thinking day and night of the options open to me.

As I have said, to stay in Wales is impossible for me, and Otto was not surprised and I think he understood why I cannot go back to Germany. Having him here these past few days, and thinking out loud in his presence, has been an immeasurable aid to me. Otto has the ability to get into my mind a little and has made a suggestion which I forward to you for your consideration.

I sit here at the desk which David gave to me for our wedding anniversary, and it, and my other beautiful possessions, are the only material reminders I have of twenty-four years of marriage. I realise I would like to have these things with me always, and to this end I propose that I have built a small house in your grounds. This will mean that while I am near you and able to watch your dear children grow, I will also still be mistress of my own home, which will not interfere with your household and will make it easier for us to maintain our present amicable relationship.

I have spoken with my housekeeper, Gerda, and she is prepared to come with me and look after me when, and if, I come to live in Ireland.

I eagerly await your response to this proposition and send kisses to Henrietta,

Your affectionate mother,
Matilde

Chapter Seven

Charlotte made her swift entry into the world in the early hours of a balmy September morning. The first time that Nanny held Charlotte in her arms her native intuition, beyond understanding, told her that she would have to carefully guard this child's destiny. She was beautiful from the moment she was born, and her smile lit her tawny eyes with points of light that glinted like gold. Flaxen curls, which contrasted strikingly with her dark eyebrows and eyelashes, made a vivid impact. Her father would dotingly say, 'In her come together beautifully the Irish, Welsh and German of her heritage.'

As Nanny took over the needs of this new baby, Jessica spent more and more time with Henrietta, who persistently called herself Ria, and who treated her sister as an intruder. This normal phase in a child's development was never to pass. Henrietta's extreme ego, wilfulness, bad temper and biting tongue were frequently vented against Charlotte.

Over the next couple of months, the house was in continuous upheaval preparing for Lady Matilde's removal to Ireland, with her possessions, whilst, at the same time, preparing for the christening of Charlotte Jane, who was to be named after her two great grandmothers.

The two important decisions, the baby's names, and where Lady Matilde would build her house, were discussed by Jessica and Michael. The question of names was easily solved; the other matter proved much more difficult. It remained a puzzle for many weeks, until Henry Moore, Michael's father, staying at Blackrock on his way to Dublin to attend Parliament, came up with an answer. He suggested that they should use the deserted ruins of the old priory, which had given its name to the house, and build on its foundations, to create a new Priory Lodge. Jessica and Michael thought this was a splendid idea. It was just near enough to be a pleasant walk through the orchard, and yet far enough away to give each household its own autonomy.

'I have been thinking for some time, Michael, that we should build a gazebo in the garden. The hill near the orchard would be an ideal situation, a perfect resting place for Mama on her way to see us.' Michael thought this a wonderfully romantic suggestion, and they joyfully conjured up pictures of picnics and luncheons on summer days that the whole family would participate in. In later years, it was also to become a trysting place for the young Moores and their friends.

On the day Lady Matilde arrived, it was wet and windy. The roses, full-blown and drooping, were burdened with rain. The seed pods were forming on spent flower heads, and berries on the trees were turning red, preparing to cheer dark winter's days and provide food for the birds.

Nanny had insisted that the house should be thoroughly turned out, and had everyone cleaning and polishing in preparation for the arrival of her former mistress. She had young Seán, who was being trained into service by Eamonn, polish the silver until it gleamed, then she had him perched on ladders, shining the windows inside and out until they looked like mirrors in which the sky was reflected.

'It's spite!' said Nanny to Cook, in her Welsh lilt. 'The rain came in spite today to destroy the lovely clean windows and doorsteps. Her ladyship will think I have surrendered to the easygoing Irish ways.'

Mrs Mahony laughed and said, 'Life goes by anyway, easygoin' or not, but I agree, its the divil's own luck it would rain today of all days. But I can't be standin' here all day gabbin' and listenin' to your fluster. Throw a bit of sackin' on the ground in front of the carriage to save her skirts draggin' in the mud. I must get on with the cookin' or they'll all be in on top of us, and me with not a bite to put in their mouths.'

'Sacking indeed!' snorted Nanny. 'I'll see that Seán finds some decent mats for her ladyship to set her feet upon.' Leaving Mrs Mahony grinning from ear to ear at her fussing and fuming, she padded out of the kitchen.

An hour later, Nanny was sitting at the window, joggling Henrietta on her knee to keep the child clean, anxiously peering down the drive for sight of the carriages. At long last they appeared. Picking the baby up, and taking the little girl by the hand, she made her way down the stairs to meet Lady Matilde, Jessica and Michael, all the while admonishing Henrietta, 'Be a good girl and behave yourself. Remember, children should be seen and not heard. Your Grossmutter will insist on that.' Immediately Henrietta set up a wail, sat on the stairs, and refused to budge, screaming that she did not want to meet that 'cross mutter'.

Nanny in panic did not know whether to tuck Henrietta under her other arm and to advance, or retreat, 'Like Napoleon at Waterloo', as she often said when recounting the incident. The decision was taken out of her hands. The front door swung open and the three adults entered, spearheaded by Lady Barker-Grey, who, seeing the woeful picture of Nanny and the children, rapped the ferrule of her umbrella on the tiled floor several times. The noise so startled the trio on the stairs that Henrietta stopped sobbing, Nanny sank onto the stairs beside her, and the baby took up where Henrietta had left off.

Michael, forestalling any further furore, sidled past the two women and gathered his little girl in one arm, and with the other helped Nanny to her feet. He ushered them straight into the morningroom, to give Nanny time to recover her composure. Eamonn and Gerda, Matilde's maid, having brought the luggage into the house and taken the ladies' coats, disappeared, and Jessica placated her mother and took her to the drawingroom, where tea was set.

Michael managed to mollify Nanny, who kept repeating over and over, 'Her ladyship will think I do not have the ability any more.' Michael, hiding his great amusement, thought that all the best-laid plans for the day had gone awry and that neither Nanny nor Matilde would ever see the amusing side of the situation. He made a mental note to point this out to Jessica when they were alone. He calmed his two daughters and, taking both of them in his arms, crooning soothingly, carried them into the drawing-room to their mother and grandmother, followed by Nanny, who was still inclined to hold her head down, ashamed that she should, in her opinion, have let everyone down so.

Henrietta, wriggling out of her father's arms, ran to her mother, and, hiding her face in Jessica's lap, mumbled, 'I don't want dat cross mutter.' Jessica laughed and explained to the others what was being said. Michael and Nanny joined in the laughter with relief as Jessica gently took the small girl onto her knee and carefully explained that it was 'Grossmutter, like Grandmama', and not 'cross mutter', and that Matilde was not cross, but kind and gentle, and had a beautiful gift for her. Henrietta looked at her German grandmother from the safety of her mother's knee, but she did not seem to be too reassured by the expression she saw on that lady's face.

Matilde enquired what all the preceding 'noise' was about, and then it dawned on them that she had not understood the meaning the child had put on the Germanic form of 'grandmother'. When it was explained to Matilde she smiled and, extending her hand to Henrietta, said, 'Come with Grossmutter, we will find your present in my trunk.' These were magic words and the tall lady and the tiny child left the room hand in hand. Michael looked at Nanny from under his eyebrows as he poured himself a whiskey and said, 'A successful opening gambit by Lady Matilde I think.'

The winter passed very quickly. Michael's parents and family came to spend Christmas at Priory House. Matilde took charge and organised everyone beforehand, to the point of distraction. The amount of pickling and jam-making, and the heavy German dumplings she insisted on with everything, made Jessica say in despair, 'Cook will either explode from aggravation, or leave, and then where will we all be?'

On St Stephen's Day Jessica and Michael hosted a party to introduce Matilde to some of the neighbours whom she had not met previously. Henry Moore announced during the evening that both his daughters, Margaret and Elizabeth, had become engaged to be married, on dates to be announced by their mother, but he added with sadness, 'Unfortunately for Florence and myself they will both be living in England with their husbands.' There were lots of good wishes extended to the two blushing girls, as toasts were drunk to their future happiness.

In March 1905, Priory Lodge, Lady Barker-Grey's new home, was completed, and Gerda was installed to polish the furniture, air the beds, and generally make the lodge ready for its mistress. Jessica filled the house with wild daffodils and bluebells that she and Henrietta gathered from the surrounding woods.

The main household breathed a sigh of relief as her ladyship walked out of Priory House. She had not made their lives easy in the past months, and Nanny was on the verge of becoming demented trying to keep the baby and Miss Ria from being a nuisance.

Things gradually returned to a more relaxed and happy state, except on Sundays, when 'Grossmutter' came to join in luncheon and supper with the family.

In the following six years, two boys, Owen David and Darragh Henry, were born. Their mother and father seemed more in love with each passing year and each new child. Lady Matilde had settled into her new home, the gazebo on the hill had been built and was used regularly by all the family. The only discordant note was Jessica's growing concern about the amount of spirits Michael drank, and how irritable he became with the children at these times. She spoke to him on several occasions and suggested that he should be more abstemious, but he always brushed her off, saying that he only took a little now and then to unwind. But in her heart Jessica knew it was rather more than that, and she kept a vigilant eye upon him.

The Christmases were spent, according to Jessica's state of pregnancy, either in Priory House, with family joining them there, or at Glenavon, where as many of the Moore offspring as could travel would also spend the holiday.

Otto and Hannah von Zeit visited twice, with Rudi and Ava. Jessica's aunts, the Misses Olwyn and Bronwyn Barker-Grey, spent several long summers in Ireland, touring around the country or staying with Lady Matilde at Priory Lodge. Most summers were divided between a month at Delahunt's Hotel in Wicklow, when all the families were united, and going back together to Glenavon for the remainder of the season, where the comings and goings of fathers, brothers and brothers-in-law were, according to the dictates of their work life, an endless round of meeting boats and trains.

In 1910, both Ava and Rudi von Zeit were married within weeks of each other, in Hamburg. Ava was married to a Jewish man, Hyman Urbach, and Rudi to a Christian girl, Katerina Becker. Matilde and Jessica represented the family at both weddings. Michael regretted that it was not possible for him to accompany them, but he requested that Jessica should explain to both of the brides and grooms that, as he was at an important point in negotiating with manufacturers, it was impossible for him to be away from Ireland for any length of time.

Dr and Mrs Ryan had become very close friends of the family. Although they had not been blessed with their own children, they were kind and affectionate with the Moores, perhaps showing a little bias towards Darragh, who was their godson, and named after Dr Ryan.

Following a particularly virulent local outbreak of consumption, in which he lost several patients, young and old, Darragh Ryan asked both Jessica and his wife Joan to join the Women's National Health Association. This group had been set up by Lady Aberdeen as a direct result of the Great Exhibition of

1907. Its aims were to promote cleanliness in the homes of the ordinary people, to ensure that shops selling food were hygienic, and especially to monitor that the greatest care was taken in the cleansing of utensils and persons in the dairies, as milk was considered the greatest source of tuberculosis, a disease that was a scourge in the land and a prevalent cause of death.

Late in 1912, Dr Ryan confirmed that Jessica was again three months with child. From the beginning, he was uneasy about this pregnancy, for what reason he could not quite formulate, but he made a note to speak to Michael and advise against any more children.

At six months, twins were diagnosed. Jessica began to suffer severe back pains and swelling of her hands and legs. Darragh Ryan became more and more concerned about his patient, and he asked Michael to come and see him at his home. As gently as he could, without showing his own growing fears, Darragh explained to Michael that Jessica's body was not reacting to this pregnancy in the same way as it had done previously. Michael at once jumped to his feet, his voice pitched high with anxiety, 'What does that mean? What are you trying to say? I don't care what you do, you must see that Jessica is safe and restored to full health, do you hear? I want you to think of nothing else but Jessica's safety.' He suddenly collapsed in his chair, ashen-faced and strangely still, as dreadful thoughts passed through his mind. 'What does this really mean, Darragh?' he said in a very soft voice. 'Do you think she should have more rest? I know the children don't realise her condition and take a lot of her energy.' Darragh Ryan stopped him, and again gently but firmly told him, 'Jessica needs a great deal of rest and quiet, and a free and peaceful mind, if nothing is to go badly wrong.'

Darragh poured a stiff whiskey for Michael and gradually the colour returned to his face. Sitting down again beside Michael, he placed his hand on Michael's shoulder, and said, in his soft south Dublin brogue, 'What I am about to ask you is going to take a great deal of courage on your part, but, if we are to have a happy outcome, it is vitally necessary. I don't want you to breathe a word of what we have spoken about today to any other person. If Jessica is to be protected, she must have no inkling that there is anything amiss. She will have to remain completely immobile until her confinement. We can explain that this is to alleviate her back pain and swellings. In view of there being twins, we should have a second opinion, as I may very well need help with the delivery. I would also strongly recommend a nurse to attend to Jessica, to protect her from the rest of the household and its constant demands.'

Michael nodded his head, and in a choked voice whispered, 'Anything, anything you say, Darragh. You can depend on my doing anything that is within my power to alleviate the situation for Jessica. She is the most important person in my life. In fact, she is my life.'

'I realise, Michael, that you must be filled with all sorts of apprehension and fears, but from the depth of my affection, friendship and experience, I would like to reassure you that, with care, we will pull both her and her babies through this difficult time. I want you to feel that if you should need me, you must call on me at any time of the night or day, both in my professional capacity and also as a friend. In the meantime, I will arrange for a very eminent obstetrician from the Rotunda Hospital and Fitzwilliam Square in Dublin to come out and visit Jessica this week.'

Michael got into his Panhard Lavassa automobile. He had been extravagant and had bought the car the previous year, when he had gone to London to visit his patent agent. As he drove slowly along the road home in the September sunshine, he felt a heat suffuse his body, as if it were keeping pace with the burning thoughts that flickered through his brain like a fever. 'Pull yourself together, man,' he said in a loud voice, talking to himself. 'You cannot help Jessica by behaving this way. She will know there is something wrong the minute she sees you if you continue with these fruitless thoughts.' The shock of hearing his own voice in such an uncharacteristic manner brought Michael to his senses, in the same way as a jug of cold water poured over his inflamed face and eyes would have done. He went over his conversation with Darragh again and again, and gradually formed a plan of action. He would tell Matilde, Nanny and the children that Jessica would need complete rest to gain strength for the delivery of the two babies. To Jessica, he would explain what Darragh had told him about rest helping her discomfort, and that the doctor coming from Dublin to see her was to assist Darragh at the delivery. Explaining the necessity for a nurse was going to be more difficult, and Michael decided to wait until the obstetrician from Dublin had been, and then talk to him and to Darragh about the best manner in which to broach the subject.

At that moment, he saw Eamonn rushing towards him on a bicycle, and he shouted above the noise of the motor to attract his attention. Eamonn looked in the direction of the voice and, swerving to meet his master, blurted out, 'I've been sent to fetch Dr Ryan and yourself, the mistress has been took bad.' Michael told Eamonn to continue to Dr Ryan's, as he put the car into gear and, stepping on the throttle, made as much speed as possible to Priory House.

As soon as they heard the motor, the children came rushing to meet him, all shrieking that Nanny was cross with them and would not let them see Mother. Michael, so distraught that even with the children he could not control himself, completely lost his temper with them, and gathering them up in an impatient scoop of his arms, shouted for someone to come immediately. Ita appeared, and taking in the situation quickly, said, 'Sir, leave them with me, I'll take them to the gatehouse to Missis Eamonn.'

'No!' said Michael. 'Take them to Lady Barker-Grey, and stay with them, but do not dare say why for the present until I find out exactly what the matter is. No need to worry her ladyship. Just say your mistress has a very bad headache, and that Nanny is putting cold compresses on her head and, as the children were very noisy, it was decided it would be better if they were not in the house. I'll tell Nanny where they are.'

Having dispatched his brood, Michael then made his way to his wife's bedroom. As he entered the darkened room, Nanny and Cook were gently placing Jessica on a wad of towelling, and covering her with the bedclothes. Not seeing anybody but his beloved, he reached the bed and, with concern, asked her what happened. She looked at his face and held out her hands to him, 'Michael, Michael, the waters have broken, we have sent for Darragh. O Michael, I am frightened. O God, help me, help me!' Michael could not bear the anguish he saw on her face, and gently taking her hands in his own, he tried to soothe her. 'My own dearest, God will help us, I know he will, we must have faith. Try to be calm, Darragh is on his way.'

As soon as he arrived, Darragh cleared the room. He told Michael that he had already telegraphed for Professor Josephs to come at once.

After what seemed an age, Dr Ryan called Michael back into the room and reassured him that, as far as he could determine, there was no cause for immediate alarm, 'but I intend staying with Jessica to wait for Solomon Josephs to arrive.'

Jessica lay on the bed listening to the two men talking, still very frightened at what was happening to her, but also concerned that Michael should not become too stressed and resort to the decanter. She called him to her and, in a feigned calmer voice, said, 'Darragh seems to be confident that both myself and the babies will be all right.'

Nanny and Cook both came back into the room carrying trays of tea, which were a welcome relief to the tension. 'Mr Moore, Sir,' said Nanny, 'we will have her ladyship down on us like a mountain of coal if we don't fetch the children back. She will come to find out what is going on, if we don't satisfy her curiosity.'

'Very well, Nanny, send Seán to fetch them, but make sure they are quiet and do not disturb their mother.'

Late that night, Professor Solomon Josephs arrived by motor car. After examining Jessica, he consulted with Darragh Ryan, and they both came to the conclusion that Jessica would be more comfortable and just as safe at home, with a professional nurse, and Darragh within reach, rather than being cut off from her family in a private hospital, among strangers. What they did not tell Jessica or Michael was that the chances of her having her babies delivered at full term were minimal.

In the months that followed, Jessica's long days were punctuated by curtailed visits from the children at bedtime, and longer visits from Lady Matilde and Michael during the day. Her sleepless nights were spent in long conversations with Nurse Philips, a very caring woman with whom Jessica soon developed a sincere bond, a bond which grew out of her own dependency, and Amy Philips' compassionate devotion to this gentle woman who had been placed in her care.

Chapter Eight

Jessica lost touch with the reality of her normal life, and again felt like the little girl that Nanny used to cosset, not having to think for herself or to lift a hand to help herself or any of the members of her household. Her present experience ended at the sides and foot of her bed. She still loved her family, and knew she was beloved by them, but she was, for the time being, apart from them. Their routine was not part of this time of suspended living, and when they appeared daily with their stories, she smiled politely and pretended an interest that she hoped hid the gnawing agony of fear which was her constant companion. Michael was with her each evening, either reading to her or just sitting quietly in the armchair in front of the fire, lost in his own thoughts. Jessica wondered what would happen to Michael and to her children if she were to die. Who would listen patiently to Michael while he rambled on for hours about the inventions he was working on, and those he was struggling to give existence to? Who would lift her beautiful but humourless daughter, Henrietta, out of her petulant sulks? Who would gently chide the wilful Charlotte, and teach her how to keep her wayward hair and impulsive nature under control? Who would comfort her little boys when they fell and hurt themselves, and who would give them little treats to help cure the hurt? Who would give the filial love to her mother, who had made her life amongst them? And who, the biggest who, would croon and cradle and love the little unborn babes who lay under her heart? She never spoke of these fears to Michael, but Amy knew of each one, and tried to soothe her patient as best she might.

The little routines that had gradually built up began each day when Michael and Nurse Philips lifted Jessica onto the Ottoman daybed by the window, whilst her own bed was aired, the mattress turned, and fresh linen, smelling of lavender, crisply thrown upon it, Nanny on one side and Amy Philips on the other, pulling the sheets tautly, tucking in the ends. Jessica faced this part of her day with mixed feelings. She hated the helplessness of having to be carried, the uncomfortable, and sometimes painful, pressure caused by the lifting as the babies moved within her, and, as she got heavier, the anxiety of being dropped before reaching the couch. But on the other hand, she loved the moment, because it gave her the opportunity to watch the seasons change. The blustering winds of late winter, the flurries of snow, some escaping to land on the grass or gravel, and melt or become slush, and other flakes that landed on bare branches and twigs, sometimes bending them under their fleecy weight. She saw the spears of the wild daffodil leaves gradually appear, following the carpet of snowdrops, and slowly open their golden trumpets, which changed colour as they were tossed by the lighter winds of spring.

She made sure that one of the children scattered crumbs each day for the wild birds that roamed the skies, flying from the bird sanctuary in Booterstown. She envied them their free flight, and could only soar with them in her imagination, seeing the white caps on the waves as they splashed on the sea shore, or the blue of the heather on the hills of the Dublin Mountains. She held these images as she was washed and changed, and then carried back to bed, trying to ignore the humiliation she felt at being unable to perform the most basic needs for herself. Lying back on her pillows, she felt a lassitude creep over her, and mercifully escaped the remainder of the morning in sleep, during which time Lady Matilde made it her daily task to put fresh flowers in Jessica's room.

On May 17th, 1913, Jessica, who had fallen into a fitful sleep around 4 am, woke to the sounds of her own screams. Nurse

Philips jumped out of her cot, which had been placed beside Jessica's bed, and turned on the main light. As she stooped over the patient, she heard Michael approach from his dressingroom. She saw that Jessica was bathed in sweat, that her colour was poor and that she was labouring for breath. 'Send for Dr Ryan immediately,' Amy said as she felt for Jessica's pulse, 'and ask Nanny to come to me at once please.'

She fetched a basin of water and a cloth, and bathed Jessica's face and hands. She tried to soothe her as Jessica rambled and mumbled, 'Papa, Papa, take away the pain, tell me a story, tell me about your school again, Papa, why don't you take away the pain like you always do? Sing to me Papa! Papa! Papa! story, sing, pain. Papa, don't go . . . Papa, don't go . . . come back . . . back. Pa . . .' At that moment, Nurse noticed Nanny had come into the room and was standing looking down at Jessica, her knuckles between her teeth and tears in her eyes. 'My pretty little one. When she was a child and sick, only Sir David could comfort her when she was ill. Where is she now? Is she slipping away from us and going to her dear Papa? O dear God, keep her safe for us. God help her in this moment of need.'

'Amen. Amen,' intoned Amy Philips.

At that moment, Jessica screamed again as another pain wracked her body, and she clutched Amy's hand so tightly that she left imprints which took days to fade.

Darragh Ryan had arrived by now, climbing the stairs three at a time. His presence calmed the dread in Amy's heart enough for her to compose herself, get into her uniform and regain her professional demeanour. Dr Ryan had met Michael on the stairs and had dispatched him to rouse Cook and Ita, to instruct them to put on lots of water to boil, and tell them that first thing in the morning they were to take the children to their grandmother's. Having given Michael something to occupy him, and to get him out of their way for the moment, he sent Nanny to dress herself. Dr Ryan examined Jessica, then gravely turned to Nurse Philips, informing her very quietly. 'I do not know how things will turn out, I can only hear one foetal heart at the moment. I have telephoned Professor Josephs' home, but he is out at another delivery. He will be reached as soon as possible. Until then, we will have to hold the fort and deal with each event as it occurs as best we can.' He then went back to a semi-conscious Jessica and said to her in a determined voice that he hoped would penetrate her awareness, 'We will pull you through, Jessica, we will pull you through together.'

As the hours went by, Darragh noted the changes in Jessica, her pulse weakening, her sweat-soaked body becoming more and more exhausted with each painful contraction. Most worrying of all, her gradual withdrawal of communication during her short periods of rest, more so than he would have expected, even under these circumstances. Soon he realised that she would be incapable of helping them to deliver the babies, and that he would have to apply forceps. He waited as long as he could for Solomon Josephs to arrive, reaching the point finally when he faced the inevitability that, if he did not act immediately, both mother and children would be lost.

He strode briskly to the table where his sterilised instruments were laid out for him, and moved it over to the bedside. He checked that a gauze mask and chloroform were also in position. He was so intent on going through the procedures that he was startled when he felt a hand on his shoulder, and the relief flooded through him when he turned and saw that it was Solomon Josephs. The professor edged him to one side so that he could examine the patient and judge the situation for himself. Darragh filled in details of what had been happening as Professor Josephs scrubbed up in preparation for the deliveries.

The professor then took charge, and Darragh and Amy obeyed his every instruction during the frantic hours that followed, sustained only by hurriedly drunk cups of tea and hastily eaten sandwiches, until, late in the afternoon, the first boy was born, followed shortly afterwards by his brother.

Nanny offered up a silent little prayer of gratitude when she heard each in turn give lusty cries, and, swaddling them in flannelette, she carried them off to the nursery to bathe and dress them. Michael, who had been on the landing for hours, rushed forward when he heard the door open. Nanny, seeing him, called, 'Boys, both! Fine and healthy!', and giving him no chance to ask the questions about Jessica to which he so vitally needed the answers, she disappeared. Frustrated, he again took up his vigil at his wife's door, waiting for the summons to come in.

Inside the room, all was far from over. Jessica was not responding. The effect of the anaesthetic should have worn off, but Jessica still lay white and silent, her breathing shallow. Professor Josephs, who had been listening to her heart, looked up with a grave face, and turning to Darragh Ryan he said very quietly, 'Ask her husband to come in, and then send for her clergyman!' As he went to the door, Darragh heard Matilde's voice raised in uncharacteristic hysteria, demanding to be allowed in to her daughter, and before he could reach it, Matilde burst into the room, brushing him aside, and made straight for the bed. '*Mein kind, mein kind.* I am here. It is Mama. Answer me! Answer me! Do you hear me? Answer me. Got in Himmel!' and her voice trailed as she saw how pale and pathetic Jessica looked. But, to everyone's astonishment, Jessica's eyes flickered and opened, as if years of obeying her mother had penetrated her deep sleep. Michael, who had followed his mother-in-law closely, went to Jessica and looked at his wife with all his anguish written on his face.

Gesturing to Nurse Philips to move Matilde and Michael aside, Professor Josephs quickly went to his patient again and felt for her pulse. Darragh could tell from his face that he was not reassured by what he found, and drawing Michael to the corner of the room, he gently said to him, 'I think it might be time to send for Reverend Acton, Michael, with your permission.' Michael looked at Darragh blankly, repeating his words, 'Reverend Acton?' Realising that Michael had not grasped the gravity of the situation, he put his arms around his friend's shoulders and explained very slowly, 'Jessica is leaving us Michael, the Lord is taking her to her final rest. We who love her must make her final hours as peaceful and comfortable as we can.'

Michael made no reply to Darragh except to shake his head 'no'. He turned on his heels and went back to his wife's side. He was oblivious of the hours that followed, of the movements in and out of the room. He sat in a trance holding Jessica's fragile hand, with only one thought in his mind – I shall will her to live. How can I let her die? How am I to exist without her laughter and tenderness, her patience and love? No. No. I will not let her die. I shall will her to live. No one saw any of these thoughts on his face, only the love with which he looked at Jessica.

As the pale dawn light appeared in the sky, Jessica's breathing began to sound easier, and the deathly pallor on her lovely face was warmed by a slight flush. The two doctors looked at each other, and each in turn felt her pulse, and then went to the corner of the room to consult together. They returned to the bed, again checked Jessica's pulse, and turning to Michael and Matilde said, 'We don't know how, but Jessica seems to have come through a crisis, and is now sleeping naturally!'

In the weeks that followed, Michael learned that, whilst his beloved Jessica would live, she had lost the use of her legs. Professor Josephs explained that the pressure on the spinal area during the birth of the twins had caused extensive bruising and that with time and patience, there might be a hope, even though a faint one, that Jessica would walk again. He suggested that Nurse Philips be persuaded to stay on so that Jessica could benefit from her expert nursing. Nanny also requested that an under-nurse be hired, as she could not look after the new babies as well as the bigger children, even though they would be occupied quite a lot of the time with school, other lessons and activities.

Michael shut himself into his study and went though his ledgers to see how his income could be stretched to pay for extra staff and the equipment Jessica would need to make her life more comfortable. He quickly realised that he would have to find other supplementary sources if he was to provide adequately for all these added expenses, even if it entailed borrowing from the bank or selling some of his land.

Jessica lay uncomplainingly, day after day, but she noticed the increasingly worried expression on Michael's face and his impatience with the children. When she felt strong enough she asked Michael to sit down beside her, and coaxed him to speak to her. 'My darling, you have so many burdens to carry, please let me be of some use and share them with you. Tell me why you are constantly looking so distraught. You know that I have come to accept what has befallen me and I am full of hope, so on that score you must not worry. What else is it my dearest?'

'I have tried to keep you free from worry, Jessica, but I am afraid we are running into financial problems. Our income is just not large enough to encompass all the extra staff we are maintaining, and yet I know they are necessary. Maybe I will sell one of my new machines, or one of my other patents will mature, or if all comes to all, I will have to ask Father to help a little more.'

'O Michael, I'm afraid I never thought of that aspect of things. I have been so sheltered all my life from matters of finance. I am so sorry that I have been the cause of your problems.'

'You the cause? You, the bravest, most wonderful girl, how can you even think such a thing? You must forget all this. You must concentrate all your energy upon getting well again! I will manage somehow. Promise me you will not worry. As I say, I will manage!'

'Why not allow me to ask Mother to help us?' Jessica responded. 'She has no money difficulties. Quite the opposite I think. She would be only too happy to help.'

Michael sat up straight and, in a very quiet and determined tone that brooked no argument, said, 'You will do no such thing, and neither will I. I am quite capable of looking after my own family. I will just have to work harder, and I am afraid it cannot be helped, but, my dear, you will see very little of me over the next months.' For all his brave words, Michael felt a tremor of fear in his heart, which he could not hide from Jessica. 'You know I will spend as much time with you as I can, you know how precious each moment we are together is to me. I know I can rely on you to understand and be patient.' Jessica looked at him and nodded.

Jessica was now well enough for Amy Philips to leave her at night, and Michael moved back into their bedroom. They found comfort in holding each other, and feeling the intimate warmth of their bodies, although any physical act was forbidden. At these moments, despite Michael not wishing to discuss such an eventuality, Jessica insisted that they should talk about a life in which she might not participate. 'Michael, my darling, I don't want you to be lonely. Wherever I am, I will understand and be glad if you find someone else to love. The children will need a mother. I know how much you love me, I have been a most fortunate woman, I have had the whole world. But, my dearest, we must face reality.'

'Jessica, I know we will be together for many years. But if we are not, if my worst nightmare is to happen and you are not with me any more, I have had a lifetime of love with you. No one could come near you, or fill the void you would leave, or take your place in my life. I have loved once, and once only!'

As the days grew warmer, Michael and Eamonn carried Jessica into the morningroom for short spells, and later on, to sit in the shelter of the porch in a bath chair. On the hottest days of July and August, she was wheeled onto the lawn under the shade of a large copper beech tree. Her children playing round her, the new babies sleeping near her and Michael and her mother taking tea with her daily gave her a new strength, and lulled her family and household into thinking that she was recovering. But as autumn came to a close, Jessica's heart gave out, she lost her valiant fight and went to her final sleep as the leaves fell from the trees.

The rains of October and November reflected the gloom in the hearts of all who had known her, and the letters, which spoke of her gentleness and goodness, poured through the postbox. Amy Philips took charge of the household, as everyone else seemed incapable of doing so. She intended to stand by the promise that Jessica had extracted from her. 'Look after my family for me, my beloved Michael, my mother and my darling little ones, for they will need you after I am gone.' Even Matilde seemed to have lost her usual fortitude, and went about her daily routine in a mechanical way, as if to say, 'It is not true. My daughter, she has only gone away, and will soon return to us.' Nanny wept for her darling, her cariad, daily, and even though she looked after the poor motherless children with her usual mixture of gruff love and efficiency, it was with an ever-damp handkerchief clutched in one hand.

When they heard the news, Otto and Hannah von Zeit came immediately, on the first ship available, to be with Matilde and Michael at this terrible time. Florence and Henry Moore came to Priory House so that they could assist Michael in making arrangements for the funeral. Cook, Ita, Eamonn and all the other staff were like rudderless ships, floundering from one routine task to another.

The desolate black-clad figures of her two small daughters, as they stood, lost, beside their father and grandparents at the graveside, illustrated more about the general feeling of the tragic young mother's death, than all the funeral trappings and numerous wreaths sent by the large attendance. Lady Barker-Grey, who had been silent since the event, stood, supported by Henry Moore and Otto von Zeit, vulnerable and yet dignified in her grief. The black clouds of autumn silhouetted the scene and etched it into the hearts of all present. After a moving eulogy by Reverend Acton, the family and close friends returned to Priory House.

The headlines of the London *Times*, which fell through the letterbox each morning, spoke of Home Rule. The comments in the House of Commons by Mr Asquith were lost to Michael in the tragedy of his bereavement. Even the outstretched arms of his little daughters and sons failed to raise his hitherto ready smile. He could not shrug off the heavy burden of guilt that he carried. His, he felt, was the load of a man who had put his own carnal desires before the well-being of a dearly loved wife. His strength seemed to have left him, and he spent the winter sitting in the bedroom he had shared with Jessica, staring into the flames of the fire, drinking whiskey. The only time he left the room was when he was persuaded by Nanny to come downstairs for meals, which he then pushed around his plate. Even the weeks of Christmas which he had roused himself to spend with his parents at Glenavon failed to shake him from the deep depression into which he had fallen. He felt that he had reached the nadir of his life, he had never realised that a house filled with people could feel so empty. As spring pushed its shoots through the black soil, and weak shafts of sunlight glanced off weather-grimed windows, the members of the Moore household, in response to the change of season, began to emerge from the cocoon of depression that engulfed them.

Nanny, who was becoming very philosophical, also came to grips with the continuity of life. While lying in bed one night it occurred to her that in a few weeks' time, God help and bless them, the twins would be one year old. 'Indeed to goodness, it is not their fault they are motherless, little innocents. They are all the more to be pitied. They shall have a birthday party. After all, their Christening was not much of an affair to dwell on in memory. Tomorrow, I will start to organise a lovely birthday; the children can all help. I will think what task each will do and maybe even the master and her ladyship will rally round.' She put her finger to her lip as another thought struck her. 'Perhaps they will hold one baby each as the candles are lit?' On that thought, Nanny fell asleep.

When she woke in the morning, she felt happy as she recalled her dream. In it, Jessica had become young and well again, and was gathering flowers in the garden in Neath. 'This one', she had said, cutting a lily, 'is for Miss Henrietta to carry', then, gathering daisies, she entwined them into a coronet, 'to be worn', she had said, 'by Miss Charlotte.' She had handed Nanny a basket filled with a myriad of flowers 'for the boys!' Now Nanny felt she had Miss Jessica's approval of her plans.

When Nanny saw Cook later, she told her of her idea. 'I have first to talk to the master and Nurse Philips. I wasn't sure if this was the right time for such a celebration, but Miss Jessica came to me in a dream and said all the things I was thinking, so now I know it is right.'

'Jasus, Mary and Holy Saint Joseph!' said Cook, as she crossed herself. 'If that don't beat all. So that was what me own dream was about last night. There I was kneadin' dough, fit to bust, the flour was flyin' everywhere and every way, and the bread would not come right, and then, I don't know why, I split it in two and put each piece on the weighin' scales, and they would not balance, and, right suddenly, instead of that dough, there were two black goblins dancin' a jig! Wasn't that a quare one Nanny?' Cook said, folding her arms across her chest with a look of great satisfaction.

The magic of the birthday party worked a small miracle. For the first time in months, Michael was seen to smile. Mr and Mrs Moore and Kit came up from Wicklow, and Michael's two sisters, Meg and Beth, came from England with their husbands and children for the occasion, and the house was once more filled with laughter.

Jessica had left sadness, and an irreplaceable sense of loss in everyone's heart. But she had also left, as her legacy, a happy and united home and a family who, in the years to follow, would always remember her, and benefit from all the things she had taught them during the brief years she had been with them.

BOOK II

Chapter Nine

Dovid Minsky received a letter in Riga, Latvia, from his brother Shmuel, who had settled in Dublin, Ireland, where he had been duped into landing by the captain of the boat on which he had booked passage to the 'Golden Land', America, as had many of his co-religionists, some of whom also landed in Scotland or in England.

In the letter, written in Yiddish, he read, 'Dovid, life is good in this city, where we Jews are treated like everyone else, and we can own our own businesses alongside those of the Gentiles. A Jew can walk in the streets, proud, without fear, without looking over his shoulder to see if gangs of hooligans or Cossacks are ready to pounce on him, without fear of a pogrom beginning during morning prayers, or afternoon devotions in the prayer house or synagogue. The monies that I realised on the sale of my home and drapery shops in Riga have been sufficient to set up a similar lifestyle in this, my adopted country, of which, I am proud to be able at this moment to announce, I am now a full Irish citizen, and where I, your brother Shmuel, am now called Samuel. All this by the will of God.'

Dovid decided that this was also where the future of his family lay. To his wife Sarah, imparting his decision, he said, 'Our eldest son, Joseph, will soon be called to the army. We have seen what happens when boys of fifteen or sixteen years go. They come back after twenty or thirty years, broken, in body and spirit. I don't wish to do what the families here have to do to protect their sons from such an army, to chop off fingers or toes so that they are useless to be soldiers. This can maim a mind as well as a body. So!' he said, his pointing finger raised in the air, 'I have decided! First Joseph will go to his Uncle Samuel and his Aunt Bertha in Ireland. We will send money with him. He will, with the help of God, buy a house and furniture. Then, next year, God also willing, we will follow with the other children when Solomon has made his Bar mitzvah.'

So it was that in the year 1886, the Minsky family followed their eldest son, Joseph, to Dublin.

From the outset, Samuel insisted that everyone should speak in English so that they could practise until they became as 'goot as I am!' Each day, for four months, there were heated discussions between Samuel and Dovid, with Samuel trying to convince Dovid that Ireland was not America, that it had nothing to do with America, that it was across the Atlantic Ocean, three thousand miles from America, but that it was also a *medina*, a golden country, and from what he had heard, a better place to have come to. Whilst Dovid would argue, 'You, Samuel, left Riga for America, and now you're telling me dis is not America? How comes it you could miss so big a country as America by three tousand miles?' Dovid finally agreed that he would remain in Ireland, set up a business and learn to speak English, and perhaps eventually go to America.

As well as Joseph, born in 1870, Dovid and Sarah had four other sons, Max born in 1871, Frederick in 1872, Ivan in 1873 and Solomon in 1874. Sarah, like all women of her generation, had miscarried or stillborn several children after that. The family was complete when a daughter was born in 1887, the year after they arrived in Dublin, whom they named 'Anna', not 'Anya', as she would have been in the Old Country.

For once, Sarah agreed with Samuel, insisting that they should all speak English, even in the home, until such a time as they were proficient. When she enquired from Dovid as to when he would start a business, he would answer, 'Ven I have goot Anglish, so I vill be understoot.' But when she was several months pregnant, she worried that soon there was going to be another mouth to feed and their only income was from their capital. 'Noo Dovid, don't you tink it's high time you started your business? You're not getting any younger, and soon all our money vill be gone. Don't you tink it's time already?'

Dovid and his older sons looked around their new city to decide on a business in which to invest their capital. They noticed that in Dublin, as in Riga, there were plenty of very poor people, whose children ran barefoot in the streets in all weathers. The rich merchants wore fine clothing and travelled in carriages driven by coachmen. Ladies of quality were seen in the better parts of the city, in the emporiums and bazaars that provided them with their finery. Dovid felt they could not compete with these established fashion houses, or with London and Paris, where often these ladies would travel to purchase their fashionable apparel. Then they learned that the wives of the soldiers garrisoned in Dublin, and housewives from north of the city's River Liffey, were always looking for new shops to supply them with the materials and patterns to copy the dresses of the rich. Dovid went to Samuel with this information and was amazed when Samuel said, 'So! I happen to have a small property in the High Street, near the Christ Church Cathedral. I vill let you have it for a small sum each veek. You can go vit me now to look?'

Joseph accompanied Dovid and Samuel to see the premises. Father and son both thought it would suit their purpose admirably. 'Of course, ve vill need to spend money to make shelves and some cupboards,' Dovid said to Joseph. 'A vindow vit shelves, de name over de door. So, Samuel, how much rent do you expect from your poor brudder, vit seven mouths to feed and no money, except vat ve managed to bring into dis Ireland? How much, noo?'

'Vell, to tell you de trut, Dovid, I could make a lot of money on dis fine property, but you are my brudder, my blood. So a bargain, tvelve und six per veek, and I'll get for you a handyman I know.'

'Are you *meshuga*? Mad?' said Dovid. 'For tvelve und six, I can rent a palace! Do you vant to see your nephews like de little kinder, de poor children of de city, vit no shoes, barefoot in de snow? Joseph, I esk you, talk to your Uncle, de big shot.'

Before Joseph could open his mouth to speak, Dovid brushed him aside and continued haranguing his brother.

'De place is all right. Vit hard vork, ve can do tings, but at tvelve und six! umpossible! At a farding here, a halfpenny dere, vere does a fortune like tvelve und six come from? I vill make you an offer, tree und six, and at dat ve vill break our backs.'

Samuel's eyes shone as he rose to the battle and, laughing, he said, 'Und you say I am a *meshugana*, a madman? You left your brains in Riga. Joseph, talk to your father, tell him I must also a living make, but for family, ten shillings. Take it or leave it!'

Joseph by now stood to one side as he realised he was watching a game with set rules and patterns. 'If ten shillings is for family,' said Dovid, 'tank God I'm not a stranger! Five shillings und I am cutting my troat at dat.'

'Oy yoy yoy, Dovid. Vat I vill do vit you? Okay, you vin! six und six und dis is final,' and he turned to walk away. So!'

'All right already, Samuel, I agree. Six und six, und if business is goot, I vill look for more shops from you, and now, vere is dat handyman?'

Joseph and his brothers were to witness many such scenes over the years, and later they learnt that both men knew that the figure was to have been six shillings and sixpence from the beginning, but the 'play' had to be acted out for the mutual enjoyment of the participants.

Chapter Ten

The next decade dealt kindly with the Minskys. Through determination and hard work, they made a success of their business. The house that Joseph had bought when he first came to join his Uncle Samuel in Dublin was now too small for the adult family. Early in 1896 Dovid came home and made an announcement. 'I have decided! Ve are moving to a bigger house. Ve can afford it now, and vit such big men, ve need more room. Anna is growing, and it is not good for a girl to have no privacy. I have a fine house bought on the South Circular Road. Samuel found for me a bargain. Und you, my Sarala, vill have a maid to help you like de fine ladies in Fitzvilliam Square.'

'You have decided,' said Sarah, bristling. The family saw the familiar signs of an approaching storm. 'You have bought a fine house? No doubt your brudder Samuel has made a profit somewhere? But I'm only your vife who vill have to live in it, clean it und look after it. I am not against a bigger house, but I vant the pleasure to see it first before you buy! Und, you have decided, I vill have a maid, noo? A *cutzpah!* A cheek! I vill have a maid ven I am goot und ready to have a maid, not ven your brudder Samuel says so.'

'But, *bubbula*, dolly, of you I vas only tinking. Vouldn't it be nice not to vash de dishes und peel de potatoes? Only of you I'm tinking Sarala.'

'Don't *Bubbala* me,' she said, giving him her famous stare. 'Tinking of me? Tinking of your own importance more like. So dis house is not goot enough for your lordship now? It isn't clean enough for you maybe? Vell I zuppose if you have bought and paid for this new house, I better take a look!' Everyone breathed again. Sarah approved of the house, and, at the good aspect of a new moon they moved in.

The South Circular Road, where the new house was situated, was near what was rapidly becoming a Jewish area of the city. There were several small synagogues in the area, and in Clanbrassil Street, shops selling kosher Jewish food. Large barrels of pickled meat, pickled cucumbers and salt herrings stood outside the shops, and the smells of spices in their jars, inside, brought an Eastern European village atmosphere to the neighbourhood. In the style of all villages, the gossip of marriages, births and deaths was relayed each day, as the women of the community lined up against the counters, jostling for position, to purchase what they needed to feed their families.

Sarah found that the work of cleaning and running the new house was too much for her on her own, and, as if it were her own original idea, she went to Dovid and declared, 'Right Dovid, dis is a big house, und a maid I vant!'

Nora Deignan was a fresh-faced girl of thirteen when she first came to work for Sarah Minsky. 'Now my girl, you vill have our Jewish vays to learn if you are to be of any help to me, und vat is more, you vill have to learn to do dem my vay, und I have to varn you, I am very particular.'

At first Nora was so flummoxed and scared that she finally went to Sarah, saying in her rough Dublin way, 'You know, Ma'am, there is so much, I'll never learn all of it if I live to be a hundred.'

'You vill my girl. In time you'll learn, und it vill stand to you ven you your own home have.'

'But many nights Nora went to bed and cried herself to sleep, not because she wasn't treated well, but because she was always so tired and felt so stupid. And even forty years later she could never understand the mad panic that filled the house each Friday in winter, to have everything ready before the Sabbath began. The samovar filled for tea, the food cooked for the next twenty-four hours, and the men shaved and ready for the Sabbath candles to be lit and blessed before leaving for the synagogue and evening service. 'For', as she said, 'yer God would not mind if I work. He won't strike me down for breakin 'yer Sabbath'. As Sarah had predicted, in time she did learn the Jewish customs, and even enjoyed the preparations for the various festivals, each with its special recipes. Unleavened bread for the Passover, honey cakes for the Jewish New Year, dairy foods for Pentacost and so many more. She looked forward to each new dish as her first year with the Minsky family passed. She even learned, although this took longer, to cope with Sarah's fussing and, more importantly, that 'urgent' and 'immediate' did not quite mean that. 'I vant you should know, Nora,' Sarah would say to her, 'orthodox Jewish vomens always strickly observe de laws of keeping de house Kosher. Ve do not mix de milk foods vit de meat foods in any form vatsoever. Since de days of Sinai, ve keep strict, only meaty food on its own, or only milky food on its own, at a meal. Derefore ve must also keep separate, in deir own compartments, all de utensils und pots und pans ve use to prepare und eat everyting. Of course,' she would continue, 've never, never eat de flesh of de pig, it is strickly forbidden. Nor do ve ever, ever eat fish dat has come from a shell.'

'God, Ma'am, you don't know what you is missin'.'

Sarah threw her hands in the air. 'Are you listening at all Nora or learning anything?' she said in exasperation.

Nora would nod, her eyes wide with wonder, fascinated by all she was hearing. 'God, Ma'am, aren't yiz great knowin' all dem tings. I don' know if I can remember it all, but sure all I can do is make mistakes.'

The fierce look of horror on Sarah's face at this made Nora quake in her boots. 'Mistakes! Oy vey, von mistake und ve have again to make everyting kosher. Now listen goot, my girl. Anyting, no matter how small, you are not sure about, to me you vill cum at vonce, and ask. Do you understand me clear?'

Nora also learned that what was done on other days was not done on the Sabbath, which began when the first star appeared in the sky on a Friday evening. There was no work performed by Jewish men or women, including the kindling of fire. Traditionally men attend service at the synagogue for worship on a Friday night, Sabbath morning and evening, the women only going if they so choose. The Sabbath concluded when again the first star appeared in the sky. Nora was taught that the holiest day in the Jewish calender was 'Yom Kippur', The Day of Atonement, on the eve of which all the family put on their finest clothes and went to the synagogue. The following day was spent there also, in total fasting, prayer and repentance, only ending when a ram's horn was sounded in a series of rhythmic notes. Most of the other Jewish festivals were joyous, when friends and family would visit each other to celebrate together.

After a year, a charwoman was employed to take some of the heavy work off Nora, which boosted her social image among her peers. On her days off, if she did not go home to her family, Nora would meet with girls from other houses, and she soon realised that in their eyes she was in a very superior household. Her mistress was considered a lady, who wore 'luvly' clothes and always looked like 'quality', when she went to do her shopping. Often, as she grew wise in the ways of the family, the boys first, then Anna, would come to Nora and ask her to intercede on their behalf with 'Ma', for they knew they had a staunch ally in her, who understood Irish ways. 'Janey Mac,' Nora often said, 'Dey wud be lost entirely without me.'

Sarah now found that, with the two women servants for the house, and another coming in to do the washing, ironing and mending, she had a lot more time to spend on herself, and instead of the utility sewing, knitting and embroidery she had to do in former years, she could now indulge in fine needlework for her own pleasure.

'My dear, I have decided!' announced Dovid one day, 'I am buying for you a pony und trap und hiring a driver, who can also the garden look after.'

'Vat, I esk you, vould I do wit a pony und trap?'

'How, I esk you, do I know vat vimmens do all de day,' said Dovid.

Sarah thought about it for a moment. 'All right already den, I suppose I can make visits to people und go to de important shops in town.' And she folded her hands in front of her and smiled in secret anticipation. In keeping with her new status and to swank to the other women, Sarah often took Nora with her when she went shopping in Clanbrassil Street. As most of the Dublin Jewish comunity were of Russian, Latvian or Lithuanian origin, there were several families who were related. Often one woman would call to another across a shop, in Yiddish, 'Had a letter from my sister in Akmenai . . .', or Riga, or some other town, '. . . she said your cousin will be leaving for America soon.' Or, 'I was so sorry to hear that your family were lost in a pogrom.' Or, very often, 'I am sorry to have to tell you I just heard from my mother that your nephew has been taken for the army.' Nora's soft heart often felt like breaking as she heard translations of these letters from the homeland, letters that were the lifeline with those left behind, nearly always telling of the suffering that was being endured and of the worsening conditions that prevailed for Jews in Russia.

Chapter Eleven

Dovid Minsky made many journeys to England, Scotland and various countries in Europe to meet with mill owners and lace makers in order to fill his shelves with silks, satins, bombazines and wool of the finest quality, as well as beautiful braids for trimmings. One such journey was scheduled for June 1899, to Bradford in Yorkshire, when Dovid fell and sprained his ankle.

The visit was important, as they were in the process of obtaining the exclusive rights for Ireland of a new weave. After a family conference, Dovid 'decided' that Joseph would go as his representative to the business house of Theodore Zucker & Sons.

Armed with letters of introduction, and lists of instructions on how to conduct all the business affairs, Joseph, at the age of twenty-nine, was permitted, for the first time, to make a business trip on his own. In previous years, he had either been a travelling companion for his father, standing on the sidelines during transactions, or he had been left in charge in Ireland during Dovid's absence. Joseph had never thought of questioning this order, his whole interest being in the finances of the company, planning ways to extend and enlarge their resources, including the acquisition of more premises in Dublin and now Cork, where his brothers, Max and Frederick, were settled with their wives. The business there had taken a new turn, and included 'Gentlemen's Ready to Wear'.

The train slowed, and Joseph lowered the carriage window by its leather strap. He put his head out as the train approached Bradford Station. He was pleasantly surprised to see Irving

Zucker, with whom he was acquainted, standing on the platform to meet him.

When he alighted, they warmly clasped hands, and Joseph was led to a waiting motor carriage, which whisked them at 15mph to the family mills outside the town.

After the purity of the Dublin air, Joseph found the smoke-laden atmosphere of the industrial town heavy and difficult to breathe. As always, he felt grimy and filthy from the moment of arrival, impatient to complete his business and leave the blackened buildings, drab northern landscape and sunken-looking people of that part of Yorkshire.

At the mill, Irving took Joseph to see his father, Theodore, and his brother Jacob. 'We are very sorry, lad, that your dad could no cume. Be sure to send ower best wishes for his speedy recuvery,' said Mr Zucker, shaking Joseph by the hand in a pumping motion. 'But we're right glad to see you.'

After eating a light lunch they took Joseph around the mill. He selected the materials as his father had instructed, albeit using his own judgement at times.

When their business was concluded, Joseph asked to be taken to his hotel. 'As yow'er on your own lad, we've taken the liberty of arranging for you to stay with us at ower home. It would be more comfortable for you to be with other Jewish people.' Joseph, though unhappy with this situation, did not wish to appear ungracious and thanked them for their thoughtfulness. If only, he thought impatiently, I could just sink into a hot bath, have a tray brought to my room, and quietly go through my order book and the arrangements for the transportation of the goods back to Ireland.

On his arrival at the house, Joseph was taken up to his room, which was spacious and comfortable. He bathed and dressed, and was ready when Irving tapped at his door to take him down to meet his mother and sister. As Joseph walked down the wide, thickly carpeted staircase, he felt a little oppressed by the heavily embossed wallpaper, which ran all through the main body of the house. The large arched hallway was filled with sombre Victorian furniture and paintings. He followed Irving into the vast drawingroom, where Mrs Zucker was sitting in state in front of a glowing fire, which, even on a June evening, seemed necessary.

'Mr Minsky, it is a pleasure to meet you, and welcume you to ower home. M'usband has spoke of your father. So unfortunate bout 'is foot.' Mumbling some suitable response, he was interrupted by Gertrude Zucker continuing, in her high-pitched voice, all in one breath, 'And 'ave you met ower daughter, Fanny? Fanny, see that Mr Minsky 'as summat to drink. I always say, a drink before dinner sharpens the appetite. Not wot my lads 'ave any trubble with appetite. You a good eater, Mr Minsky? 'nd 'ave you met my daughter-in-law, Irving's wife, Elsie?'

Much to Joseph's relief, at that moment a maidservant approached her mistress to say that dinner was ready. Gertrude Zucker stood up in a great hurry, and, rustling her way to the door, called over her shoulder, 'O dear, and you never did get your schnapps, Mr Minsky! Well, nowt to do about it now. We mustn't keep Cook waiting, must we?' And, keeping up an inconsequential chatter, this plump little woman, like a mother duck, led her family out of the drawingroom, across the hall, and into a very gracious diningroom.

During the meal, Gertrude, at whose right hand Joseph was seated, kept up a flow of banalities, at which he was only required to nod his head now and then, whilst he sipped the excellent homemade raisin wine from a delicate goblet. As the monologue continued, he began to realise why the rest of the family were eating in such detached silence, and the events of the day, and the fatigue he now felt, were quite soporific, and everything that was going on around him had a hazy air of unreality. He was suddenly brought back to his senses by a shriller exclamation from Mrs Zucker, as she said to the maid, whom for the first time he saw standing to one side of her shoulder, 'Oh, aye, show Mr Bacherim into the drawingroom, and say we will join him shortly. Isn't that nice Theodore!' she shrilled to her husband at the head of the table. 'Young Frederich Bacherim has cume visit us,' and turning back to Joseph, she laughed excitedly. 'Freddy is quite smitten by ower Fanny y' know.'

Joseph looked over at what had, up to now, been a shadowy figure across the table, and was quite startled to realise that Miss Fanny Zucker was a beautiful young lady, who at the moment was blushing, covered in confusion by her mother's tactlessness. He was further startled by the strange dart he felt as her black eyes met his own dark brown ones, in a mutual sympathy for the embarrassment to which they were both being subjected by the good-natured but impervious chatter of Gertrude Zucker, who now made the momentous declaration, 'We will take coffee in drawingroom. Fanny can entertain us with sum o' that poetry she learned at elocution school, which she attended to learn to speak like the toffs.' She rose, and, at this signal, the family left the table.

Chapter Twelve

Bradford
October 1899

Dear Mrs Minsky,

I hope this finds you, your dear husband, and your fine family, in good health. The last four months have been a whirlwind in our home. Your son Joseph has been arriving each weekend to see our only daughter Frances, woo her, and now become her betrothed. It is all so romantic. I know he has told you of this event, and Mr Zucker and I hasten to acquaint you with how delighted we are at the match, and, of course, Fanny will have a substantial nidan. *Joseph is a gentleman, never arriving without flowers for Fanny, and boxes of chocolates for us. Fanny has never looked so happy. As you know, it is every mother's wish to see their daughters marry successfully, and although Fanny has had her fair share of suitors, Joseph is the first one that she has chosen.*

And now I am going to be so busy making all the arrangements, as the chosan *and* calla, *bridegroom and bride, are so in love, they have decided to marry soon, possibly in June, after* Shavouth, *Pentacost, and then, dear Mrs Minsky, we will be one family. I am sure we will write to each other many more times, and have many things to discuss.*

Regards to your husband, Mazeltov, Mazeltov,
Your machateneste *to be,*
Gertrude Zucker

South Circular Road
October 1899

Dear Mrs Zucker,

You will forgive that I am writing to you in Yiddish, but my English is not so good for letters. I have received, through Joseph, the daguerreotype of your daughter, and I must say I think she is a pretty girl. Joseph tells me that she is as good and clever as she is beautiful. He too is very happy. Mr Minsky and I will welcome Fanny. We have hoped for so long that Joseph should meet a nice Jewish girl.

We too have been told the wedding will take place in June. It is a good time to travel, and not such a busy time for my husband and family to leave the businesses.

You will write and tell me what colour you are wearing. We shouldn't clash. Dovid sends his best to you and Theodore.

Mazeltov *to you too,*
Your nearly machateneste,
Sarah Minsky

Bradford
January 1900

Dear Mrs Minsky,

I hope this letter finds you all well, as it leaves us. Now that Chanucka *and the Gentile Christmas and New Year celebrations are over I can get down to* tachlas, *business, in my preparations for the wedding. It was no use before as the birth of the new century put every other event out of everyone's mind.*

I have booked the synagogue, and the hall, for June 15th, and Fanny, my daughter-in-law, and I have chosen our gowns. Mine will be wine red. Fanny asks me to ask your daughter, Anna, to be her chief bridesmaid. If she agrees, will you please send her measurements, and when she comes in June the dress will be ready for a fitting. This week I have an appointment with the caterers and the florist. My husband and I are presenting a new chuppah, *wedding canopy, to the synagogue, so your son and my daughter will be the first to be married beneath it. There is so much to do and so little time.*

Goodbye for now.

Best wishes from Theodore and Gertrude

South Circular Road
January 1900

Dear Mrs Zucker,

We are fine, how are you? I am sending you enclosed Anna's measurements. She is so excited to be maid of honour, and received the letter from Fanny asking her in person. She says it will be lovely to have a sister-in-law in Dublin. The others are in Cork city.

By the way, my brother-in-law, Samuel Minsky, has found a big house for Joseph in a good part of the city. Joseph will be bringing back the colours Fanny would like before it is decorated. They will stay with me for a few weeks while they buy the furniture, curtains, and all the fittings for the kitchen.

We are getting our gowns ready also. I have picked a nice shade of dark blue, which I have been told will complement your maroon.

All the best from the family in Dublin,

Sarah

Bradford
March 1900

Dear Sarah,

Thank God the winter's nearly over, and we can all emerge into the town again.

Thank your brother-in-law, Mr Samuel Minsky, for finding the house. Of course, Fanny, as I have said, will have a good nidan, *and we expect to pay for furnishing the house. I will come over and help her. I have now completed all arrangements where everyone will stay. You and Mr Minsky and Anna will be with us. Your brother and sister-in-law, and their son and daughter-in-law, will stay with my* machutan, *my daughter-in-law, Elsie's parents, Mr and Mrs Marcus Glazer.*

Joseph and his brothers, Frederick and Max, and their wives, will stay with Irving and Elsie, and your other sons will stay with Elsie's brother William and his wife Martha. Their little girls, Marcia and Zena, are the only other bridesmaids. They are six and seven years. As everyone lives nearby it will be very handy.

The colour of your gown sounds very nice. We look forward to meeting you soon, you, Dovid and your family.

Your machateneste *to be,*
Gertrude

Dublin
June 1900

My dear Gertrude and Theodore,

Well, here we are back home after all the festivities. What a wonderful wedding it was, and Fannila, bless her, looked like a princess. Dovid and I, and all the family, were very proud of her. Now she and my son are abroad, as you well know. You certainly have a good head for organising, Gertrude. Everything to the smallest detail you thought of, even in the shul *you thought to have flowers in front of the* chuppah, *the marriage canopy, and on the bimah. What an inspiration you had, lilac muslin for the bridesmaids, with cream roses for their posies to match Fanny's dress.*

I could hardly believe that the bride's gown was made in Bradford, by your dressmaker. It looked like a Paris model, which is where mine came from. Anna will get some good wear from her bridesmaid dress. I agree, the necklets and bangles I picked to give, from Joseph, to the two little girls and Anna, did look very good. Well Gertrude and Theodore, Dovid and myself, and all the mishbocha, *extended family, would like to say a big 'thank you' for all your wonderful hospitality to us. You need not have thanked us so much – it was a great pleasure to us, to send to all our hosts, the baskets of fruit and the chocolates.*

Well, I hope to reciprocate such hospitality to you when you come to Dublin to see our children. By the way, we have, as a surprise, my Dovid and I, sent to the house two large Persian rugs for the chosan *and* calla, *as our wedding present.*

By the way, you have a wonderful cantor, he sings like an angel. And also by the way, you and Theodore made a very handsome couple.

Best wishes from your now machateneste,

Sarah

Chapter Thirteen

Fanny and Joseph were married in late spring of 1900. After the ceremony, Gertrude and Theodore Zucker held a luncheon and afternoon tea dance for the wedding guests. Later in the evening Fanny's brother, Irving, saw them off, by train, for London, where they were to spend the first stage of their honeymoon, and from where they would travel on to Berlin and Vienna. In Berlin they stayed at the von Zeit Berliner Hotel, and in Vienna at the von Zeit Staad Hotel. Each day was filled with interest. In Berlin they went to see the famous galleries and museums, and visited members of the Zucker family, several of whom held receptions in their honour. In Vienna they attended the Opera, and were fortunate to see a special display by the Lipizaner Horses of the Spanish Riding School. They waltzed to the music of Strauss, and they took long, romantic carriage rides through the beautiful Vienna Woods.

Late one afternoon, returning to their hotel, the concierge handed Joseph a telegram. Taking it, with the feeling of apprehension that such envelopes always evoked, and moving closer to Fanny, he tore it open. Joseph's hand shook as he read the contents, and passing the slip of paper to Fanny, in a very slow and controlled voice he said to the concierge, 'We need to return to Ireland immediately, will you please make the necessary arrangements.' To Fanny he said, 'We must pack now. As you have read, my father is dangerously ill.'

The journey back to England, and thence to Kingstown, seemed to take forever. Fanny fancied that the rhythm of the wheels of the train repeatedly said, 'Let Mr Minsky survive, let him survive, dear God, please let him survive.' They changed trains at Preston, and continued on to Holyhead, where arrangements had been made for them to have passage home on the next boat departing for Ireland.

The funeral of Dovid Minsky had already taken place when Joseph and Fanny arrived in Dublin. They were met from the boat train, at Westland Row Station, by Joseph's cousin, Chiam Minsky and his wife, Ilsa, who took them directly to Joseph's mother's house on the South Circular Road.

There, a member of the Holy Burial Society met Joseph and, with a blade, made a small cut in the vee of his waistcoat, a ritual in which Joseph then tore it further, while repeating a prayer, thus symbolising the rending of garments in times gone by. Joseph went to his mother and, kissing her, in the traditional manner of such occasions, wished her 'long life', which she reciprocated. He then went to his sister, brothers and uncle Samuel, repeating the same words and actions.

Returning to his mother and holding her tightly, he broke down and sobbed bitterly. She comforted him as she had when he was a small boy, crooning '*Kindela . . . Kindela . . . Kindela . . .*' over and over, until his crying stopped. He then took his place next to his mother on the empty stool, which had been left vacant for him, as her eldest son, and held her hands, as if afraid she too would disappear from his life.

Ilsa now brought Fanny to express her sorrow to Sarah, Samuel and the other members of the immediate family. Sarah took Fanny's hands and said, 'I vish ve could velcome you to your new country in a happier time, but Got villed it dis vay, and dat's life! Oy, oy, oy vey! I cannot understand vy God should vant to take such a gut man so soon, a gut husband, a gut fader, a gut grandfader. So young. Never did no one a day's harm. Oy yoy yoy! vey's me're . . . !' And she wept bitterly, her daughter Anna trying to comfort her through her own tears.

Rabbi and Mrs Chanaan, who were present, spoke wise words of comfort, the rabbi adding a blessing, 'May the good Lord make his face to shine on you, and from now on there should only be *simchas*, happy events.'

Fanny was feeling very lost, and was grateful when Ilsa took her arm and steered her from the room. Ilsa Minsky, who had come from Germany to marry Chiam, only child of Samuel and Bertha, had also been through the difficult process of settling in to a new country, and, in her case, learning a new language. The similarity of their experience made her feel and show deep compassion for Fanny, who responded gratefully. A firm bond of friendship was established between the two young wives.

It was the first time that Nora had experienced the traditional Jewish seven days of initial mourning, Shiva, which is observed by Jewish people who have suffered the death of parents, siblings or offspring, in the tradition of Job. After the funeral, Bertha Minsky informed Nora that 'the mourners will sit on low stools, which will be sent to the house by the Holy Burial Society. You will cover the mirrors, so that the vanities will not be observed. The men will not shave, and a minimum of domestic duties will be performed by Mrs Minsky and Anna. Family, friends and acquaintances will visit the house during the week of mourning to console, converse and absorb the attention of the families away from their sorrow. Visitors will bring food to keep up strength and morale, so you, Nora, will not have too much extra work to contend with. Prayers will be chanted three times a day, in the presence of a "*minyan*" (ten men over the age of Bar mitzvah). The entrance door to the house is to be left open; all who wish to extend their condolences must be allowed to enter and give comfort. A traditional meal, on returning to the house after the funeral, consisting of hard-boiled eggs, bagels and tea, will be prepared and served to the mourners. I will arrange this. During the week you will not be required to make refreshments for anyone who comes to visit.' Nora crossed herself involuntarily and, eyes filled with tears, said, 'You can count on me, Ma'am. The master was a lovely man, very generous in his tips to me, and I will do everything I can to help the poor missus!'

The following year, 1901, a son was born to Fanny and Joseph, David, named after his grandfather Minsky. And the year after there was a daughter, Sybil, and two years later another girl, Hilda.

Chapter Fourteen

Fanny never knew quite how it happened, but she gradually fell out of love with Joseph. When they had been married twelve years and he suggested they no longer share the same bedroom, she could only feel relief.

Joseph spent more time at the Jewish Men's Club in Harrington Street, when he was not involved with his growing businesses, than he did at home. And although he dearly loved his children and was generous to them, not one of them felt as close to him as he had to his father, of lamented memory. They would always rush to Fanny with their childish troubles.

Fanny took pride in running her large home on the Rathmines Road. She was aware of the severe criticism of her mother, Gertrude, during her frequent visits, if matters did not meet with her approval. But Fanny listened and learned, for she took pleasure in knowing that her children were well cared for, and that her husband always had a well-starched collar, and well-pressed clothes, shining shoes and spotless spats.

She filled her days with charitable work within the community, always making herself available to see to the needs of the poor, whether it was to nurse the sick or to provide a trousseau for a bride whose family could not afford one. This was all done with the minimum of publicity, for to a Jew, charity which is boasted about is not charity of thought, word or deed. She was fortunate in having the wealth to employ good staff in her own home. Her amiable nature made her cook, maid and nanny loyal, until, in turn, they married, at which time they would train in a younger sister or cousin to take their place and continue the smooth running of the house. Joseph was proud of the way Fanny managed their domestic affairs, and their connubial arrangements did not interfere with their friendship. He followed her example, and he too became involved in communal activities, particularly in the management of the recently built synagogue in Adelaide Road, where he aspired, one day, to sit in the warden's box.

Ilsa, Chiam and their son Harold were frequent visitors on Friday nights, to celebrate the inauguration of the Sabbath. The candles were blessed by the woman of the house, bread, salt and wine were blessed by the man of the house, and the first of the three meals of the Sabbath eaten. Other members of the family also found a welcome on Fridays, and the house soon became the centre of such gatherings on High Days and Holy Days. Anna had married a cousin, who had come to Trinity College from South Africa to study and qualify in medicine. She now lived with him in Johannesburg, where her mother, Sarah, journeyed each year before Rosh Hashana in the autumn, and stayed until after Pesach in the spring. Sarah then returned to Dublin for the summer months.

Over the years there were many visits between the families in Cork, Dublin and Bradford, to celebrate a circumcision, or a Bar mitzvah. Chiam Minsky was now a well-established solicitor in the city of Dublin, and there were rumours that, one day, he would be elected to the judiciary.

These were difficult years in Dublin, years of unrest. Ilsa and Chiam came to the house in Rathmines one day to discuss an important decision with Fanny and Joseph. 'I have made up my mind to change my name,' said Chiam. 'I feel that Minsky is not one to sit well on the tongues of Gentiles. Especially if I am, as is expected, to be in a position of prominence.' After much discussion on how both Jews and non-Jews would react to this idea, it was decided that 'Charles Minns' would be a suitable compromise. Joseph was so taken with the idea that he too decided, 'as a cousin of a judge', that he would, henceforth, be known as 'Joseph Minns'.

Despite the disapproval of Samuel, Bertha and Sarah, as well as of Joseph's brothers, who felt that the name Minsky had stood them well, the legal formalities were concluded, and both the Chiam and Joseph Minskys were, by deed poll, now known as the 'Charles Minns' and the 'Joseph Minns'.

In 1907, several events of note took place in Dublin. The first Irish Motor Show was mounted in the Royal Dublin Society grounds, and several members of the family purchased new cars at the exposition stands. The 'Great Exhibition', an international event, was built on grounds between Ballsbridge and Donnybrook. Joseph Minns joined with other firms to organise an Irish stand, to display Irish wares. Returning home one evening he fascinated Fanny by telling her that he had actually seen King Edward and Queen Alexandra, although the weather had been so bad that he had not been able to stand for very long in the pouring rain.

Fanny went to the opening night of John Millington Synge's *Playboy of the Western World*, with Ilsa and Charles. She had been very frightened by the feelings of violence which the play seemed to arouse in the audience.

Chapter Fifteen

In 1913, the year of the big lockout of workers in Dublin, and of severe union unrest, David Minns had fast reached his thirteenth birthday, the age to make his Bar mitzvah, Confirmation.

The Sabbath morning on which he was to recite a portion of the Torah, the Jewish law, arrived crisp and dry. David, his father and grandfather Zucker, who had come with his wife and family to Dublin for the occasion, walked to the synagogue early in the morning.

From his vantage point in the front row at the side of the synagogue, David observed the large number of men who came regularly to worship on each Sabbath. Several times during the morning, he raised his eyes to the ladies' gallery, where he saw his mother, two grandmothers, sisters, aunts and girl cousins take their seats. They were dressed specially, and fashionably, in his honour, and for the occasion.

At long last he heard his name called, in Hebrew, to the reading of the week's portion of the law. 'Dovid, ben Yosef.' David, son of Joseph. As he mounted the steps to the elevated platform, in the centre of the House of God, from which the service was conducted, he nervously put his hand to his head to make sure his skull cap was in place. Standing in front of the large lectern, on which was placed the holy scroll from which he was to read, he settled his prayer shawl. Glancing from his father on one side of him to the Cantor on the other, who was holding a silver pointer to mark the passages, he touched the corner fringes of his prayer shawl to the scroll, kissed them and commenced.

His mother looked down anxiously at the slight figure of her son. She saw his pale face and large brown eyes, now so solemn, where normally they twinkled with mischief; his mouth, set now in a serious line, which usually smiled and showed dimples at the corners. She felt an agonising nervousness for David in case, in spite of all the practice he had had, he should now make a mistake. Knowing he was feeling the same, she offered up a silent prayer. Please God, help him through, and I'll give money to charity in your name. But she need not have worried. His voice rose pure and clear, well practised, confident and filled with all the emotion the ancient words evoked.

Outside, in the bright winter sunshine, he was wished '*Mazeltov*' and 'Good luck'. Many of the men said how proud they were to accept such a fine fellow, now a fully fledged male, into Judaism.

The family and their guests walked back home along the banks of the Grand Canal, to the luncheon that Fanny and Joseph were holding in celebration at their home. A toast was drunk to the occasion, to David's health and to his future.

The outbreak and duration of the First World War did not seem to impinge on the young boy, but the events in his native city in 1916 were a constant subject of discussion at the Protestant school which he attended, St. Andrew's College on St. Stephen's Green. At school, there was a division between those who said that an independent Ireland was just and deserved, and those who still upheld the rule of the British. David saw merits in both arguments, but his own sense of history and fair play swayed him in favour of his compatriots. He felt that were he from another familial background, he would take his place at the barricades, which stood the length and breadth of the city. He resented the fact that he should have to observe a curfew, and was not free to roam his city at will. But, he considered, if he were to rebel, it would put pressure on his community.

During his senior years at school he realised that, like his uncle in South Africa, whom he had met several times, and greatly admired, he too would like to pursue a career in medicine. In 1919 he sat the entrance exam to Trinity College, Dublin, and he and his family were filled with jubilation when he was notified that he had been accepted to begin his course in the following autumn.

BOOK III

Chapter Sixteen

At long last the Great War was over. Lady Matilde Barker-Grey and her young granddaughter, Charlotte Moore, had returned safely to Ireland in April 1919.

Despite all the years that had passed, it was very evident to Lady Barker-Grey that Michael Moore still mourned the death of his darling wife, Jessica. His elder daughter, Henrietta, had been of no real comfort to him, and he had been more than grateful when his mother, Florence Moore, had suggested that Henrietta should stay with them at Glenavon until Charlotte returned home. With Kit in France fighting, and Meg and Beth living in England, they were very lonely. This made it a little easier for Amy Philips to fulfil her promise to Jessica to stay and supervise the household, and for Nanny to look after the four boys, who at thirteen, twelve and eight, were very mischievous.

But now it was summer, the first summer of peace. They were all together again in Delahunt's Hotel, near Wicklow town.

When Ria had heard that Grossmutter and Charlotte were returning, she complained bitterly, and whinged continuously, to anyone who would listen to her. To Grandmama she said, 'I suppose Lotte will lord it over everyone, now that she is so experienced in travelling and living abroad. Well, I won't listen to her prattling on about her experiences. It's not fair that she was taken to Germany. It should have been me. I am the one who should have been taken. I am the eldest, and it should have been my privilege to go.'

'My darling girl, we all felt that your place was here with your father,' said Florence, 'and do remember that Lottie has been through a terrible war, an experience from which you have been saved. She was probably very frightened, and often hungry, and further remember, she did not have you, or the boys, or your father near her, to comfort her.'

'I don't care, I still say it's not fair. She has been away and I have not even gone, as planned, to stay with great aunt Olwyn and great aunt Bronwyn in Wales, and to attend mother's school.'

'Now Ria, I think that is enough. Be glad your sister and Grossmutter are safe.'

When she got no satisfaction from Grandmama, she turned to Nanny. 'Well, I won't share my things with her, Nanny. She probably has lots of gifts anyway! It's not fair, Nanny, she seems to get everything.'

'Now Miss Ria, don't you talk like that,' Nanny reproached her. 'If your poor dear mother was alive she would be most upset to hear you talk so, cariad.'

'If Mother were alive, this whole situation would never have arisen. She always treated me as the eldest.'

'That is enough, Miss Ria. Go this instant and attend to your studies.'

Amy was the most patient. 'You know, Nurse Philips, that little monster has had all the adventures, while I have been shut away in Wicklow with Grandmama, oversupervised, no diversions, with only lessons to occupy me and country bumpkins to mix with. No fun, no social outlets. It's not fair, it's not fair at all,' and she stamped her foot.

'You know, Miss Ria,' said Amy politely, 'you are growing up now, and if you spoil your face with such grumpy expressions, no one will want anything to do with you.'

Finally, finding no one to be as sympathetic towards her as she expected and needed, Henrietta vowed to herself that she would get away from them all as soon as she could, and do better than them, and then they could have their precious Charlotte. She wouldn't care if she never saw them again.

Chapter Seventeen

Charlotte lay at the edge of the water, the ripples of the sea lapping around her. Her brothers were playing on the sand, their shrill voices carrying to her on the light breeze. Henrietta and Amy were sitting in deckchairs, under an umbrella. Henrietta always sat in the shade, being afraid, like all redheads, that the sun would freckle her fair skin.

At fourteen, Charlotte was beginning to develop into a beautiful woman. Her long tanned legs emerged from her woollen swimsuit. She was young enough to defy the convention of the day and allow the exposed portion of her body to bask in the summer sun. She had learned, during her years in Germany, the value of a healthy mind in a healthy body. The physical freedom expounded by this philosophy suited her own freedom of spirit. She gave a sigh of contentment at the perfection of the moment. The sea spread out limitless in front of her, and she stretched her toes, as if trying to reach some unknown point beyond the horizon.

As she turned her head to the right, she could see other groups of people further along the strand, and further back again, the buildings of Wicklow town, outlined against the sun. To her left, there was more beach, and beyond, the railway station, and the beautiful Georgian building of Delahunt's Hotel, to which her family had been coming to stay, every summer, since her father was a child. In the early years, Jessica and Nanny had brought them, but now Nurse Amy Philips was in charge of all expeditions, as Nanny had become plagued with rheumatism and was finding it very difficult to move as quickly as was necessary to keep the twins out of harm's way.

Grandma Moore, or as her grandchildren called her, Gran, had initiated this annual month of the year with Michael's children at Delahunt's, the year following Jessica's death, as she felt that they needed some special attention. They all looked forward to being there, and the letters that had reached Charlotte in Germany during the war years, telling her of this idyllic month, had made her more homesick than she was already feeling. Now that she was back, she was fulfilling the promise she had made to herself during those years, 'I will love even Henrietta and, of course, my little brothers, and I will get to know them and be kind and gentle and patient with them.'

With Henrietta, this was proving to be more difficult than she had thought. They were so different. Henrietta was very cool and disciplined, her hair always tidy, her dresses pristine and uncrumpled, and her manners perfect, far beyond her years. While Charlotte, a hoyden, could never tame her wilful curls, or keep her skirts smooth, and her impetuosity was always getting her into trouble for blurting out her thoughts unasked, and often at the wrong moment. It was evident that Henrietta did not approve of, or welcome back this sister, who always stole the limelight from her.

Charlotte found the little boys much easier to be with. She was so filled with love herself that she could not fathom Henrietta's attitude towards her. Charlotte would gather the four boys, a twin in each hand, and an older boy holding the twins' other hands, and she would march them along the beach, and sit them in semi-circles around her, and drawing pictures in the sand, she would spin yarns to them, until their eyes would widen with wonder and shine with delight. They would clasp their hands, enthralled by this big sister, who would spend endless time with them like this. Or else she joined them in tumbling down grassy slopes, or helped them to ride their ponies, hoping they would become as proficient and as good at horsemanship as Uncle Kit had told her she was.

Florence Moore was happy to sit in the well-kept gardens on fine days, under the shade of the trees, or in the plant-filled conservatory on days when the weather was inclement. She never tired of watching the different moods of the sea, and could sit happily for hours, staring out to the horizon, her needlework or book forgotten on her lap. She wrote stories in rhyme for her grandchildren, illustrating them with amusing, mischievous sketches. On rainy days she kept the children enchanted by reading to them from these little books, and showing them the drawings, pointing out each child as she had depicted them. They would shriek with laughter when one of them was held up to gentle ridicule, and, on the other hand, hotly deny that it was them when the others laughed at some ridiculous pose or gesture by which they were easily recognised.

At the end of the month, the carriages came to Delahunt's to convey the holidaymakers back to Glenavon, where their cousins from the north and south of England would be joining them for the remainder of the summer. Grandfather Moore was there to welcome them back, and Michael was due to arrive the following week.

Michael, Beth and Meg enjoyed the long days spent out of doors together as much as their children did, and when they all played they would reminisce together, each savouring their particular favourite memory of an idyllic youth.

Lady Matilde did not join the family at Delahunt's, feeling that she should use the time when the children did not need her, to return to Wales, to visit with her sisters-in-law, dear Olwyn and Bronwyn. On her return to Ireland, she usually travelled directly from the boat at Kingstown, to Glenavon. She spent hours telling her host and hostess of all the many changes that had taken place in south Wales, of the new people she had met, and the sad news of friends who had passed on. Florence listened with politeness, and clucked and commented where she felt necessary. Henry

Moore, on the other hand, promptly fell asleep whenever Matilde began another Welsh saga, but she was so lost in recounting her memories that she never noticed.

Some of the grimness that had become part of his usual expression slipped away from Michael. His family noted that he was responding to their love, and looked younger and fitter than he had for some time. He even, occasionally, instigated outings and events, as he had in the past. Amy Philips found she could no longer put off approaching Michael Moore about Ria's resentment of Lotte, and one morning, finding him alone on the lawn, she spoke to him of what was worrying Nanny and herself. 'Thank you, Amy, we are lucky that you are so watchful. Now that you have appraised me of the situation I will take it from here.'

Michael had no idea what he could do to rectify the problem. Michael Moore, you are a fool, he thought. For the first time you are faced with a decision, and you have no idea how to tackle it. Jessica left me the sacred trust of our children, and I have abrogated it to others. My darling, I did not mean to let you down, but I have felt so lost without you to help me, and to be with me, and now, our first-born child is at a crisis in her life, and needs me, and I have not even been aware of it. Forgive me Jessica, I love them so much, not only because they are the expression of our love for each other, but because each one, in their own individual right, is precious. I did not even stop to think if it was the right thing for your mother to take Lotte away, or for me to send Ria to Glenavon. I have no real knowledge either of the boys and their needs. All I have done is pay bills and sign my name when necessary. O God, Jessica, what kind of man and father have I been! Now I don't know where to begin.

He walked along the paths of the woods and tried to put back some meaning into his life. When he returned to the house, he asked his mother and Matilde to join him in the drawingroom.

'Dear O dear!' said Florence Moore. 'I must confess that I took very little notice of her sulks. My goodness! Although now that you come to mention it, she made very little reference to Charlotte all the time she was abroad, but then, she is a child who keeps all her thoughts to herself.'

'It is not so much zat she keeps her soughts to herself,' observed Lady Matilde, 'It is zat our dear Henrietta has always been a little surly. I have often pondered on zis, and tried to sink from whom she gets zis trait.'

Michael and his mother exchanged glances. 'Yes I know,' murmured Mrs Moore soothingly, 'but for now, our concern must be how to address the situation at hand. Michael darling, will you allow Lady Matilde and me to try to find an equitable solution to this problem? I promise you that we shall.'

'No thank you, Mother, I will no longer avoid my responsibilities, we will work this out together. But I do feel that you, my dear ladies, with your experience and wisdom in such matters, will find a solution in a much more expert manner than I ever could on my own. Therefore, I will listen to your advice and counsel, and take all you say into consideration when I am making my decisions.'

Florence crossed the room and joined Lady Matilde on the window seat.

'Matilde, m'dear, the things that we three must now speak about and decide are not easy. Our beloved Jessica is not here to guide her eldest daughter through this difficult period in a young girl's life, the transition from childhood to womanhood, when the guiding hand of a mother is so vital. We, as her mentors, who have only Henrietta's best interests to the fore, who have a natural affection for this lovely child, must make the best possible decision for her future. On thinking everything over, I believe, through the years of Charlotte being abroad, Henrietta's most constant resentment was that she, as the eldest, had to remain in Ireland. Therefore she did not have the opportunity to be the first to travel, in particular, to attend Jessica's school in Wales, as had always been promised by her dear mother. Do you not think that if she were to go there now, it would help to redress what seems to Henrietta to have been an injustice?'

'I am shocked and grieved Florence', said Matilde, 'to hear of zis emotional suffering by my first, sweet granddaughter. I feel a little to blame, but I truly felt her place was wiz her fazer, and zat we would be home in a few weeks. Of course, Florence, you are zo right, to Wales she must go, and because of her age, she will only be zere a short while. Afterwards, Michael, I would suggest, she must also go to Switzerland or France, or bosz. I will write to my sisters-in-law in Wales at once, if zis meets with your approval. Zey must arrange to visit Henrietta often at ze school, and take her to zeir home as much as possible, for ze weekends. Oh, so much to do! We must send her equipped, as a young lady should be, and of course I insist, Michael, zat my estate shall pay all expenses zat shall be incurred. May we call ze child now to us and tell her ze good news?'

'Matilde, you are most generous!' said Mrs Moore, 'but I too would like to make some contribution. However, before we call Henrietta, should we not make sure that there will be a place for her at Pentylla Hall?'

'Zat will only be a matter of a letter, as my late husband's family have been patrons of ze Hall for many years, and several of his family have been pupils zere.'

'One moment,' said Michael, 'I appreciate your offers, but this is my daughter and I will be responsible for her schooling. Your suggestions are absolutely right, and if it is what Ria wants, so it shall be, but I don't want her to feel that she is being pushed away by me once again.'

Both women gave great sighs of relief that a solution had been found, and for a moment they all relaxed and looked out at the rose garden, bathed in late afternoon sun, before Florence went to summon Henrietta. When Ria was told of the discussion, a flush of excitement came into her normally pale cheeks, and she quietly said, 'Oh yes, please, please may I go!'

Two days before her departure to Pentylla Hall school, Henrietta sat in her bedroom in Priory House whilst Nanny busily packed her trunks, calling out to her to check the items on her list of belongings, which she would paste to the inside of the lids before they were closed and strapped for the journey.

Henrietta had spent several weeks being fitted out with new clothes to see her through the following year, and her fingers were sore from sewing name tapes to each and every garment, inner and outer. Although most of the items were made of serviceable materials, the girl felt a thrill when she looked at the three party dresses and their accessories, which she would wear for social occasions. She sat in a daydream, building castles in the air, thinking of her new friends who would invite her to their homes during the short school vacations. For Henrietta knew, with every fibre of her being, that she would not live out her life in the confines of Irish society. She loathed the house parties for the hunting, fishing and shooting seasons, and even more, hated the provincial musical evenings she had to attend on her rare visits to Dublin, when she would have preferred theatre and parties. She knew that, even the Aladdin's Cave interior of Minskys' emporium in George's Street, where they had made many of their purchases, was but a pale imitation of those she would see on mainland Britain, and later, in the capital cities of Europe.

She was rudely interrupted from these thoughts by Charlotte bursting into her room.

'Don't touch anything! Your hands are probably filthy from your precious pony!' said Henrietta through gritted teeth.

Charlotte looked at her sister with an air of assumed innocence. 'Don't be silly, *liebchen*, I washed them . . . look!' And she lifted a bundle of snowy white underwear and plonked them on her sister's lap. Henrietta controlled herself with great difficulty, knowing that soon she would be leaving, hopefully forever. 'I am glad, dear Charlotte,' she said, 'that finally you have learned what the combination of soap and water is used for. What do you want?'

At that moment, Charlotte's attention was drawn to the dressing table, and crossing to it, she picked up a silver hair brush and accusingly turned on Henrietta. 'What are you doing with

Mother's things? Put them back in her room at once! Nanny, tell her to put them back!' Two tears ran down her face in a mixture of vexation and upset.

'Cariad,' said Nanny, understanding Charlotte's distress. 'Your father gave them to her.'

'He had no right to, they belonged to Mother. I am going to tell Grossmutter,' and she went to leave, only to be checked by a laugh of triumph from Henrietta.

'Don't be a silly fool! Father felt there are some things that are special to an eldest daughter, and now a lot of Mother's things are to be mine,' and she held out her hand to show a golden and pearl bracelet that Jessica had worn every evening to dinner, and opened a box to show other trinkets that had also belonged to Jessica, but which were now hers.

Charlotte ran from the room before Henrietta could see any more tears. 'She is rotten and cruel. How could Father have done such a thing? I don't want anything to change any more . . . I don't! . . . I don't!' And she ran through the hall door, and continued running until she reached the gazebo on the hill, where she had always gone to hide and find peace, where the sunshine fell on the spiders' webs, spun, as she spun her dreams, dreams of always staying with father in Priory House, and one day, of being old enough to be Father's right hand, and greet his guests, and be hostess as Mother had been. To always be there to watch the boys grow, and to teach them all about horses, and the wild things that lived in the woods. Let hateful Henrietta have Mother's things. She would not have the gazebo, and Father. She at once felt comforted, as if by her mother's arms, and she took a solemn vow that she would never desert her family, but would be a rock for them to cling onto.

The next morning, being Sunday, the family all went to church to ask for a safe and happy future for Henrietta. There they were joined by Darragh and Joan Ryan, who, though not of the same religious persuasion, felt that they, as an adopted part of the family, would like to join in the prayers for Henrietta.

Reverend Acton, when he had finished his sermon of the week, gave a special blessing to Henrietta. 'May life keep you in God's path, and remember for always the righteous family from which you spring. Always bring credit to them.' He also mentioned how happy the congregation were to welcome Mr and Mrs Henry Moore, up from County Wicklow, and that Mrs Moore, formerly being a Miss Green from the locality, was always most welcome. 'I remember as a young man, being invited to Priory House, the 'Green' family home as it was, which was always as welcoming and gracious then, as it is today.'

As the family left the little church, Henrietta went to the vestibule where she had left a bouquet of flowers, and on her own, she went to the little graveyard attached to the church, where Jessica had been buried, and laid the flowers on her mother's grave.

'My dearest Mother,' she whispered, 'I miss you always, but especially today, as I go on the most important journey of my life. I truly wish I were more like you, and I will try to be. I will love your memory and honour you always.'

After lunch, for which Cook had made all of Henrietta's favourite dishes, the family, along with the Ryans and Actons, gave Henrietta small tokens of their affection to remember them by. Henrietta was excited by all this attention, though very dismissive of the hard work, and many hours, spent by the children in making their offerings, including the pencil case, so painstakingly sewn and embroidered by Charlotte, under the careful eye of Nanny. The box which Michael had helped the boys to make, to hold Henrietta's hair clips and ribbons, painted in their own individual style, was shyly presented, as were the bookmarks of canvas, threaded with coloured wools, that nurse Amy had watched the twins make, their tongues sticking out with their concentrated effort. Henrietta, however, was much more interested in the mother of pearl and ebony music box she had always admired in Grossmutter's house, which was now passed on to her, and the set of beautifully bound books of poetry from

Gran and Grandy Moore. The Ryans' gift, her very own writing box of Killarney work, was something she really did prize all through her life, and the Book of Daily Prayer from Reverend and Mrs Acton was to be a great comfort in the years ahead. Nanny presented her with a lace handkerchief that she had worked herself, admonishing her to use it on all social occasions, and to remember 'A lady always carries a handkerchief'. Amy gave her gloves, with a similar comment.

Michael then stood in front of her and said, 'I have given you things that are your right, which belonged to your dearest mother, so that they will be a reminder of her gentleness and goodness, and so that you may emulate her. But now I wish to give you something that is new, and therefore yours alone.' He took a small box from his pocket and handed it to her. She opened it and found inside a fob watch, and turning it over she read 'To my darling daughter, Henrietta'. Reading this moved Henrietta, and for the first time in many years, she felt that perhaps she was loved, and with the only impulsive action in her life to date, she flung herself first into her father's arms and then ran to each of the others and thanked them warmly for their gifts, and kissed them. The boys blushed with embarrassment, but looked proud that Ria seemed so pleased with their efforts. Florence Moore was happy that Charlotte was included. Charlotte, who had been wondering could Ria have pretended to like her gifts, changed her mind when she saw the girl's gesture, and felt that perhaps it was nice to have a sister, even if she was frightful at times!

Chapter Eighteen

In the autumn of 1918, when Henrietta had left for school in Wales, Charlotte was enrolled at the Alexandra School for Young Ladies in Earlsfort Terrace, Dublin, situated opposite the recently opened National University of Ireland, an establishment for young Catholic students, who were forbidden by their Church to attend the Protestant Trinity College Dublin.

Every Monday morning Charlotte would travel by train to Harcourt Street Station, and come home by the same route every Friday. Michael had taught Eamonn to drive the motor car, and he would leave her at the station and collect her in it each week. The smell of Cook's baking which greeted her at weekends was one of the memories that sustained her through many stormy times in the years ahead.

Charlotte made friends easily. She had a special chum, Constance Wall, who was an awkward, mousy, bespectacled young woman with a serious turn of mind, who hung onto every word and gesture of the vivacious Charlotte. Nobody could understand the friendship between them, but the two girls, so different, could be seen, heads together in a corner of the assembly hall, or passing notes to each other and giggling. Charlotte was invited to join some of the extracurricular activities, to which she loyally and resolutely brought Constance. Charlotte had the wit of both grandfathers, which made her a leading light in the Debating Society. She excelled at all sports and soon was a permanent member of the school hockey and lacrosse teams.

'You know, Amy,' she said over and over, 'I find my life stimulating and happy. Weekends at Priory House, devoted to father, Grossmutter and the boys, and during the week, school and my friends.'

Little by little the family heard about her years in Germany, and the cousins they had only seen when Owen and Darragh were very small, and before the twins were born.

'Soon after the war started, it became clear that Grossmutter and I would be unable to return to Dublin. It was then decided that the whole family should move to the von Zeit schloss in the mountains. You could never believe how cold it was in the winter, and how much snow there was everywhere. Sometimes it was up to your knees, and even though we wore big boots, with heavy alpine stockings underneath, our feet would pain so much with frost that it made us younger children cry. There were huge fires everywhere, burning half a small tree at a time. But the rooms were very big and high, with lots of windows, and at nights we had covers made from fur on our beds over thick eiderdowns to keep us warm. Great Aunt Hannah was very unhappy there because, Grossmutter said, the news of the war was slow to get through to us, and she was always worried and afraid about Great Uncle Otto and her son Rudi, who were in the army, and also for her daughter Ava's husband, Hyman Urbach, who was in the navy. Finally, Uncle Otto came back, although we were shocked to find he had lost a leg at one of the battles and had been in a hospital for several months. Then the other two men arrived together one morning, without any warning. You never heard anything like the shouting and crying and laughing. Immediately a large party was organised to celebrate, and Uncle Otto made a speech to say how grateful he was to have been spared, and that the family as a whole had been more fortunate than many, for, even now, distant relatives were losing their lives in the revolution that was going on in Russia, and we must pray for them. Then Grossmutter made a speech, in which she thanked everyone for being so kind to me, and to her, and looking after us so well, and she said she sincerely hoped that the Great War had really been a "war to end all wars". And I remember looking out my window that night, and seeing the moon shine on the snow, and thinking that all of you here would see the same moon.

'But by now the roads had become too bad to travel back to Hamburg, and we all had to stay in the mountains. I learned to ski on the higher slopes. I felt sorry for Uncle Otto that he could not join us, for I was told that he had been very good on skis before he lost his leg. But he did go hunting on horseback through the forested slopes, and often came back with wild game for the table. He spent a lot of time with Ava and Hyman's children, his grandchildren, our second cousins, Renata and Ernst, and of course I was included always. At last the weather improved . . . and the rest you know.

'Father, it is awful. They are so fine. I will never be able to think of Germans as the enemy. I do love our family and friends there. Why should it be this way? Why can't people see the good in each other, and live in peace, and see all the beauty in the world?'

Michael tried to explain that sometimes events happened that were beyond understanding. 'People are greedy. They are poor, and live in poverty, and this breeds envy, and plays a large part in human unrest. I know these are concepts that are, as yet, beyond your comprehension, and I hope your intrinsic values will remain as they are.' Though he doubted it, as life had a way of sullying that which was pure.

Charlotte found her father's words comforting, even though she did not fully understand what they meant. Putting her own feelings into words to herself, she thought, 'I am content now to be the eldest at home, and Father talks to me about everything. I know Henrietta would never have been able to respond to, and understand him as well as I can, and whenever Father needs me I will drop everything else, and go to him, for a man needs a woman by his side. Besides, although men are leaders in the world, at home they would be really quite helpless if they did not have women to run things, and make the home comfortable for them. It is all right for them to come back when they have been away at meetings, and commerce, and other pursuits, but they are useless at anything domestic. We women are much better able to organise, and to be there to talk to, and give them their good ideas in the first place.' Thus, having worked out her scheme of the roles of men and women, she set about preparing herself for her future, as she saw it.

Lady Matilde found in her a willing pupil, eager to learn all the social skills and keep up her fluency in the German language by speaking it when they were together. She felt that Constance Wall, whom the family had met on several occasions, was a good influence on her.

Nanny was puzzled, but pleased, that her little tomboy was trying so hard, though not always successfully, to be tidy in her habits, and in her appearance, brushing her unruly locks until they behaved for short periods, brushing her skirts of all spots and stains, and generally attending to her grooming. Amy also found her willing to take an interest in all household duties, and to amuse the boys, and to be with them, when she was at home.

At fifteen, her world was almost complete. She felt secure in the love showered on her by her family, and she in turn made every effort to please them, so that they would know how much she loved them. In school she had the special friendship of Constance who, also living in Dublin with her own family, fully understood Lotte's devotion to everyone at Priory House.

All her life, Charlotte had been bringing small animals home to nurse back to health. A bird with a broken wing, a puppy with a sore paw, and once, a cat which had lost an eye in a fight. So it caused no surprise when she came home from school one weekend with a petite girl from her class, whose home was in the west of Ireland. 'And Nanny, she never goes home for the weekends, and has to stay at school with the teachers . . .' said Lotte, by way of explanation.

The school had been in touch with Mr Moore to see if Charlotte had his permission to invite guests. They explained that Mrs Bailey, the girl's mother, had agreed that, should such an invitation be extended, and if it met with the teachers' approval, their daughter might accept.

'So here we are,' she said to Amy, when they were deposited by Eamonn at Priory House. 'My very dear little friend from school. I like her very much, and so will everybody else! Where are the boys?'

'In the orchard with Seán, picking the last of the apples and pears.'

She grabbed her friend by the hand, and before Olive knew quite what was happening, she was running across a yard, down a hill and into an orchard. As they pulled up and looked around, they saw no one, and Charlotte called out 'Hello-o-o, yoo-hoo!' and was greeted by a chorus from the tree tops. 'It's potty spotty Lotte! Potty spotty Lotte! Yoo hoo hoo-o-o!', and four figures dropped to the ground in front of them. 'You beasts!' said Charlotte, 'You know I have no spots, and yes, I must be potty to love a lot of rascals like you. Meet my friend, Olive Bailey. Olive, meet the four worst-behaved boys in all of Ireland. Owen, the eldest, Darragh next, and then the terrible twins, Laurie and Jimmy. The two dogs jumping all over us are Finn and Oisin,' and she patted the two red setters, stroking them affectionately.

Eamonn appeared with empty baskets he had fetched on his way to join in the harvesting. 'Come on Master Owen, don't be standin' dere gawpin',' he said, seeing the young boy hanging back. 'Bid yer sister's friend welcome, or has the cat got yer tongue?' At Eamonn's instruction, Owen David Moore wiped his hand on the leg of his knicks and extended it very formally to Olive. The other boys followed his example.

Before anything more could be said, Charlotte challenged them all to a race back to the house, where she knew that Michael and Grossmutter would be waiting.

It was the first of many such weekends for Olive Bailey, who was a little dark-haired girl, with enormous black eyes and a deluge of freckles over her tiny, turned-up nose.

Priory House buzzed each weekend. Charlotte and Olive arrived on Friday afternoon, and often, on a Saturday, Constance, or one of the other girls would come to tea or supper, or stay overnight. On many of these occasions Charlotte would include one of the poorer girls who, coming from genteel families that could not afford the fees, were in the school on grants or charity. She always made Constance responsible for seeing that they were put safely on the train to Blackrock, or that she accompany them. Charlotte, Constance and Olive, so different in appearance and temperament, soon became known as 'The Terrible Three'. A title, if truth be told, that at times they richly deserved. They became the ring leaders of most of the escapades schoolgirls commit, often being sent to the headmistress to be punished for 'conduct unbecoming to young ladies'. It was only that each of the three was a good student, that saved them from a more rigorous form of discipline, and even expulsion, for some of their more daring exploits. Constance was particularly assiduous in her studies, as she had ambitions to go on to Trinity College and pursue a degree, which would enable her to be financially independent and thus free to lead her own life. Charlotte thought this a wonderful idea and she decided that when she had finished her course at Alexandra College, she too would go on to university. Olive felt left out of these plans, as she knew that such ideas were not to be thought of for her, as her family's finances would not stretch to providing third-level education for a girl – her brothers' education would be given priority and she would have to earn her living.

Nanny began to wonder why, on a Friday, she never had trouble in making Master Owen wash, and brush his hair, and she even caught the whiff of Mr Moore's hair pomade. Michael Moore, who had caught the same scent, smiled, suddenly remembering the first time he had been enamoured of a young lady, the joy and the pain that such emotions brought, and, a little sadly, he acknowledged that his eldest son was reaching the end of childhood, and that he would have to consider plans for his further education.

Chapter Nineteen

The topic of conversation in diningrooms, sittingrooms and kitchens all over Ireland in the winter of 1919/20 was about the difficult times Ireland was going through. Henry Moore, one of the sitting MPs for the county of Wicklow, travelled to Dublin for meetings much more frequently than he had previously. He and Michael talked for many hours about Éamonn de Valera, Michael Collins, William Cosgrave and all the other members of Sinn Féin, who seemed hell-bent on achieving independence from British rule, and in Ireland becoming a Republic.

In March 1920, Michael's brother Kit returned to England from the front in France. The following month, on his way to Wicklow, he broke his journey in Blackrock to see Michael, who felt that the return of his only brother, safe and sound from the war, should be marked with a celebration. Michael enrolled Lady Matilde to organise a dinner party, to which friends and neighbours, as well as some of his father's political friends, should be invited. Now that hostilities had ended and the economy was improving, Michael had sold some patents, and that, along with a slight increase in his income from Glenavon, made him feel that just this once the extravagance of a party was justified.

When she heard of the event, Charlotte begged that she and Olive should be allowed to attend their first grown-up dinner party.

'Please, Father. We are old enough now, so do say we may come.'

‘ Yes, I think that the occasion is appropriate, Charlotte, and what is more, Owen shall be included also.’ Michael seemed greatly pleased with his decision.

The house was busy for days beforehand. Extra staff was hired, both for the kitchen and to serve at table. Cook and Lady Barker-Grey discussed the menu. ‘Ma’am, how about some home-honeycured ham and quince jelly, beef broth and wheaten bread, haddock puffs and tartar sauce. Me speciality, roast spring lamb, and I’ll stuff a couple of capons for them that won’t take meat. We can have braised onions, carrots, boiled potatoes, mint sauce from the store cupboard, and, of course, the gravy from the roast. Then, queen of puddings and caramel sauce,’ said Cook. ‘And, if they’re not satisfied, they can have preserved plums, and pears, and vanilla custard.’

‘I sink zat sounds very nice, Cook. Quite adequate, and also, zere will be nuts and fruits to be put on ze table, along with ze cheese. Wines, dry white, and a light red. Madeira with dessert, I sink. Port and brandy afterwards for ze gentlemen to have wiz zeir cigars. I will consult wiz Mr Moore about ze wines and spirits. I have written it all down now, and will make a copy for you. Sank you, Cook.’

Charlotte drove them all to distraction, even Amy’s patience was sorely tried the weekend before the party, with her fussing about her dress. ‘It is, after all, my first grown-up party, and everything must be perfect.’ Exasperated beyond endurance at her teenage self-absorbtion, both Nanny and Grossmutter had to tell her to behave, that the party was for Uncle Kit, and not for her, and would she please remember that, or she would not be permitted to attend at all.

Lady Matilde raided the flowerbeds and shrubs, and filled the house with sweet-scented lilacs, and bowls and bowls of golden daffodils. The tables were splendid with newly laundered linen, fine silver, and crystal stemware. The epergnes were filled with lily of the valley, and ferns from the nearby woods. Michael went to his cellar, and having selected his bottles, watched as Eamonn filled the decanters from them. Amy saw to it that fires were lit, and with their subtle glow, and the homely aroma that the turf sods and logs of wood sent out, the entire effect was welcoming on that special April night.

The guests had assembled in the hall. Ita took their cloaks and Eamonn handed trays with glasses of preprandial drinks to each one, as they arrived. Michael greeted them, and introduced Kit to those whom he had not previously met, whilst the family gathered around him, outdoing each other in their eagerness to welcome him home.

Michael stood a little to one side, his usual glass of whiskey in his hand, as the guests mingled. It had become his habit to do so at social gatherings since Jessica had died. He watched Joan and Darragh Ryan, Reverend and Mrs Acton, neighbours Major and Mrs Townshend, cousins of Mrs George Bernard Shaw, who often partnered Lady Matilde at whist, the late Colonel Fitzgerald's son, Willie Fitzgerald, and his sister, Blanche, a young woman who had rather a reputation for being sympathetic to the women's suffragette movement, and Mr Seamus O'Byrne, the second Member of Parliament for Wicklow. Michael's own cousins, Eleanor and Anne, and their husbands, Dr George Watson and Mr Roger Campbell, had also arrived. Kit's friend, Kevin Carey, and his sisters, Kathleen and Moira, with whom Kit had grown up in Wicklow, were among those present.

Lady Matilde whispered in Michael's ear, 'Everyone is here now. Cook is anxious for dinner to commence before the food is spoiled.'

Michael answered, 'Of course, we will go in at once. I will instruct Eamonn to sound the dinner gong.'

Lady Matilde made her way up the stairs to where the three children were waiting to be summoned. Lotte, predictably, was fuming and stamping her foot with impatience, saying that she could not fathom why they had had to wait for the gong, and, that they could easily have gone down earlier, as if they wanted those silly drinks anyway! Nanny gave them a final check to see that everything in their dress was perfect. With a last injunction from her, to mind their manners, they accompanied Lady Barker-Grey down the stairs.

As she entered the familiar diningroom, Lotte was unprepared for its transformation. She could not remember how it had looked when her mother had entertained. The lustre of the room, and the luminosity of the table, filled her with enchantment. Through the firelight and the candlelight, she saw the assembly in a nimbus as she slipped quietly into her seat between Olive and Mr Willie Fitzgerald.

Mr Acton said a short grace, and Matilde signalled to Eamonn to pour the wine. The first course was already on the table, and Michael, as host, commenced. The company, following his example, also began to eat.

Eamonn, making his way around the table, caught snatches of conversation. 'The little shop in Dalkey is going very well now,' Mrs Campbell was saying, 'I never realised so many people needed buttons, zip fasteners, needles and threads, and now that I am keeping some of their patterns, *Vogue* magazine is being sent to me, and I must say, the clothes they show are very exotic.'

'Oh!' Matilde replied, 'my sisters-in-law have been sending me a copy each month since it was first published in 1916. Had I known you would have been interested, I should have given them to you.'

'Then, my Lady,' said Mr Campbell, 'You will appreciate how my commodity, ladies' stays, have improved. And how, if you will pardon the subject at the dinner table, these new-fangled brassieres will revolutionise the whole industry. What was that for?' he said, looking at his wife, who had kicked him under the table, while she blushed with embarrassment.

At these remarks, a total hush fell, which Mr Moore quickly broke by asking Kit, 'Did you come across our own local seanachai, Willie Duffy, in France or Flanders?'

'Indeed I did, Sir,' said Kit. 'He was organising everything in sight out there, as if he had never left the banks of Lough Dan. Ballad singing and step dancing. He should get a medal for personally shortening the war by scaring the Bosche with both the wailing of his uileann pipes, and the roars from the football matches he organised.'

'I would like to return to the topic of ladies' undergarments,' said Blanche Fitzgerald, breaking into the general laughter that followed Kit's story. 'Why should we be trussed up like a Christmas goose? We women are harnessed from all sides, either being a domestic drudge, or a pretty ornament, never given credit for intelligence, or an ability to meet men on an equal footing. It's time we were set free, from stays and everything else.'

'I am sure you are right my dear,' said Mrs Moore gently, 'but perhaps we could postpone the discussion for some other time?'

'No, Mother,' said Kit. 'Miss Fitzgerald has a valid point. I have just returned from a war about freedom, and seen men lose their lives to preserve it, and women risk theirs to care for our wounded. These women saw more horrors in a day than most men see in a lifetime. Freedom is a most precious possession, and we in Ireland should know that better than most. I know you agree, Kevin.'

'Look here, young man!' bellowed Major Townshend, 'I also fought for king and country, and feel that I too have a point of view, and the right to express it. This land, this West Britain, has benefited from the protection of England, and now Ireland is showing its ingratitude, and biting the hand that feeds it.'

The ensuing silence was like a blanket, almost palpable with emotions of discomfiture, anger, frustration and aggrievance, until very slowly and quietly, Mr Thaddeus O'Byrne said, 'Major, Sir. Yours is the attitude that has brought this Ireland to its present pass. You, and all like you, have been so concerned with the glory of your Protestant England, you have forgotten that the Catholic Irish are a much older people, a people who have fought for you in your wars, who have starved to provide wood and grain for your ships and armies, and who have been degraded, ignored and belittled in this their own country, by the oppressive yoke of English imperialism.'

'Gentlemen,' said Lady Matilde, 'perhaps politics can be reserved for your port, when we ladies have retired to ze drawingroom,' and turning to the Misses Carey, she enquired, 'Are the hens laying well in Wicklow zis season?'

'I don't see why they should wait until we ladies leave. We can think, and we have opinions, in Wicklow or anywhere else!' burst in Blanche Fitzgerald. 'But oh, Mr O'Byrne, do not lump all Protestants together. Some of us are Irish first, and care beyond all else for our country and its poor benighted people. We are ready to join, or lead, like Mr Parnell, our compatriots, to raise our flag on the highest pole possible. Don't try to stop me from saying what I must, Willie dear!' she snapped at her brother, who had been making signs at her to calm down.

'I must beg your pardon for abusing your request, my dear Lady Matilde,' said Mr Moore, 'But I feel that I must make some response to my co-parliamentarian, Mr O'Byrne, in the interest of fairness. I am on record in the House for promoting the ideals of a more Irish point of view being regarded at Westminster, as well you know. But I really cannot go along with the seditious views you have just expressed. The English have made many mistakes in Ireland over the centuries, but that is just what they were, honest mistakes, which any fair-minded Englishman would wish to see righted. But we must march slowly. A tidal wave would swamp any progress that has been made. I must ask you, Sir, to apologise to my son's guests for your intemperate language, and for forgetting how much has been accomplished for Ireland by having England's protection, commercial outlets and legal system.'

At this, Dr Ryan leaned forward, and in a hesitant voice said, 'Because of our great friendship, Michael, it grieves me, especially on this joyful occasion, to have to say that Mr O'Byrne owes neither Joan nor myself any apology. My own good fortune in life has not blinded me to the history of poverty and suffering of my co-religionists in this once wealthy land. Whilst I am pledged to save life, and will not take up arms, I am also pledged to see that this nation will march forward, further into the twentieth century, able to carry its head high, with learning and courage.'

'Please, gentlemen,' said Reverend Acton, 'we are trying to resolve our differences in peace. In the name of God, who guides us all, irrespective of creed, let us leave politics for now, and I propose we raise our glasses, and drink to the return of our neighbour, Kit, and couple it with a prayer for harmony for all who live on our fair island.'

The assembly rose, and saluted Kit, who, in response, thanked Michael, said how proud he was of his beautiful niece and her equally lovely friend, and that he hoped to get to know his nephew a lot better over the coming years.

The ladies then retired to the drawingroom, and no one noticed the looks that were being exchanged between the hired servants. But Eamonn, during the tragic events of a year later, was to remember a conversation he had overheard in the kitchen passage later on during that same evening.

Chapter Twenty

In 1921, on a clear May night in County Wicklow, a band of men gathered beneath newly leafed trees at the edge of a large estate. The spring breeze brushed through the long grasses and scuttled the wispy clouds over the waning moon. As the dark hours before dawn approached, the men crept forward, and, breaking into the servants' quarters, which had been left unlatched for them, gagged and carried out the faithful retainers, before setting fire, with coals from the ever-burning ranges, to the piles of brushwood they had brought with them and now placed strategically around the hallways and stairs. The fire crept along the rush mats and attacked the wooden floors and doors. Soon the rugs and curtains were smoking. The acrid smoke crept through the cracks in the ceilings and was fanned into flames by the breeze blowing through the windows. The arsonists waited until they saw the flames engulf the upper storeys, then they left, confident that no house could survive such a conflagration.

This was a scene that was repeated that year in every county in Ireland, where property was destroyed, annihilating forever a glorious legacy for the future. Warnings were always given, so that life was not endangered. On this occasion, however, the staff, lying trussed and gagged on the lawn, were unable to tell the attackers that the family was still in the house, that this year they had decided not to make their usual trip to Dublin for the Spring Show. Had the IRA volunteers waited by the burning house in Wicklow, they would have seen one lone figure crash through a window and land on the ground beneath, to lie silent and still.

The local constable, who was cycling to his work at the police station, saw in the distance the unusual light in the sky. He quickly made his way over the fields towards the house, and jumped off his bike when he discovered the bound servants. He quickly untied them and sent a young lad to fetch the farmhands, and hosepipes. Duffy, the butler, as soon as he was free, ran to the figure he had seen coming through the window. It was Mr Kit, who was thankfully still alive. Duffy bellowed to a maid to send for the doctor. By now, it had become apparent to those who were left to witness the devastation, that no other members of the Moore family could have survived.

Michael Moore was working at his desk in his study when Eamonn came in to tell him that Mr Carey from Wicklow was here to see him.

'Oh! show him in Eamonn, and please ask Cook to send in a tray with coffee for two.'

The door opened again, and Kevin Carey entered. Michael rose and held out his hand in greeting. 'How nice to see you Kevin, all well at home? Are you up for the Show?'

'Michael,' said Kevin, his face grey. 'There is no easy way to tell you what I must.' He hesitated for a moment, then before he lost his courage, went on. 'Glenavon was targeted last night by the IRA. Your father, mother, Beth and her two little girls, perished in the fire. Kit was badly hurt jumping through a window, but he is alive. He has a number of burns, and both his legs are broken. The servants were let out by the 'lads' beforehand, but the dogs had been drugged. The horses in the stables were badly burnt, and the vet had to destroy them. Jesus Christ, Michael, I am so sorry . . . I am ashamed betimes to be Catholic and to see what is done in the name of Mother Ireland.'

Michael stood stunned and silent, as if unable to absorb the news. Kevin became frightened by his silence and shook him by the shoulders. 'Did ye hear what I said, man?' he shouted into Michael's face, 'Your family in Wicklow has been murdered, even though they weren't meant to be at home, but in Dublin. It was a mistake. D'ye hear me, it was a mistake. Talk to me, will ye?'

'Did you know it was going to happen, Kevin?'

'God, no, on me honour. D'ye think I would have stood by and let them do it if I had?'

'The bastards. O dear God! my poor family. O God, I can't bear to think of it. Their poor bodies burnt.' And he put his head into his hands as if to shut out the picture he had conjured up.

Eamonn came in with a tray at that moment, and quickly Kevin explained the situation. 'I'll send for Dr Ryan. The master will need a friend,' said Eamonn, leaving the two men.

Michael lifted his head, and in a voice filled with hate, and eyes cold as ice, pointed to the door. 'Go, Kevin. Go back to Wicklow and tell those who are responsible for this black deed that they have not heard the last of it, that good, caring families cannot be murdered in their beds, and the perpetrators get away with it, no matter what the cause.'

Kevin took one look at his lifelong friend, and saw that it would not help now to try and argue the matter. Taking up his hat he left the house, uttering a silent prayer to the Virgin to comfort the tormented soul he left behind.

By the end of the day all the family had been notified of the tragedy. Henrietta, Beth's husband Arthur, and Margaret and her husband Bert, were now all on their way to Ireland. Michael had gone to Wicklow, accompanied by Darragh Ryan, to be with Kit, who had been brought to the local hospital for surgery. They then went together to one of the cottages, where the remains of the victims had been taken. Their bodies had already been sewn into their shrouds, being unrecognisable after the carnage of the fire.

Michael wept unashamedly, and the loyal workers from the estate stood by, caps in hands, and hard men though they were, they too had tears for the gentle lady, kind master and their lovely daughter and her little girls.

Amy had contacted Charlotte's school and asked that the girl should be told the terrible news as gently as possible, and then be accompanied home by one of the teachers. When the news was broken to her, Charlotte looked at her headmistress in disbelief and said, 'They can't be dead . . . they can't have burnt Glenavon . . . I would have known . . . I would have felt it! Please say it isn't true. Please! Please, please!' And she burst into tears, her shoulders shaking with sobs.

'I am sorry, my child,' said Miss Pollock. 'I only wish it were not true. Miss Scott will help you get ready and go with you to Priory House, where Lady Barker-Grey is waiting for you.'

When they heard the news, Constance and Olive were stunned. They tried to comfort Charlotte, but for once she did not seem to want the presence of her two closest friends. They realised she was too distraught to act rationally, and so they remained quietly in the background, in case Lotte should need them.

At Harcourt Street Station, Miss Scott left Charlotte on a seat while she purchased their tickets. Charlotte was in a daze. Between her uncontrollable sobbing and her unfocused thoughts going round and round about the incredible events that had taken place, she was unaware of her surroundings, and of the people who glanced in her direction. In particular, a handsome dark young man who hovered near, and who, when Miss Scott returned, approached and enquired if he might be of some assistance. He explained that he was a medical student, and that if the young lady was unwell, perhaps he could be of help. He was, he added, travelling on the same train, and would be with them as far as Bray, County Wicklow.

Miss Scott's first reaction was to rebuff the young man, but the weight of her mission sat very heavily upon her. She thanked him and replied, 'I will be glad to have your company, Sir, but we are only going as far as Blackrock.'

On the journey she learned that the young man's name was David Minns, the same family that owned the large departmental stores, Minskys. His parents had a summer home in Bray to which the family moved each year, from May to September, and he was on his way now to join them.

Miss Scott told him of her mission. There was something about the young man that invited her trust. 'Miss Moore has suffered a great loss. Her grandparents and other members of her family have died in a fire in their home in County Wicklow. I believe it was the work of those Fenians, tch, tch, and, as you see, she is in shock, and could not travel alone, so our principal has sent me to escort her to her home.'

As they alighted at their station, Miss Scott thanked David Minns for his solicitude, and bade him farewell.

In the early hours of the following morning, the household was woken by sounds of terrified shrieks coming from Charlotte's room. Nanny and Amy were the first to reach her door. Going in, they found the young girl crouched up against the headboard of her bed, her knees drawn up, her arms clenched across her chest, and her eyes wild and staring. Nanny took the frightened figure into her arms and tried to soothe her, whilst Amy shepherded everyone else out, organising Cook to give the boys some warm milk and biscuits and to put them back to bed. 'Lotte will be fine now boys,' she said. 'She was just having a bad dream.' And with that, she went back into the room and closed the door.

Charlotte was a little quieter now, responding to Nanny's soothing comfort. But, as she saw Amy, she became very agitated again, and kept repeating, 'Where is Father? Is he dead too? Where is Father? Was he in the burning house? Where is he? I want Father. You are not telling me everything! I want Father.'

'Now Lotte,' said Amy, 'Your father is fine. He has gone to be with Uncle Kit, who was hurt. We will all go to Wicklow tomorrow for the funerals, when Miss Henrietta comes home, and then you will see him, see for yourself that he is perfectly well. You must understand, he had to go on ahead to make all the arrangements.'

'Oh, will I?' said Charlotte in a desperate voice. 'Will I see him? I need him, I am so frightened. Will they burn this house? Will we also all be killed? I loved Gran and Grandy Moore so much, and now I will never, never see them again.' And her wailing resumed.

Eventually she quietened and fell asleep, exhausted from all the emotional experiences of the day. Amy stayed with her for the rest of the night. Nanny went to see how the boys were, and then she tried to get some sleep herself.

The weeks that followed carried many unhappy memories. The travellers being met by Lady Matilde, Lotte, Owen and Amy at Kingstown, and having been joined by Joan Ryan, proceeding to Wicklow. The poignant meeting with Michael, and then with Kit in hospital, swathed in bandages and in a great deal of pain. Going to see the remnants of the once happy and gracious home in Roundwood tore at their already broken hearts. Most harrowing of all were the funerals at the family plot at Dunlossary graveyard, beside the little Protestant church. On the first day, Henry and Florence Moore were buried, and on the second day the young mother, Beth, and her little girls.

These memories lived forever in the hearts and minds of the families affected, and were to become a blot on local history, which made the people of that part of the country feel shame for such a deed, even though most agreed that it could not have been the intention to cause loss of life, but rather the destruction of property.

As soon as possible, most of the family returned to Blackrock, unable to be in the proximity of the ruins of what had been the heart and anchor of the Moore family.

Darragh Ryan felt that Kit would also make a better recovery if he was moved to a hospital in Dublin, nearer to Michael, and he made the necessary arrangements for Kit to make the journey as comfortably as possible.

To make space in Priory House for the extra guests, Lotte and Ria shared a room. The sense of loss that both girls felt, and the pity for their father, and for Uncle Arthur, who had lost a wife and two little daughters, drew them close for a little while.

Lotte told Ria of the dinner party of the year before. 'Olive and I were so excited, and then there was such a fearful row, it was not at all what we had expected. In the summer, when we all went to Glenavon, there were more differences of opinion. Uncle Kit and Grandy were shouting at each other, and Gran was so upset, and now we will never go there again, and we will never be together again, either in Delahunt's or Roundwood. Why, oh why Ria, is life like this? Why do all the good people we love have to die? I know Father has tried to explain it, but I will never understand.'

'Well, I'm very glad I was not in Ireland to witness such unpleasantness, and I wish I had not had to come and see the ruins of the house. What happened to all the furniture and pictures, and Gran's jewellery? She always promised me some special pieces.'

'Everything was destroyed in the fire,' said Lotte.

'Oh no!' said Ria. 'Now I won't have those lovely things to remember them by,' but seeing the look of disdain on her sister's face she quickly added, 'Of course, I will remember them without things, and miss them, and, of course, I am very sorry about Aunt Elizabeth and the girls, although I did not know the children very well, as they were so much younger than I.'

Charlotte felt that she could not stay and listen to such selfishness and hard-heartedness any longer. She ran out of the room, as she had done many times before, so that Henrietta could not see the tears that were running down her cheeks. She went, as she always did at times of great distress, to the gazebo on the path to Grossmutter's, and shutting herself in, drew on her own memories, one by one, dwelling on them, as if they were tangible treasures, to be preserved and taken out at intervals, to be looked at and then carefully put away again.

Chapter Twenty-One

David Minns was very disturbed by the memory of the beautiful, haunted young girl, with whom he had shared a railway carriage the previous week. She came, unbidden, into his thoughts at moments when he was occupied by other activities.

The following month, when he returned to Dublin to see his grandmother, who had just returned from one of her frequent trips to Baden Baden, he made a detour to visit Miss Scott at Alexandra School to enquire after Miss Charlotte Moore. He requested her home address, so that he might write a note of condolence to her. He was a little taken aback when Isobel Scott said that if he left a note with her, she would see to it that it reached Miss Moore. It was the first time that he had been made aware of the code of etiquette that surrounded young Protestant ladies of the time, and he knew he had made a social gaffe in seeking the address. Knowing the strong moral shield that surrounded Jewish girls, he realised that he should never have tried to breach the code in such a gauche manner.

'Thank you, Miss Scott, for your courtesy. I apologise for my lack of good manners in asking you for the address. I promise I will post the note to you, for you to forward at your discretion.'

When Charlotte read the brief words of sympathy, and the signature, she could not, try as she might, recall who David Minns was. She showed the letter to her father, who also had no idea of the writer's identity. 'But I feel that such a kind thought should not go unanswered, Lotte, so will you please write to Mr Minns on behalf of all of us, and thank him for his kind expressions of sympathy. By the way, I am writing to your von Zeit and Urbach cousins in Hamburg – do you have any special messages you would like me to convey.'

'No thank you, Father, I am writing to them myself, and will enclose my letter with Grossmutter's, as I usually do.'

As she wrote to him, Charlotte felt curious about David Minns, and impulsively invited him to come to tea at Priory House on the following Sunday, so that the family could thank him again, in person, for apparently being so kind to her when she was in such distress.

When she told her father and Grossmutter about the invitation, they were very angry at her lack of decorum, explaining that although they were sure the young man was of impeccable character, it is more usual to know something about a person before inviting them to your home. However, as the invitation had already been sent, Mr Minns would be made to feel welcome. But in future, Charlotte was to consider matters more carefully, and act with more circumspection. Michael received a note in reply to thank him for the invitation to tea, and that David Minns would have great pleasure in accepting.

After lunch on Sunday, Lady Matilde and Michael retired to the drawingroom. The boys disappeared out of doors and, as it was Cook's afternoon off, Charlotte and Amy went to the kitchen to prepare tea. But Cook had already prepared platters of tiny sandwiches, sultana scones, accompanied by a dish of butter and a cut-glass pot of homemade gooseberry jam, a jug of whipped cream, and some delicious small cakes, all of which were set on a three-tiered cake tray, covered with damp muslin to prevent them going dry. A cool earthenware bowl of freshly gathered strawberries, and a large jug of yellow cream, from the jersey herd of a neighbouring farm, stood, keeping cool, on a marble-topped sidetable. There had been a discussion at lunch as to whether tea should be served in the drawingroom or, the weather being so beautiful, in the garden. Lotte voted for the garden. Lady Matilde protested, 'Zose dreadful insects! Zey will eat us up.' Michael agreed that it would be rather pleasant to sit in the sunshine, and, begrudgingly, Lady Barker-Grey gave in, saying, 'Well, when you are bitten to pieces, don't forget zat I warned you. I am very curious to know why a young man, a stranger, should go to zo much trouble for, and accept an invitation from, a mere schoolgirl?'

'You forget, Grossmutter, that I am seventeen next month, and that I have finished at Alexandra School and will be going into Alexandra College.'

'I forget nozing Miss! Alexandra School, Alexandra College, to me, one is an extension of ze ozer. Now, if you will excuse me,' and with that she swept out of the room.

David Minns arrived promptly at four o'clock, and was shown into the drawingroom by Eamonn. Michael rose to greet him and introduce him to Lady Barker-Grey. He extended his condolences and said that at such times, a Jewish custom was to wish the bereaved 'long life', which he would like to do now. Michael thanked him and said there was a similar Irish custom to which was added 'With no more sorrow'. David informed him that the Jewish custom was similar.

Charlotte came into the room. Seeing the dark handsome young man, she hesitated, for once shy. Her father made the introductions.

'I believe you were most kind to me last time we met. I am afraid I have no recollection of that journey at all. I suppose I was in a state of shock,' and she looked at him with her open and friendly smile, which took any sting out of the words.

'Please don't mention it, Miss Moore,' David replied. 'I am only too glad to have been of some little help, and to see you so well recovered now.' Turning to Michael he said, 'I read with horror in the newspaper the report of what happened. The reality of being involved must be devastating. I gather that your brother, Mr Christopher Moore, has survived. May I enquire how he is?'

'Thank you for your sympathetic understanding of our loss,' said Michael. 'My brother is recovering from his physical wounds quite well. He is now in Sir Patrick Dunn's Hospital in Dublin. But I fear there will be emotional scars, which he will always bear.'

'Sir Patrick Dunn's!' exclaimed David, 'but that is the hospital to which I am attached for my medical studies. How extraordinary. I will, if I may, call on Mr Christopher Moore from time to time.'

'Whilst we appreciate your very kind concern, Mr Minns,' said Michael, 'we would not like to impose on your precious time. After all, we are strangers.'

'Perhaps if I explain, Mr Moore, Lady Barker-Grey, that the reason my own family is in Ireland today is because too many Jews were victims of similar barbarities, and in order to save those that could be saved, we were forced to leave our former homes. When I saw you, Miss Moore, in such distress, and heard the story, I thought of the members of my own family who are still in danger.'

'It is refreshing,' said Lady Barker-Grey, 'to meet a young gentleman today with such sensitivity of feeling, and we sank you for it. Now, shall we go into ze garden and see if tea is ready?'

Later that week, on his daily visit to Kit, Michael learned that David Minns had called in to see him, as promised. Kit thought he was a very nice fellow, and that he seemed very clever. Mr Minns promised to call again, and to bring some of the other students with him next time, as it would help to break up the long tedious hours to have some bright company. Michael never stayed very long, as his brother tired easily and was still in a lot of pain. He heard more and more of David Minns from Kit as the weeks went by, and it became clear that a friendship had developed between the two men, in spite of their age difference.

Chapter Twenty-Two

'I am arranging, wiz your approval of course, to take Lotte and ze boys to stay wiz my dear sisters-in-law in Wales. Ria can join us zere. I feel a month will be enough,' continued Lady Barker-Grey to Michael. Ita and Amy can go ahead and make sure ze beds are aired and everything else is in order. Zen I will follow with Nanny and ze children. It will also give Amy and Nanny an opportunity to see zeir families. I too would like to renew old acquaintances during the summer months, although it will be sad to see my old home, and all ze memories zat will live again. Also, I sink, it will be a good time, if I may suggest it, while the house is quiet, for you to bring Kit home from ze hospital. He needs now his heart and mind to heal. His body is soon going to be well. Michael, you are very dear to me, I may never have ze opportunity to say such sings to you again. You made my Jessica very happy, for zis I sank you. You made me welcome to your world. Srough you I have ze joy of my six angels, although sometimes I sink zere is a little of the devil in zem as well! I feel for you, Michael, you have so much to bear, and you have to be so strong, and at times you must be very lonely. What I am trying to say is, I am a strong woman. If I can help you, please ask.' And she put her hand on Michael's forearm and looked into his eyes, which had unexpectedly filled with tears. 'Thank you, Mama,' he whispered, 'I know your worth and I thank the dear Lord for your presence here.'

When the school term came to an end, everything was ready, and in a few days, highly excited, they were on their way to Holyhead, and from there, to Neath.

Michael brought Kit back to Priory House, with the help of David Minns. The two brothers settled into a routine, looked after by Eamonn and Cook and visited each day by Darragh Ryan. Soon there was a steady stream of visitors, the most regular being David Minns, Miss Blanche and Mr Willie Fitzgerald, and friends and neighbours, all of whom had been at the fateful dinner party the previous year. Blanche, who had lost none of her feminist fervour, did much to stimulate Kit's adrenalin, providing good arguments for him to rage against some of her strongly held views.

The three friends took turns accompanying Kit, who now walked supported by his crutches, on his daily outings. Even though there were times when his armpits were raw from pressure, he persevered, as the exercise was helping him to regain his strength.

Letters and cards came from the family in Wales. Reading between the lines, Michael gathered that the visit wasn't going as smoothly as planned. Ria seemed to be irked by the quietness of their life, and talked incessantly about the friends with whom she was going to stay in France for the rest of the summer, before going straight back to school. She nearly drove her two maiden aunts to distraction, apparently, with her complaints of how 'dowdy' the dressmaker was, whom they had employed to make her several dresses, as their gift, for her forthcoming trip. When Grossmutter had spoken to her about her ingratitude, she had thrown a tantrum and said, 'In my final year, I need better clothes. Please ask Father to send me money, and I will buy them in France! If Grandmama Moore were here, she would understand, but now there is no one, and if only Father can send me the money, I will be so happy.'

Michael, though hurt by Ria's decision to go to France rather than home, promptly sent her the money when he received her letter, knowing he would have to face his mother-in-law on the matter later.

Nanny was upset to find she was quite a stranger in her home village, now that, with the exception of one niece, her friends and family had either died, moved, or were too young to remember her. Amy on the other hand was so taken over by her family that very little was seen of her in Neath.

The boys loved everything. The long golden beach, the pony rides, and the picnics which they took on their adventure outings. They had made friends with some of the local children, and were all as brown as berries from hours spent each day out of doors at their various activities.

Lotte loved her two great aunts, and she listened for hours to their stories about her mother as a child, and of their own and Grandfather David's childhood. Lotte even won over the rather dour cousin, Jasper Barker-Grey, who had inherited the estate, and she befriended his wife, Miranda, and baby daughters, Iris and Caroline. They gave her the freedom to roam their house and gardens whenever she liked, to see her mother's room and all of the other places Jessica had told her about, which up to now she had only been able to imagine.

Lady Matilde found she had very little in common with the people she knew when she was married to David Barker-Grey, and, to her great surprise, she realised that she had become accustomed to the Irish way of life, and that was where she now felt most comfortable.

One morning, at the end of July, Kit received a letter from his sister Meg, in England, informing him that her bank had told her that her allowance from Glenavon had not arrived for some time, and asking Kit did he know the reason why, and if Beth's allowance was still being paid to Arthur, her husband.

When Michael came back for lunch, Kit showed him the letter. 'Can you cast some light on the matter?' he asked him. Michael crossed to the sideboard and poured them both a drink before answering.

'I did not want to worry you with financial matters yet, Kit. But when I spoke with the bank in Wicklow, the manager informed me that, for several years now, the only money that was in Father's account was what came in from the horses and the farm. The outgoings have consistently been outstripping the income. Now, with the horses gone, and the farmhands too afraid of the Fenians to work the farm, there is nothing. As the furniture, paintings, silver and mother's jewellery were all lost in the fire, there is no way to raise any money. I have sold off the far field. I had to, so please don't look so shocked. I had to pay outstanding wages before dismissing everyone. But now there is nothing left, no income for Meg or you, or for that matter, myself. Only debts and the land, which is at present fallow, and we will have to find ways and means to pay the death duties.'

'Good God, Michael . . . but what happened to Dad's shares and stocks and bonds?'

'I too wondered that,' said Michael. 'Apparently, they have all been realised over the years to fill the gaps in Father's income. I believe there is one lot left, but the dividend is not due for some months, and when we sell them, there will be just enough to get the farm going again. Even then, you will have to live in a guesthouse, or a rented cottage, when you are well enough to go home, as there will not be sufficient money to rebuild Glenavon. And while I will help all I can, I too will be in very straitened circumstances, with Ria's fees to find, and now, no extra income. All I know is that there may, and I stress may, be a small sum from the insurance company, but how much I can't say, and I have been advised that there is a faint possibility that the death duties may be waived, because of the circumstances of Father's demise.'

Kit stood straight as a ramrod, his hands balled into fists at his sides. 'As sure as my name is Christopher Nathaniel Moore, I vow, one day, Glenavon will be restored, and the stables filled with the finest breeds of horses. Our family fortunes will again be able to support all they did in the past. I mean this, Michael. I also swear that those who have harmed us will bloody well pay the price!'

Michael, looking at his young brother's pale and pain-racked face, knew that for Kit, the ease and charm of his former life had disappeared forever.

As the weeks went by, Kit seemed spurred by his bitterness and the need to redress the tragedy that had befallen them, to make quicker progress than Darragh Ryan had predicted. His desire to get back to the land was the carrot that lured him through the painful exercises and treatments. That, and the increasingly devoted attention and companionship of Blanche Fitzgerald, who, whilst never pandering to Kit, kept his spirits from flagging, with her good sense and encouragement. They sat and talked for hours in the drawingroom, or walked, first in the woods by the farm, and then, as Kit grew stronger, along the seafront. It did not seem to matter when silence fell between them, it was not awkward at all, just companionable. It was Blanche who, when Kit was vociferous about the revenge he would wreak on the Fenians, made both him and Michael see that such plans would be a waste of precious and much-needed energy, and that the best revenge of all would be to rebuild the estate, and their lives. They acknowledged her good sense, but she was left with the feeling that they still brooded, and hatched plans, when they were together. When Kit spoke to Michael and said that he thought Blanche would suit him admirably as a wife, and that he had asked her to honour him in marriage, Michael was not at all surprised, nor at the news that the said lady had consented.

As it was so important to be in Wicklow for the autumn planting, it was decided that the couple should marry in church, and then have a quiet reception at the Fitzgerald home after the ceremony. The 1st of September was the date set. It was further decided that the couple would go straight to Roundwood and defer a honeymoon until the following summer, if finances then permitted.

Kevin Carey, who had long forgiven Michael for his outburst when he had come to Priory House to break the horrendous news, had found a small house for Kit and Blanche to rent, furnished, in good order and near the estate.

Everyone was surprised when Henrietta agreed to come home to be maid of honour, which rather put out Charlotte, as she had seen herself in that role. Lotte's curiosity was roused when she heard that Francis Thompson, Uncle Kit's friend, who had been present when her parents had first met, was to be best man. She overheard Michael and Kit talking, and was surprised when Kit said, 'Obviously my first choice would have been Kevin, followed closely in second place by David Minns. It is a shame that all three religions stand in the way of friends participating in church ceremonies of other faiths.'

The vicar and his wife tried to make the church and ceremony as cheerful as possible, but the missing faces of so many members of the family was too grim a reminder of what recent events had brought about. Lady Matilde stepped in, where more sensitive angels would not dare to tread, by remarking, 'Out of every tragedy some good must come, such as zis marriage of Blanche and Kit today.'

When the party reached the Fitzgerald home, Henrietta noticed that her father was missing, and she was relieved, but shocked, when he arrived some time later, very red eyed and distinctly 'in his cups'. Michael, as usual, stood and surveyed the scene. Yes, he thought, it is much better to view things through a haze, which blurs the sharp edge of memory, and pain, and where everyone looks younger, and more lovely. He thanked goodness he did not have to make a speech, as good old Francis Thompson had been primed on what was needed to be said.

Charlotte had seen her father enter the room, and she ran over to meet him. 'O Father, there you are. Where were you? Wasn't it a lovely ceremony, and doesn't Aunt Blanche look a picture? Father, are you all right?' Michael, who had been swaying backwards and forwards, stumbled, and Charlotte caught his arm. Francis, who was standing nearby, saw that Charlotte was having problems, and he quickly went to her aid. He realised at once that Michael was quite drunk, and he said to Charlotte, 'I think perhaps we had better bring your father into another room.'

'Are you ill Father?' Charlotte asked anxiously.

‘Leave this to me,’ said Francis, ‘I think he needs to be on his own for a little while.’

Her intuition told her that her father was in safe hands.

When he re-entered, Francis saw that Charlotte was in conversation with a young man. He went over to them, and excusing himself, said to Charlotte in a low voice, ‘Everything is all right now.’ Charlotte was grateful and introduced him to David Minns. Turning back to the best man, she said, ‘You know, I had not fully realised how much strain Father would be under today. . . I should have looked after him better.’

‘Of course, it is a terrible strain for him,’ David said. ‘Your father usually seems so strong. We are inclined to forget how he must be feeling.’

Charlotte, aware of the two handsome men, one on either side of her, preened with pride at their attention. David, with his mane of blue-black wavy hair and dark eyes, and Francis, with his thick fair hair and deep-set piercing blue eyes. She was torn between which type she most admired. She felt a new sensation, a quickening of her pulse, and her voice, when she spoke, did not sound like her own. She was breathless, and to her chagrin, gushing! Her two companions, however, did not seem to notice anything, and she answered all the questions that Francis put to her about her interests and ambitions with vivacity and charm. ‘I am going to university soon, to Trinity College Dublin. Grossmutter, my grandmother, feels it is the right thing for me to do.’

David was content to stand back and watch this new-found poise that Charlotte was exhibiting, and he determined in his own mind that one day, soon, he would marry this beautiful girl, in spite of all the difficulties which he knew lay ahead. He was glad when, a few minutes later, Francis Thompson was called upon as best man to make toasts to the bride, groom and maid of honour.

When all the speeches were finished, and good wishes had been read from those guests who had been unable to attend, Charlotte said to David, ‘Let’s go and congratulate Francis on the way he has conducted the ceremonies.' Charlotte took David's arm and propelled him towards the best man, who was making his way back to her. After some more pleasant conversation, Francis was once again called upon to finish his duties. He was to escort Kit and Blanche to the station and to see that their luggage was put safely on board the train.

'Your family have very kindly invited me to Priory House for supper,' Francis said to Charlotte before leaving, 'so I hope to have the pleasure of continuing our conversation then. Shall I see you there, David?' he asked.

'Oh, indeed,' said David. 'Indeed you will.'

'Good,' came the answer. 'I will be staying a couple of nights with Willie, packing the wedding presents, which I shall then personally escort to their new home, on my way back to my own family in Waterford. So we shall have ample opportunity, Charlotte, to carry on these fascinating conversations.'

Later that night, as Charlotte and Henrietta were getting ready for bed, they chatted about the day.

'I thought Aunt Blanche made a very stately bride, even though she wasn't wearing a white bridal gown and veil,' said Lotte. 'And I think she was very brave defying superstition by wearing an apple-green costume.'

'Huh!' cut in Henrietta. 'Either very brave or foolish, wearing any kind of green with her complexion, and that hat was dreadful. It looked more like a platter of carrot greens.'

'O Ria, you're so cruel, but of course, you're so right.' And the two girls burst into giggles.

'I was quite mortified walking down the aisle behind her. What a waste of my beautiful primrose silk. I only hope none of the photographs come out,' said Henrietta.

'Oh, that is too cruel, Ria! How awful not to have any reminder of your wedding day, I couldn't bear it if it were me. Did you meet Francis Thompson and David Minns?' she asked, rather hesitantly.

'No I did not,' said Ria. 'They were far too busy with you, and you with them. Whatever do you want to be bothered with them for? Francis Thompson is an old man, he must be thirty-six or seven if he's a day, and the other one is a Jew! My dear, I ask you!'

'Well, I think they are both very handsome and charming,' said Lotte, who had thrown herself on the bed, and lay on her stomach with her head propped on her hands. 'So what if David is Jewish? His family own Minskys' emporiums in Dublin, and they are kind and generous people, and David is going to be a doctor. He has been wonderfully kind to Uncle Kit . . . and thirty-six is not old! Oh, you are horrid! Why must you always spoil everything?', and she got into her bed and pulled the sheet over her head so that she barely heard Ria say, 'Jean Louis de Ville does not think I am horrid. He thinks I am very special. He is from a good old Huguenot family, so tosh to you Lotte Moore!', and she put the light out and got into her own bed.

The next day, when Henrietta had left for the mailboat, Charlotte felt relief that she would not have to listen to her sister's spiteful remarks about everyone, or hear the endless list of Jean Louis de Ville's virtues. With a rare flash of spite on her part, she thought that he probably was greasy and ugly, and a prig, and therefore he and Ria would suit each other very well.

As she crossed the hall on her way to help Grossmutter with some letters, the doorbell rang. 'I'll answer it,' she called over her shoulder, as she walked to the hall door. Her heart gave a flutter when she saw Francis Thompson on the step. He looked so handsome with the sunlight on his golden hair. His broad shoulders made him look so dependable and solid.

'I have come to say "Adieu" to your father, and to thank him and Lady Barker-Grey for their kindness and hospitality,' he said.

'I'm afraid Father is not here. He has gone to take Henrietta to the boat. She is on her way to England and then to France for a visit, before she returns to complete her education. I am on my way to Grossmutter's, if you would care to come with me. I know she will be at home.' And she held her breath until he answered that he would care very much to accompany her. She felt her cheeks blush with the implied compliment, and she was very glad that she was wearing her new shirt and skirt, that her hair was brushed and tied with a becoming bow, and that her skin was still glowing from the past weeks of good weather.

They set off along the path from Priory House to Priory Lodge. Charlotte almost skipped, she was so filled with excitement at having this scrumptious man all to herself. She chattered happily about the weather, and how some of the trees were starting to show a little yellow. 'My favourite season is nearly with us. I adore the russet leaves and pine needles making a carpet to shush through. Hallowe'en is such fun.' She prattled on about going to university, and all the wonderful things there were in the world, as well as the horrid. She asked him about his friendship with Kit when they were boys, and all he could remember about her mother and father when they were young. He did his utmost to reply, but the questions came with such rapidity that he could barely sort them out. When they came to the gazebo, she told him, 'It was my darling mother's, and when I am very lonely for her, and need to talk to her, this is where I come . . . a very private place. No one else ever comes here these days.'

On one of her impulses, she asked him if he would like to see inside. 'I keep my favourite toys and books from childhood here, and the rug that Mother used when she was ill. There are other keepsakes various members of the family have left here over the years.'

With a gentle understanding of the honour being paid to him, Francis thanked Lotte and said, 'If you are sure I will not be intruding, I would very much like to go inside.'

Without speaking, she led the way in. They stood, while their eyes adjusted to the darker interior after the bright light outside. She watched him as his glance took in the surroundings, trying to see things as he must, the wicker chairs and table, the built-in benches, the loose cushions with their faded chintzes, shelves filled with a jumble of knickknacks, and cupboards that would not close properly. She stepped towards him at the moment he turned. He never knew how he came to take the exquisite young girl into his arms and kiss her. He felt her tremble, and then her arms went around his neck. She pressed into him, returning his kiss with an ardour that roused a passion within him that he knew he must control. He gently pushed her away, but keeping his hands on her shoulders said, 'I am old compared to you, who are very young. I wish it were not so, but there you are.'

'No, my darling Francis. You are not old. You are so handsome, and I have never felt like this before. Can I have fallen in love with you? Do kiss me again.'

And he did, and for a brief moment they were lost in the midst of feeling and emotion. But again he pushed her away, and in a voice that was gruff and gentle at the same time, said, 'Forgive me, remember me kindly, live your life to the full', and strode swiftly away, closing his ears to her sobs as she tried to follow him, calling to him to come back to her. When he did not, she sank to her knees on the ground, and pressing her face into her hands, wept and wept. She did not understand what she had done wrong, and she yearned for him, yet she felt humiliated by this man who had aroused such unknown feelings in her breasts and limbs, in the very core of her being, feelings which were unsatisfied, disturbing and frustrating.

Chapter Twenty-Three

Every Friday, Joseph Minns came home in the afternoon. It was his habit to sit with Fanny over a cup of tea, and to discuss the events of the week, before getting himself ready to attend the evening service at the synagogue to inaugurate the Sabbath. When at home, David would accompany his father, and then they would walk together to his grandmother Sarah's, where Fanny, Sybil and Hilda would have preceded them. Sarah Minsky liked as many members of the family as possible to attend the Sabbath dinner when she was at home, and as this particular Friday in November 1922 was to be the last one before she left on her annual visit to Johannesburg, she was particularly anxious for her family in Dublin to be present.

At tea, Joseph listened to the gossip and news that Fanny recounted, and then he said, 'Rabbi Chanaan came to see me in the office this morning. He has a proposition he wants us to consider . . . such a compliment to our family, such *nachas*, joy, for a rabbi to think so highly of our family that he would suggest such a thing. I tell you I could not believe my ears. *Ada rabba*, on the other hand, we are *menschen*, people of standing in the community, regular synagogue attenders. I'm on the Council, we are important merchants, successful businesspeople, our son, bless him, is going to be a doctor of medicine, *tacka*, really, what more could anyone want? So it's settled, I feel better now.'

'Joseph, what are you talking about? What is settled? What, for goodness sake, did the rabbi propose? What is all this about?'

'I told you. He has a niece coming from the Hame, and he wants for to make a *shiddach*, a match, with our David. A lovely girl, twenty years of age, a real *mavin*, expert in running a house, which she did for her father, also a rabbi, and brothers and sisters, after her mother, our rabbi's sister, died, *Olay'v Shalom,* rest in peace, and he showed me a picture, a *shane maidela*, a very pretty girl. *Mazeltov*, Fanny! Congratulations!'

'*Mazeltov* to you too, Joseph, if David will agree, and I'm not so sure he will. Modern young people like to make their own choices.'

'What's to disagree? He'll agree,' said Joseph, and rose to go to his study, leaving no room for argument. But Fanny thought she would speak to her mother-in-law about the subject later, before the men returned from synagogue.

When they arrived at the grandmother's house on the South Circular Road, Sybil and Hilda went upstairs to help set the table in the diningroom, which was only used on these occasions. The large family room, next to the kitchen, was used as the everyday livingroom, with its cheery fire and large square table, family photographs sitting on the mantelshelf, and portraits hanging on the walls.

It was here that Fanny found Sarah, resting from her labours in the kitchen, where meals for the next twenty-four hours had been prepared. She told her what the rabbi had said to Joseph, and of her own feelings, and was not surprised when Sarah burst out angrily, 'Vat does he mean, he vants? A girl of tventy. Could they not find anyvun in deir own village dat dey vant to foist her off on us? Or maybe, she is a *bissel,* a little, pregnant from a Cossack pogrom?'

'Oh Mother! What a thing to say. I am sure she is a very nice girl. But you know that David has a mind of his own. I am afraid what the outcome will be between him and his father. They can both be so stubborn.'

Soon Sarah put on her lace head covering and lit the candles to herald in the Sabbath, their light reflecting in the eyes of those present. Joseph returned, washed his hands and blessed the wine and bread. They sat and ate a traditional Sabbath eve meal.

Chopped liver pate, chicken soup with homemade vermicelli, roast stuffed chicken and potato pudding, with accompanying vegetables, followed by a fruit pudding.

David came in late, having been delayed at the hospital. He kissed his grandmother, mother and sisters, and bade his father 'Good Shabbos', said a quick blessing on wine that had been left for him, and ate his meal.

When they had finished eating, Nora put a dish of fresh fruit and nuts on the table, a glass of tea was poured from the samovar, which had been filled before the first star appeared in the sky, boiled and left on a small light to stay hot overnight and all next day. Each added lemon slices and lumps of sugar to the tea, according to their individual tastes, others preferring spoonfuls of a thick orange preserve.

Joseph then recited the Grace after Meals, and they all joined in traditional Sabbath songs of praise.

'So noo, David? How are things?' said Joseph.

'Very well thank you, Father. I have just started my term in the Accident Room and this eveni . . .'

'Good, good,' said his father, interrupting him. 'I am glad you are enjoying your work. How goes your social life? Have you met a special girl yet?'

'Stop beating about de bush, Joseph!' said Sarah. 'Get to de point.'

'What point, Grandmother?'

'De point dat de rabbi spoke to your father today. Dat is vats de point!'

David and his two sisters looked enquiringly at their father.

'The point,' said Joseph, 'is . . . ahem . . . ahem . . . is that Rabbi Chanaan, who is a great man . . . err . . . showed me this picture today.' And he took it out of his pocket and passed it to David, who glanced at it and handed it back.

'So what?' said David.

'So vat? he says, so vat?' said Sarah. 'They vant her for your *calla*, bride, dat's so vat!'

'Mamma,' said Joseph. 'Let me explain.' And he told David what had transpired.

David laughed and said, 'I am afraid you and the rabbi are too late. I have chosen my future bride, and I know you will grow to love her. I had not meant to say anything to you yet as the girl does not know how I feel, and I do not know how she feels.'

'Noo David! Tell us who it is!' 'Do we know de family?' 'Is she a friend of your sisters?' came the chorus from around the table.

'No to all your questions. She is the niece of a patient I became friendly with in the hospital. She is beautiful and clever, and I love her madly!'

'A *shiksa*! A Gentile!' shrieked his father, jumping to his feet. 'Do you want to give me a heart attack? Do you want us to sit Shiva for you, as lost? Are you mad? This is what comes of an open education. Are there not enough beautiful and clever Jewish girls for you to love madly? Oy vey! Oy vey! What vill become of us, my only son, what a disgrace – *goyim*, Gentiles. How can I tell the rabbi, my son, the *goy* lover prefers a *shiksa* to his niece, a good Jewish girl! The daughter of a rabbi. Oy vey, oy vey,' and he collapsed into his chair and slumped forward onto the table, wailing to God to take pity on him and 'What have I ever done to deserve such an ungrateful child? How can you be such a traitor to your own people and all they believe in?'

'Shush mine Zun,' Sarah said, 'I know of dis man, Kit Moore. David has told me of the tragedy his family have suffered. I know noting of dis girl. I have never seen her. Did I leave Riga to come to an unknown vorld, leaving mine own people behind, if it vas not to preserve all I love, including you, Joseph, who vas ready for de army? So listen to me goot now! David has done nothing yet for you to get so het up about. Ven he does, it will be time enough for you to bust a blood vessel!'

Fanny had sat tight-lipped and speechless. One look made her realise that all the suffering was not one-sided. She gathered her thoughts together in her mind. 'As a wife and mother I make this silent vow, that I will help David to reach a good and honourable solution. I must speak to him as soon as possible. I know I do not have an easy task in front of me, for as much as I love my son, I have no wish to betray my husband, or all my other allegiances to Judaism. Thank God our daughter, Sybil, is going to marry a fine Jewish boy from Leeds in a few weeks.'

On Sunday, when Joseph was at a council meeting, she rang David at the hospital, and asked him if he would come to see her as soon as possible. He arranged to do so the next morning.

On Monday, when she had given him a cup of coffee, she sat down opposite David, and asked him to tell her the whole story about the girl he imagined he was in love with. He did, leaving nothing out, including all he knew of the family, and all that had befallen them. When he had finished, he saw that his mother was very moved and was shaking her head in sympathy. 'It is not only Jewish people who know suffering. Wealth and position are no barriers to grief. But you know how all Jewish people feel about intermarriage. In the case of a Jewish man marrying a Gentile girl, their children can never be recognised as Jewish. Jewishness is something that is passed down only through the female line.'

'I know I am causing considerable grief. I would give a great deal not to do so, but I cannot stop the dictates of my heart. Besides, if Charlotte does not share my feelings, and I am going to do my damnedest to make her, it might come to nothing.'

'It is my duty as a Jewish mother, David, to warn you not to go against the teachings of our rabbis. Not to destroy your family, to spoil your sisters' chances, or to break your father's heart.'

'Mother, I hear what you say, but I can make you no promises.'

Later that night Fanny said to Joseph, 'Please do not cross bridges that might not be there, Joseph. David has told me again that he has made no approach to the girl so far. Nothing permanent has occurred. As sure as there's a God in Heaven he will protect us all, so have faith, Joseph.'

When David went over all the events in his own mind, he realised that it was not only his family that would have the heartbreak of such a situation. Fortuitously, he saw at first hand how these events could work out. A childhood friend from Hebrew School had gone down the same road he was contemplating. He saw the boy's parents actually sit Shiva for him, as if he had died. He could not put his mother through such heartbreak. He also knew that Charlotte would suffer, and that her family, who had already had more than their share of grief, would suffer, and that if they had children, they would also suffer, for where would they belong in this intolerant world? He could see no way out of his dilemma but to renounce his love and throw himself into his work.

As his internship in the hospital was now completed, he moved back into his parents' home. The look of love and relief on their faces when he announced his decision was some small recompense for the miserable ache in his heart.

In January, David was due to attend the Rotunda Lying-in Hospital for three months, as part of his course. He would be on call to assist at domiciliary deliveries in the city, and thereby gain practical experience, looking after the mother and the newborn infant in the patients' homes, in addition to working on the wards.

Because of the general unrest following the signing of the Treaty and the unheralded explosions and fires that could occur anywhere, Fanny was in a constant state of apprehension for his safety, and he was sorely pushed to convince her that he was not in any danger, and that if he was, he would not leave any house where he was in attendance, until everything was quiet again.

The weather was cold and wet, and very soon David and his co-students found that most babies seemed to be born at night, and especially on nights when one was particularly tired and worn out. It was absolutely awful being rudely woken by the porter and told to be ready to accompany the doctor on duty, at 2 am or 3 am on a freezing morning. As they were travelling by bicycle, they were often wet by the time they arrived at the mean flats, or houses, which were usually unheated, only to find the handywoman already ensconced, and nothing but newspapers for the mother to lie on, and pitiful, washed-out rags in which to wrap the infant.

One night in March, he went on a call to a tiny room at the top of a tenement, to find a young girl about to deliver. She had been in labour, they were told, for eighteen hours, and was very exhausted. The doctor in charge examined her, and looking at David, shook his head. 'We will be very lucky if we save either of them,' he said. 'The baby is in a breach position. I will have to try to turn it to come either head or feet first. If feet, it will probably suffocate.'

They worked together, speaking only when necessary, and they were both relieved when, an hour later, a live baby was born.

'Is it a boy or a child?' asked the handywoman.

'A fine boy,' said David. 'Now we have to save the mother.'

It was some time before they knew the mother was safe and they saw a little colour come into her cheeks, and her eyes slowly open.

'There, there, mother,' said the doctor. 'You are going to be fine, and so is your little son.'

'God bless you, Sir,' said the young girl, who only looked about eighteen years of age. 'But what is to become of us?'

The tears rolled down her face. There were no sobs, she was too weak, and soon she drifted into a sleep of exhaustion.

Part of David's duty was to see the new mother on the day after the delivery. So, after the rounds in the hospital, he went to the tenement to visit the girl and her baby son. He climbed the several flights of bare and dirty stairs to the attic of what had once been a gracious Georgian house in vice-regal days. He first attended to the mother, and then examined the baby. Having had very little experience, he could not quite pinpoint what the problem was, but he was not happy about the way the infant looked, and he told the girl that he would return soon with another doctor.

Going to the nearby Children's Hospital, he spoke to a member of the medical staff. He explained that he was a student from the Rotunda and was on a visit to a new mother, and that he felt the child needed attention. 'The best thing you can do, Mister, is to bring the child round to us. We are very short-staffed and have no one to send on District just because some clever-dick student feels something is wrong.'

David went back and told the young mother that he was taking the baby to hospital for a checkup, and would return him to her very soon. The medical officer on duty examined the young child, and looking up at David said, 'I apologise for my abrupt manner earlier. I have been on duty all night, and at that moment I was so tired I didn't know what I was saying. But you were right I fear, about the little fellow. We'll admit him now, and make him as comfortable as possible.'

David Minns went back to the girl. 'The baby is to stay in hospital for a while. A nurse will call to pump your breast milk to feed it. Try not to worry. I'm sure they will do everything for the child's welfare.'

A few days later, Matron called David into her office. 'I am afraid, Mr Minns, that the baby you helped deliver in Eccles Street a few days ago, died this morning in the Children's Hospital, of congenital heart disease. You know it is now part of your duties to break the news to the mother. Bring her back to the Rotunda in an ambulance to be admitted until her milk has dried up, and be sure to tell her that the child was baptised.'

It was the first time that David had had to go on such a mission, and it was with a heavy heart he entered the house in Eccles Street, along with the two ambulance men, carrying their stretcher. At the foot of the last flight of stairs he asked them to wait, while he went on ahead to tell the girl of her loss. The handywoman, who had gone to make a cup of tea for the patient, appeared. 'Der y'are, Sir, God luv her. She took it real hard dat she has just lost the wee babby. De woman from down de hall was at the Chill'ers Hospital with her young wan, and she heard. God, wouldn't yer heart go out to her, she's only a young wan herself. I just came t' collect me few shiller,' and pulling her shawl tightly around her, she clumped off down the stairs, shaking her head, and mumbling about 'de ways o' de Lord' being strange and unfathomable.

David was very relieved that he did not have to break such awful tidings, as no matter how many lectures they had been given on the subject, such tasks were never going to be easy to perform. He went into the room and tried to comfort the weeping girl. When she had somewhat calmed down he said, 'I am going to call the stretcher men to come and collect you, they are just outside. We are taking you to the Rotunda Hospital for the present.'

The next months flew by for David, and he soon found himself in the Examination Hall doing his finals. This was where all the years of learning, from books and through practical work, would show if he had learned all that he should have, or whether it had been a waste of studying. Only time would tell.

When he had attended his last written paper and his last oral exam, he packed a case with suitable clothes and prepared to spend the next few weeks loafing in Bray. He went for long walks over Bray Head, and into Greystones. Often on the way back, he would stop at one public house or another, for a pint of beer. The weather was warm and sunny, and he soon acquired a glowing tan from the mixture of sun and fresh sea air.

The night that he heard he had qualified as a doctor, he met some of his fellow students to celebrate. They went from pub to pub, and their obvious excitement and elation attracted the attention of some of the ladies of the town. The lads by now were game for anything, and wandered off with partners to spend the night sowing some wild oats.

His father and mother felt that he deserved some relaxation after all his years of hard studying, and, coupling this with their appreciation for his coming to his senses about the Christian girl, they gave him a graduation present of a 'touring holiday' around Europe. Nothing else presenting itself immediately, he gratefully accepted.

Chapter Twenty-Four

In August 1924, the Moore family, including Kit and Blanche, returned from France where they had attended the marriage of Henrietta to Comte Jean Louis de Ville. They had been joined there by the von Zeits and Urbachs from Germany, and Michael's sister, Meg, from England. The Misses Barker-Grey had also travelled from Neath to be with their sister-in-law, Lady Matilde.

The wedding had been held at the de Ville estate, as had been customary in that family for many generations. The Moores had been impressed by the beauty of the château, situated on the outskirts of St Malo, in Normandy.

Charlotte and the boys had been in their element. The de Ville family had a stud farm, and there were several horses put at their disposal, on which to gallop over the lush countryside and wide beaches. Everyone was charming and welcoming, except Henrietta, who went around with her nose in the air, explaining, 'As Jean Louis' father is dead, Jean Louis is the head of the family, and I will be mistress of Château Bellevue.'

Jean Louis de Ville turned out to be kind and courteous to his new Irish relatives. His mother, sisters and brothers did everything possible to make the visit memorable. Even Lady Barker-Grey could find no fault with the way they were received, and on their return to Ireland, regaled all her circle about the splendid lifestyle her granddaughter, Henrietta, would be living in France.

Charlotte, on their return, stayed in Blackrock only long enough to change her clothes, repack her trunk, see Nanny and

Amy, and to tell them all about the wedding. She quickly left for Connemara, where she was to spend the rest of the holidays with Olive Bailey and her family in their home, near Clifden in County Galway.

The Bailey home was a large Georgian house, grown shabby and in need of repairs. Since leaving school, Olive had been living in London, working as a social secretary to one of the society luminaries of the time. This was her first visit home and the first time the girls had seen each other in over two years. Constance Wall was to have travelled with Lotte, but, at the last minute, family matters prevented her doing so, and Lotte travelled alone. She jumped out of the train at Roundstone Station as soon as she saw Olive. They hugged each other, talking at the same time and laughing at everything and nothing.

All the way back to Clifden, in the trap, they chatted, trying to catch up with each other's gossip. They moaned in sympathy with each other that their threesome was not complete without Con and her acerbic wit.

Olive's parents, Elsie and Geoffrey Bailey, loved the sound of young people enjoying themselves. To celebrate their only daughter being at home again, they had invited some cousins and friends from Olive's childhood to stay. Charlotte was excited to find that a busy programme of point-to-point races, sailing, tennis, pony-trekking and parties, some in neighbouring houses, had been arranged, and was grateful that Amy had insisted that she pack some party dresses.

The house was filled to capacity, and Lotte learned that she would be sharing a bedroom with Olive. She met several attractive young men, and even fancied she had a crush on a couple of them. At one party she danced most of the night with a young Corkonian, and managed to slip away and go for a long walk with him, returning with her eyes shining, holding hands. But after a couple of days, she found someone new to partner her at tennis and dancing. 'O Olive,' she said one night as they were getting ready for bed, 'I don't know how you could ever leave this paradise of a place.' She was rather surprised when Olive answered very sharply, 'Some of us have to earn our living early in life. I am not as popular as you are. I am known to be poor, and therefore not a good catch in the marriage stakes.'

'My goodness Olive! Do they think I am rich? Is that why they court me?' And she laughed. 'Why, we too are as poor as church mice. If Grossmutter were not so generous, I also would be looking for employment.'

Olive looked contrite. 'No Lottie, I am sorry. You are so beautiful and full of fun, that is why you are popular. I am just tired and grumpy. Go to sleep.'

'Tomorrow, Ollie, you and I are going to sneak away and spend some time together, talking, just as we used to in the old days. You are one of my two dearest friends. I do understand, so please don't be upset.'

After lunch the next day, the two friends left before they were inveigled into some activity or other, and making their way along the cliff paths, they came to the ruins of an old tower, in the shelter of which they sat, facing out to sea, the broken walls acting as windbreakers and support. The sky was a clear blue, with wisps of white clouds streaked across it. Gulls sailed by, their cries mingling with the sound of the waves breaking on the rocks.

Lotte sat on a pile of old stones, hugging her knees, her face between her arms. Olive stretched out on the turf, lying on her side, propped up on an elbow, her head resting on her hand.

'Do you remember, Lotte, how we used to sit like this in your orchard, dreaming of the days when we would be grown up and have left school? Now, here we are, still dreaming, but now our dreams include what seem to have been halcyon days at school.' And this remark started a stream of memories, one sparking off another. Olive wanted to hear all Lotte's news, and Lotte asked hundreds of questions about Olive's life in England, to which she noticed she only received cursory answers.

'How is your father, Henrietta and the boys? Is your Grossmutter keeping well, and how are Amy and everyone else at Priory House? Although I only ever met them briefly, I always remember your Gran and Grandy Moore with affection. I was very sorry and upset when we heard at school what had happened, far more than I was able to express at the time.'

Charlotte confided in her, as had become her habit over the years. 'I am so very worried about Father, Olive. He is unhappy and unwell, and I have a horrible feeling that he is drinking far too much, at night, when he is by himself. But Amy and Eamonn say that I am wrong, and I suppose they should know. But he looks so wretched, and his clothes are always crumpled and soiled, looking as if he has slept in them. Some days he does not appear before lunch, and then, often he goes out, God knows where, by himself. Even his work, which he always loved, does not seem to call to him any more, and there is so little money for anything now, only a little Uncle Kit sends, what Grossmutter allows, and what Father gets when he sells a painting, or something else from the house. I worry so much about him, and what is to become of him. The boys are growing up and need their father. Maybe Ria has done best by getting out before it is too late! Maybe I should do the same. I did have one moment of romance when Kit and Blanche married. A friend of Kit's came to be best man and . . . O Olive, he was gorgeous! We were in the gazebo, and he kissed me, and I wanted to faint, but at the same time, I wanted it to go on forever. I would have given him everything if he had wanted it . . . O God! How he made me feel! It was the first time that I had the ultimate urge with a man. I was madly unhappy and felt rejected for ages after he left. You were not there to help, and neither was Con. I thought of David Minns, who was also around at the time, but somehow could not bring myself to talk about such an intimate thing to another man, even though a medical doctor. I am glad now that I did not, for we have lost touch with him. And you, my dear friend, tell me of your life in the big city, it must be so full, and so exciting.'

Olive evaded giving many details, just describing in general what her duties were, and some of the plays and musical shows she had seen in the West End theatres. Suddenly she changed her mood and, jumping to her feet, said, 'I am going for a swim, come on Lotts, you don't need a costume, no one but me ever comes here, it is supposed to be haunted!'

Both girls threw off their clothes and ran into the water. After a while, they returned to where they had left their things, and to dry themselves in the warm air. They sat in silence, holding their faces up to the rays of the sun. Soon Charlotte felt drowsy, and eased herself down until she was lying on the soft turf, her head supported by her hands. She felt she must have dozed off, because suddenly she opened her eyes and met those of Olive looking down on her. She was startled by the expression on the other girl's face, and even more by the huskiness in her voice as she said, 'Gosh! You are lovely Lotts! You look like some nymph that was created at one with the scene.' Leaning even closer she whispered, 'Tell me Lotte, have you never really been with a man, I mean really with? I have, but even more exciting, I have been with other women, and oh, it is infinitely more fulfilling. No, don't be shocked, I would do nothing to hurt you,' and she stretched out her hand and gently smoothed the wayward strands of hair away from Charlotte's face.

Charlotte made to sit up, but the soothing tones of Olive's voice and the gentle insistence of her hands as they caressed her, mesmerised her, and when she felt Olive's lips brush her eyes and cheeks, and then search for her mouth, she could not help herself, but allowed it all to happen. She felt as though someone else had taken over her body. Something in her mind said that what they were doing was not right, but the will to break away was not there, and she ached to know what was going to happen next. She was frightened by the sensations that were being roused in her by Olive's seeking hands and mouth, and when the most secret and sensitive part of her was ravished by Olive's thrusting and flickering tongue, she reached her first climax, her senses reeling, and thrills of pleasure rippling through her, and she heard a voice moaning, then realised it was her own.

After it was over she lay panting, warmed by the sun and the memory of what had happened to her, perspiration drying on her, only the warm dampness remaining between her legs. She opened her eyes and shaded them with her hands. She looked at Olive, who was watching her with a little smile of triumph on her lips, and said, 'God, Olive! Where did you learn that? It was wonderful. O God it was wonderful . . . sex is wonderful!'

'Yes, my darling girl, and I will teach you how to make the joy as wonderful for me. Now we had better get dressed and go back to the house,' said Olive.

That night when they were alone together in their room, Olive started the process again. Only this time she made Charlotte do the same things to her. This went on over the next several nights. Each time became more distasteful to Charlotte, who after the novelty had worn off, realised what was happening, what she had become involved in, until, waking one morning, she thought she would burst if she had to face one more night of being used by Olive's insatiable demands, unable to cry out in protest in case they would attract unwanted attention. Suddenly she hated herself for being weak, and Olive for being what she was. So she announced at breakfast, 'I will be catching the midday train back to Dublin. Please forgive my hasty departure, but I feel a sudden urge to return home.' Everyone begged her to stay, saying how disappointed they were she would not be with them for the Gymkhana and Harvest Ball the following week. She excused herself, saying that she was worried about her father and felt that she had stayed away too long already.

Thanking her hosts, she departed for the station with Olive. 'I am sorry Olive that I cannot be anything more to you than a friend,' she said. 'I don't know how this thing got so out of hand. Please don't let such practices spoil your life. I think it is for the best we are to be separated. No! Don't hug or kiss me.' And she quickly climbed into the railway carriage.

At home, she brushed all enquiries aside, letting them assume she had been crossed in love by a young man, and that was what had led to her early homecoming. She bathed every day, and went swimming in the sea, but she felt she would never really be clean again.

A couple of weeks later, a letter arrived from Olive, begging for forgiveness for her abandoned behaviour.

. . . It was just, dear Lotte, that I was carried away by the perfection of your lovely body, and now I know that I have always been in love with you. I realise by your disgust with me how I have hurt and disappointed you, it was never my intention to do so, and this grieves me dreadfully. I devoutly hope, as it will be some time before we meet again, that the distance of time will dim your memories of the past weeks, and that we will regain some of our past comradeship, which has always meant so much to me. One thing that is now clear to me is just how much I have come under bad influences in my present circumstances in London. On my return, I will be taking up a new position, and therefore I will be meeting a different type of people. I will let you have my address in case you ever wish to write to me again.

In the meantime, I remain,
Your devoted friend,
Olive Bailey

Chapter Twenty-Five

The cold weather aggravated Nanny's rheumatism, and limited her participation in domestic activities. Charlotte, as well as involving herself in her studies, helped Amy with the running of the house. She found life at university very much to her liking, even though women students, who had now been in the various faculties for almost twenty years, were not fully integrated into the college. They were allowed to use the library facilities, but, as they had to be off campus by 6 pm, this often meant that it was easier to go to a public library than to obtain special permission to be on any of the college premises after that time, and then only in the company of a chaperone. That irked the independent Charlotte and Constance, as did the fact that they were, as women, unacceptable members of the various college societies, with the exception of the Elizabethan Society. Furthermore, women students were only allowed to gather at Numbers 5 and 6 on College Square. The girls enjoyed wearing their undergrad gowns and being part of the campus. As many of the female students did not live in Dublin, they had rooms in Trinity Hall Women's House, in Dartry. Lotte and Con were often invited there to join their friends for study periods and all-female gatherings. They certainly were not without male companionship, for both girls were sought after and they had no shortage of invitations to the social events held by one or other of the societies. Besides, there were the cafés, where all students congregated and conducted 'world affairs' over as many cups of tea or coffee as they could afford.

The terms passed, punctuated by Christmas, Easter and summer, when, according to the season, there were parties, dances, rambling in the mountains, which were near the city, or walking arm-in-arm along the seashore which rimmed one side of it. Charlotte never regretted going to university, especially as Constance was there to share the experience and to be her confidante.

At the beginning of December, Lady Barker-Grey requested Lotte to accompany her to Grafton Street to do some Christmas shopping. Early the following Monday, she and Grossmutter set off for Dublin. As Michael had some business there, he said he would drive them into town, and then meet them later in the afternoon to have tea together before returning home.

Lady Barker-Grey was armed with a formidable list, which would take them from one end of Grafton Street to the other. Charlotte was concerned that Grossmutter, who was now seventy-one, would be overtired by the end of the day, and she determined that she would make sure that they paced themselves sensibly.

Michael left them at Dixon & Hempenstall's, where Grossmutter wished to buy some precision instruments for Owen, who had commenced a course in engineering. She bought fountain pens and bottles of Quink ink for Lawrence and James, who, she felt, were quite old enough to own them. Darragh, she had decided, should have a monetary gift. He was now an army cadet and always needed extra spending money.

As Lady Barker-Grey had an appointment at Leon's gown shop, they made that their next stop. When they entered, Madame Leon herself came forward to greet them. 'I have the coat ready, my Lady,' she said, 'Please have a seat.' She spoke to one of her assistants, who disappeared, returning carrying a tray with steaming coffee and dainty biscuits. Another assistant was sent to fetch the cherry red coat, with a high collar and deep cuffs of fur, which Lady Barker-Grey had ordered.

'Grossmutter, what a gorgeous colour, it will look splendid on you!' exclaimed Lotte.

'You will try it on for me, my *liebchen*, so that I can see how it will look?' said Lady Barker-Grey, smiling conspiratorially behind Charlotte's back at the proprietress.

Lotte put on the coat and wrapped it round her. 'Oh, how lovely! It is so soft and cosy,' she said, running her hands up and down the fabric.

'That will do very nicely, Madame, thank you. Will you complete it and send it to my home,' said Lady Barker-Grey.

The old lady said that she felt rested after her coffee, and was ready to tackle the most arduous part of the day. First Brown Thomas, and then Switzers department stores, which faced each other across the narrow but busy thoroughfare. In Brown Thomas she bought a green velvet smoking jacket for Michael, and a fairisle cardigan for Amy. In Switzers she purchased a warm flannel nightgown and a large fine-wool lace shawl for Nanny, gloves for Gerda, and a large woollen scarf for Cook, as well as boxes of fine Irish linen handkerchiefs for her friends. While they were at the glove counter, Lotte was surprised to hear a voice say, 'Good afternoon Ladies, what a welcome surprise to see you after so long, and turning, she saw David Minns standing behind them.

'Oh, how nice to see you again David, how are you? Grossmutter, you remember David Minns, he was so kind, first to me, and then to Uncle Kit?'

'Of course. How nice to see you again, and how is your family? Well, I hope?' said Matilde politely.

'They are very well, thank you,' said David. 'I am afraid I have only seen Kit and Blanche once since their wedding. I have been abroad. How are they? Please give them my regards. How are the boys? They must be quite big now. And your father, Charlotte, he is keeping well? I have so much of your family news to catch up on . . . I have an idea. If you have no other appointment, may I take you both to lunch, then we can do all our catching up. But I must tell you my most important news immediately. I have passed my examinations, and I am now a qualified doctor.'

'O David, how wonderful. I am delighted to hear such good news,' said Charlotte. But before she could say any more, Lady Barker-Grey intervened. 'I too add my felicitations on your achievement. Sank you very much for your invitation, but I am afraid we are in town to do my shopping for Christmas, and I still have quite a list of things to attend to. Perhaps some other time, or better still, come and visit us over the holiday period. We are on the telephone now. My number is Blackrock 407 and Mr Moore's is Blackrock 406,' and she held her hand out to him.

'Wait!' said Charlotte. 'Why not meet us for tea in the Shelbourne Hotel? We are meeting Father there around three-thirty, when he will have finished his meeting at the Kildare Street Club.'

'If that meets with your approval, Lady Barker-Grey, I should love to, thank you.'

'Very well, young man. Sree-sirty at the Shelbourne Hotel. Now, if you will excuse us.'

Lotte thought that Grossmutter was looking tired, and she suggested that they should go to Bewley's oriental café for a light lunch. It was one of her own favourite haunts. The aroma of the newly roasted coffee beans from the rotary drum, housed in the window, wafted through the grating in the pavement, and it was a magnet that she could never resist. Neither could she resist the freshly baked buns, which filled the interior of the large café behind the shop with mouth watering, yeasty smells. The food was wholesome and tasty, and Lotte felt that this was just what was needed to regenerate energy for the rest of the shopping marathon.

They settled into one of the wooden booths that flanked the perimeter of the room, and sank gratefully into the plush red cushions which lined the seats. The rich oriental-patterned wallpaper and the jewel colours of the stained-glass windows gave the café a unique individuality.

When they had ordered their lunch, Lady Matilde ticked off items on her list, and discovered that her only other major purchase was at Cullen's confectioners, to collect the large wooden boxes of crystalised fruits and marzipans she sent every year to the families in Germany, and now to France, to Ria. It was decided that Lady Matilde would remain in Bewley's while Lotte ran back to Leverett and Frys, in Wicklow Street, to order the hamper for the Ryans, which her grandmother had been sending to them since her first Christmas in Ireland. Lotte also volunteered to pick up their boxes of Christmas cards, which they had selected from, and had printed by, Sibley's stationery shop. She left Grossmutter with a fresh pot of Bewley's famous tea, and confirming with one of the assistants in the shop, on her way out, that the order for Priory House would be delivered on time, she proceeded with her errands.

Lotte returned a little while later, her cheeks flushed and her eyes sparkling from the frosty air, to Cullen's, where she and Grossmutter had arranged to meet. Lady Barker-Grey, seated in a wicker chair, was being shown this year's array of exotic preserves, from which to make her choices. When she had completed her order, Lady Matilde requested that a cab should be called, as she and Lotte could not possibly carry their many parcels. Lady Matilde asked the cabby to stop at Molesworth Street, where she went first into Noblett's sweet shop on the corner, and then next door, to the Misses Kennedys' needlecraft shop, to replenish her stock of embroidery threads and to buy a new tapestry and wools to keep herself occupied during the winter months.

They finally arrived at the Shelbourne Hotel, fifteen minutes late, to find that David Minns had already met Michael, who had ordered afternoon tea. They chatted for a little while, but soon Michael said that they must start for home. They all rose to take their leave.

Michael called the waiter to settle his bill and to have his car brought from the hotel garage to the front of the hotel. They were standing in the hallway, chatting in a desultory way, when David, who had been frantically searching for another excuse to see Charlotte, asked, 'Do you have any plans to attend the D'Oyly Carte performances next week? My father takes a box in the Gaiety Theatre for the whole winter season. Would you, Lady Barker-Grey, Mr Moore and Charlotte, like to join my family one evening at the opera, and to some supper afterwards?'

'It is a charming idea,' said Lady Barker-Grey, 'but we certainly would not like to impose on your family.'

'My mother will telephone you tomorrow,' said David 'and I am positive she will assure you it will be no imposition, only a pleasure.'

'Well, it would be most kind of Mrs Minns to take such trouble.'

'Here's the car,' said Michael. 'Nice to see you again, David, goodbye.'

On his way back to Rathmines, David had second thoughts about the invitation he had issued. Too late now, however, the deed was done. But he knew that the news would not be received kindly. He decided to wait until after dinner before broaching the subject, when he hoped his father's mood would be more mellow.

'I think you have taken leave of your senses,' said Joseph. 'I am sure they are as nice as you say. But you had no right to involve us with the family of your Gentile girl. I won't go. You will have to make some excuse. No Fanny, my mind is made up.' And he retired behind his paper, deaf to anything that might be said to him.

Fanny looked at her son's anxious and troubled face, and put her finger to her lips. 'Well, David, if that is how your father feels, there is no more to be said.' But she winked at him, and smiled a smile which said, as plain as words, leave it to me and phone me in the morning.

When he did, Fanny said to ask no questions, but to give her the telephone number, and she would verify the invitation for the following Wednesday with Lady Barker-Grey, and she would also make arrangements for supper in a private room in the Hibernian Hotel. 'But David, do not depend on my intervention another time, for I will not go against your father when I know that he is right.'

The following Wednesday the two families met in the Coffee Room of the Gaiety Theatre, as arranged. Introductions having been effected, they made their way to the reserved box. David presented his mother and Lady Matilde each with a casket of chocolates. Joseph handed everyone a large glossy programme for the light opera, *The Mikado*. Lady Matilde looked around to Mrs Minns, saying that she was most comfortable, always preferring a 'loge' to being in the body of the theatre.

There was a warm hum of greetings and a clatter of seats as people moved into their places. Women craned their necks to see who was where, what other women were wearing, and who was with whom. More than she had expected, Lotte felt at ease with David's mother, and although she was a little afraid of Joseph Minsky, she decided she rather liked him.

As the curtain came down for the interval, there was thunderous applause. Even Lady Matilde was smiling and clapping her gloved hands. The gentlemen excused themselves and left as a tray of refreshments was brought into the box for the ladies.

'Charming performance,' Lady Matilde said, turning to Fanny Minns.

'Yes, yes it is, and are you enjoying it Miss Moore?' asked Fanny.

'Oh, it's wonderful!' said Charlotte. 'I hadn't expected it to be so colourful. The costumes are so rich.' Charlotte looked very beautiful, her eyes shining and her hair gleaming. 'I have heard many of the songs before, but I am enjoying myself so much. Thank you, Mrs Minns, for inviting us to join you.'

Making a pretence of looking at her programme, Fanny thought to herself that she could see what David admired in this girl, she was indeed a delight to look at, and she was obviously full of intelligence and vivacity. Oy! If only she were Jewish!

The third bell rang for 'Curtain Up' and the gentlemen returned to the box.

When the performance was over, they made their way from the dress circle down to the foyer. Joseph asked David to see, before the ladies left the warmth of the theatre, if their cabs had arrived to take them to the Royal Hibernian Hotel.

In the cab, Fanny explained that the Royal Hibernian was one of the few hotels in the city which catered for Jewish guests. The management had installed facilities for the preparation of kosher food, in the prescribed ritual manner, and she and Joseph frequently availed of the private diningrooms to entertain guests after the theatre.

When they arrived, the porter came to help the ladies, holding a large umbrella to shield them from the drizzle that had started. As they went up the steps and entered the foyer, the duty manager welcomed them, and said to Mrs Minns, 'Everything has been prepared as you have ordered, Madame. If you will follow me, I will show you to your supper suite.'

He took them in the lift to an upper floor and escorted them down a lushly carpeted hall to an open door. Standing to one side he allowed the guests to enter. An attendant took their cloaks and a waiter showed them to the drawingroom, where aperitifs had been set out. When these were declined, they were shown to the diningroom and seated at the table as directed by Fanny. A large trolley was wheeled around the table from which each guest made their choice. There were hot vol-au-vents filled with flaked haddock in a creamy sauce, and rissoles of baked chopped fish in a jellied gravy, garnished with carrot rings, accompanied by chopped spinach and sautéed potatoes, with a horseradish and beetroot relish.

'Oh, gefilte fish and crane, how wundebar! I have not had an opportunity to enjoy any since I was last with my sister-in-law, Hannah von Zeit, in Hamburg,' exclaimed Lady Matilde.

'Oh, so you know something of our food, your ladyship?' said Joseph.

'Why yes. My brother is married to a Jewess, and she still observes many of the culinary practices she learned as a girl in her parents' home.'

'Your sister-in-law is Jewish?' said Joseph. 'Well . . . well . . . how very interesting! My wife's people came from Germany, also Hamburg, but they went to the north of England. I gather there is a large Jewish community in Hamburg. In these modern times they no longer stay in ghettos but integrate into all aspects of business and cultural life, and meet many people from all social levels. This was one reason my family-in-law moved to England, so that they could remain in a smaller Jewish community, and thus not lose touch with their own roots.'

As the evening progressed, Fanny watched David's face as he talked to Charlotte, and she felt that perhaps she had made a mistake in taking his part and persuading Joseph to go along with the plans for this evening. He was obviously besotted by the girl, and if the truth were told, who could blame him? She was a lovely creature to look at, and had all the charm and wit of her class and upbringing. But, Fanny thought, any further contact between her beloved son and the girl could only bring heartache and disaster. She would have to, cautiously, make David see that such an alliance could not work, and would only cause grief to all concerned.

On the way home, Joseph was very quiet, concentrating on his driving. Therefore, it took Fanny by surprise when he suddenly said, 'A very pleasant evening, extremely nice people. Lady Matilde was most appreciative of the menu you chose, my dear. Mr Moore is a gentleman of erudition and original ideas, and even the girl is passable. But here it ends, do you understand me Fanny?'

Some weeks later, Joseph asked David to come and see him in his office. 'Noo David? You are now a qualified doctor of medicine. You have travelled, and have had experience in working in your profession. Again I say, noo? What now? Do you a specialist want to be, or what?'

'Well, Father, you will probably be relieved to hear I do not want to specialise,' said David with a laugh. Then more seriously, 'I have studied and worked and played for nearly seven years. I agree that I must settle down now and think of the future. I have decided I would like to be a general practitioner, a family doctor who is always there for his patients in times of illness and stress. But I don't have enough money to just put up my plate and wait. I also don't want to impose on your generosity any more, so I have made the decision to look for a position as assistant with an established general practitioner.'

'My son . . . an assistant? I ask you, David, who do you think I run this business for? Me? I have enough money now to sell and retire. Who needs these headaches? No, my dear son. I run it so that you and your sisters and my grandchildren will have a secure future. So we will talk no more about money. Now, we must look for somewhere to buy a house, and go to see my accountant about providing you with some income, until such a time you can on your own feet stand. Then we will get some furniture for your house and consulting rooms, then . . . we will get you a wife . . . eh? Is that a good plan?'

David laughed. 'So much for the hours I have spent thinking out my future. You make it all sound so simple. Thank you, Father. You are most generous, and I am most grateful. As soon as I am making some money, I will pay you back, but a wife I will find for myself.'

'Pay back, *shmay* back! We'll see. I am glad you will look for a wife. A man needs an anchor, and in the future, children. Now we will speak with your uncle and see if he has a property for you. In fact, he mentioned a house in Baggot Street the other day. Are you interested?'

'Interested! My God, Father! Baggot Street is way beyond anything I dreamt of. Of course I'm interested. But I'm also aware that, for a Jewish doctor, it may be an area in which it will take a little longer to become established in practice.'

'Who cares. It is ideal, near the synagogue, near us and near your grandmother, when she is in Ireland. It is on a route out of the city, where, your great uncle Samuel says, it is going to become more and more fashionable. There are already a few new houses built in the last twenty years, beyond Ballsbridge. Soon there will be more, and the children of your patients will live there, so your future is well assured.'

As the house in question had been unoccupied for some time, David and his father were able to go at once for a preliminary viewing. They both felt it was ideally suitable, and accompanied the estate agent back to his office to begin negotiations for its purchase, and to arrange for Fanny to see the house the following afternoon.

The next day, Joseph stopped at the estate agent's office to collect the keys, on the way to Baggot Street. He handed them to David and said, 'There you are my son, it is for you to open the door to your house for your mother. With *mazel*,' he said, kissing David on both cheeks.

Fanny said nothing as they proceeded towards the house. When they arrived, David excitedly jumped out and opened the car door for his mother, saying, 'Welcome!' He then ran up the few steps to the hall door, and by the time Fanny and Joseph reached the top step, David had found the right key on the large bunch and had opened the door wide.

Fanny preceded the two men into the house. In her thorough way she made a tour of the rooms, from the basement to the attic, followed by her husband and son, who pointed out good features of the house and their plans for the use of the various rooms.

When the tour of inspection had finished, and they were back in the hall, David burst out, 'Well, Mother, what do you think? You have said nothing.'

'Noo Fanny?' said Joseph, 'It's quite something, isn't it. He will be the finest Jewish doctor in Dublin!'

'It is certainly a very substantial house and will be most elegant when furnished.'

'You're right! You're right! But Fanny, don't you feel it will also make a very fine home?'

'We have a long way to go before it becomes a home,' Fanny replied. 'When the *mezuzas* are in place on every doorpost, outward sign of a Jewish house, and when David brings to it his Jewish bride, then it will be a home. But for now, as I have said, it is a very good house.' And lifting her face up to her tall handsome son, she said, 'My darling, you know you have my blessing.'

With this, David bent towards her, and she kissed his cheek.

During the next three months, while decorating and carpeting were being done in Baggot Street, David noticed that his Jewish social life was becoming very busy. He received many invitations to houses where there were unmarried daughters. Even at home, in his parents' house, more often than not, his sister Hilda had one of her numerous girlfriends to join them at mealtimes. It certainly did not need a giant intellect for David to realise that the flower of Dublin Jewish girlhood was being paraded for his benefit. This amused him greatly, and when Hilda questioned him as to why he never asked any of her girl friends to go out, and only flirted with them in the house, he replied, 'Because they are too silly, and I can see through your ruses. It's all got to stop now. I must settle down to work. But, as the American saying goes, "Ye'r a nice kid, kid!" '

David now had his consulting room and waiting room ready to receive patients. His motor car stood waiting to rush to any emergency calls that might come. A brass plate, with his name and hours, was fixed onto his door, shining, to match the well-polished knocker and doorhandle. He put a notice in *The Irish Times* to announce that he was now in practice, and sat waiting for his first patient.

He sat. Day after day. The first week became the second, and then the third. He filled in time reading all the current medical journals, and any other articles on which he could lay his hands. But the hours passed slowly. Each time the doorbell rang he straightened his already perfect desk, and was always disappointed when the caller turned out to be one or other of his parents, or his sister. He became despondent, wondering how he had let his father talk him into this ridiculous establishment which was eating up money. The effort to dress himself, and to sit in his surgery, became more difficult with each passing day, and when, at the end of six weeks, nothing had happened, he made the decision that he would, to save his sanity, spend his time working for another degree.

With this in mind, he went to see his old professor at Sir Patrick Dunn's Hospital. Sir Seymour Mills, senior medical consultant to the hospital and professor of medicine at Trinity College, was delighted to see his former student and to hear all his news of what he had been doing in the intervening time since he had qualified. He was sympathetic about the weeks of waiting, and said that he remembered going through the same phase. 'You are taking the right course, Minns. Nothing like having a few extra letters tacked onto one's name . . . gives a fellow added glamour and interest. Now, let's see what you can do. What is your special interest, eh?'

'Well, Sir, the only thing that I am sure about is that I want to stay in general practice, to be a family physician. I do not feel I am cut out for hospital work, or to be a surgeon of any description. I do like children, but would like to be involved with them in their ordinary lives, and follow them into adulthood, not just in a paediatric practice. I also like women, but have no wish to specialise in their diseases. So now you see why I have come to you for advice.'

'Hmm . . . hmmm. Yes, I see Minns. There is very little left. Skins . . . what? No, you say. Well what about a diploma in public health, or a diploma in children's health or . . . No! I have the solution, you will do your MD. From there you will have all sorts of openings, including, if you should change your mind, a position such as mine. After all, I will want to retire some day I expect, go fishing, get some golf in, that sort of thing . . . eh? I will get my registrar to send you all the data, and then come and see me again. You must come and have dinner with my wife and myself one day, eh? Nice to see you, Minns.'

And they both rose and shook hands.

Once again, David was busy. He spent part of each day either sitting in at out-patient clinics in hospital or studying in the library in Trinity. He even had some real patients. The child next door had fallen off her swing and hurt her shoulder, and a frantic nanny had called him in. He was so efficient and calm that the family, impressed, became his patients, and recommended him to the other members of their families, and to their friends, who also liked the cheerful and caring way he treated people. His reputation started to grow, and he found that instead of the long empty hours of the past weeks, his days were too short to fit everything into them.

His first summer in Baggot Street was nearly over when an invitation arrived for him to attend Charlotte Moore's graduation party, on September 3rd, 1925. Fanny later spoke to him on the telephone and said that she, Joseph and Hilda had also received an invitation. They were going to decline, however, as they felt that Hilda was too young to attend and there was little chance that there would be any other young Jewish people there. She wondered to herself if it was wise for David to accept either, but perhaps he had decided not to. David quickly realised what his mother was trying to tell him, and although he knew it was foolish to risk becoming involved again, his heart quickened when he thought of seeing his lovely golden girl. He knew that he did not have the strength of character to refuse the invitation along with his family. He so looked forward to seeing her. Each time he thought about it, his whole being tingled with anticipation. Every spare moment he had, he spent haunting the shops for something appropriate and lovely as a gift, something he hoped she would cherish always, and by which she would remember him. He discarded idea after idea. One day, whilst browsing in West's jewellery shop in Grafton Street, he saw, at the back of one of the display cases, a tortoise shell and gold Visiting Card case. In his memory the colours reflected the speckled lights of Charlotte's eyes. He arranged with the assistant to have a gold letter 'C' set into one corner. He looked at the trinket again, and felt well pleased with his find.

Chapter Twenty-Six

The months of January, February and March were the longest Charlotte could remember. Owen, Darragh and the twins were in England, the twins at Michael's old school, Owen at university, and Darragh in the cadet corps. Grossmutter very seldom moved out of the warmth and comfort of her own house. Nanny found the cold more and more difficult to contend with, her joints were stiff and her fingers crooked and knobbly with arthritis. Even simple tasks were getting beyond her. Cook was grumbly and complaining, and even Ita and Eamonn were not as spritely as they had been. Amy alone stayed cheerful and calm in the increasingly shabby house. Constance was the only guest who came to stay, and that was on widely spaced weekends.

Charlotte spent all her free time with her father. He was growing thinner with each passing month, and he seemed to have lost not only his appetite for food, but also for his work and estate duties. Several times Charlotte surprised Eamonn surreptitiously refilling the whiskey decanter when it should still have been fairly full, and she realised that her father's appearance and blurred approach to life was rooted in the speedy disappearance of the contents of the decanter.

Her anxiety grew when she came across a letter from the bank asking Michael to pay them another visit, and again when Grossmutter made an unexpected appearance at Priory House one morning, and she heard angry words, which she could not quite catch, coming from the study.

Finally one day, taking his post to him, she found her father sprawled unconscious on the study floor. She immediately sent for Dr Ryan. Next to family, Darragh Ryan's place in the Moore children's lives was that of a close and dear uncle, and Charlotte had no hesitation in telling him of all her fears and worries.

Darragh was shocked when he saw Michael for the first time in several weeks, for Michael had been keeping out of his way. He felt very guilty about the great deterioration in his friend, knowing that it was partly because he had neglected calling on him. Michael recovered consciousness and Darragh Ryan examined him thoroughly, then helped Eamonn to put him to bed. He went on his rounds and, calling back later in the day, had a long talk with Michael. Charlotte, who was anxiously waiting outside her father's door to speak to Darragh Ryan, was devastated when she heard great racking sobs coming from her father, and bursting into the room she ran and threw her arms around him, trying to comfort him. 'O God, Lotte. What kind of father am I?'

'The best . . . oh the best! O Father, don't cry, please don't cry. We will make you better, won't we Uncle Darragh?' She turned her heartbroken face towards their friend, confident that he would know what to do.

Darragh thought for what seemed a long time before speaking. 'Charlotte, you did the right thing calling me, and I am sure that we are in time to prevent permanent damage. But you must realise that in the years since your mother died, your father has had a heavy load to carry alone. He has never spared himself, either physically, emotionally or mentally. All the responsibility he has had to shoulder has taken a heavy toll on his resources, and that, combined with heavy drinking, which he felt was his only solace, has weakened his constitution considerably. But with good food and good care, in a while he will be himself again. I have advised, no insisted, that he should go where professional staff can help him, and look after him. I know of a clinic not too far from here. I am going now to make arrangements for your father to be admitted today. In a couple of weeks, you will be able to go and see that he is back to his former good health. Now child, stay with him until I return.' And he went to the telephone in the hall.

Darragh came back and asked Charlotte to see that a bag was packed for Michael, just some night clothes and his toiletries. He then drove Michael to the clinic. The doctor in charge, having made it clear that there were to be no visitors until he gave permission, promised that he would give a twice-weekly progress report to Dr Ryan.

After seeing his other patients, Darragh telephoned Charlotte to ask her and Amy to meet him at Lady Barker-Grey's. He needed to explain Michael's illness to them, and it would be easier if they were all together. He reassured her that he had left Michael in as good spirits as possible, under the circumstances.

When Darragh and Joan had married, they had made a pact whereby, if patients were also involved in their social life, there would be no discussion of their medical problems. In that way there could be no breach of doctor/patient confidentiality. For the first time in all the years, he now broke that arrangement. He told Joan of the situation and asked her to accompany him that evening in her capacity as 'honorary aunt'. When they arrived at Priory Lodge they were met by three very troubled faces. As gently as possible he explained that Michael had become an habitual drinker, and that the effect of long use of alcohol on the system caused some damage to the liver, kidneys, and often the heart. 'It seems,' he said, 'that the damage is minimal, but it is too soon to be very exact. But what I can say is that we all have a very long and trying time ahead of us if we are to help Michael to regain his health and mental balance. Initially he will be in the clinic for about six to eight weeks, and then there will be months and months of a careful regime when he comes home. The most difficult part will be the continuous watching to see that he does not slip back and start drinking again, as the outcome would not bear thinking about. All the alcohol will have to be removed from general use, and the cellar secured with extra bolts.'

All were shocked at what they were hearing. Not one of them, although suspicious, had dreamed of how far matters had gone. Of course, they promised willingly they would follow to the letter of the law, everything prescribed by the doctors.

'Now, to be practical. Can the estate and other financial matters take care of themselves, or how will you manage?'

'We must send for Kit at once,' said Lady Barker-Grey in her authoritative way. 'He will know what we must do, and will keep control of everything. I do not see ze necessity of telling Henrietta. What can she do, so far away? And it will be time enough to tell ze boys when zey are coming for ze Easter holidays. But Kit, yes! We need him, and he has ze necessary experience.'

The anxious waiting for Michael to be allowed home was apparent on each member of the two households. Lady Matilde was heard to mumble that, for the first time, she felt like an old lady, and this she wrote to her two sisters-in-law in Wales. Nanny was very grumpy and nothing that Charlotte did seemed to please her. Easter came, and with it the return of the four boys, whose irrepressible high and low spirits were equally noisy, which did nothing to help Nanny's spleen. Cook, Ita and Eamonn, although willing to help Kit in every way possible, squabbled among themselves. Cook saying over and over that, 'A bad spirit, bad cess to it, was visitin' the house', which set Eamonn mad with her, calling her 'A silly, superstitious auld woman'. Ita became scared of her own shadow, and jumped and yelped every time a puff of wind rattled the doors or windows. Only Amy, as usual, stayed calm, and Charlotte spent all her time when at home in her company.

When the boys returned to England, life in Priory House settled down a little. Through the trauma of the months of Michael's illness, Charlotte felt that she would have gone crazy without the staunch friendship and support of Constance.

At long last, towards the end of May, Michael came home. The house was made as cheerful as possible and Charlotte had written little messages of welcome to him, which she placed in strategic places for him to find. They were all shattered by his appearance. His once thick and lustrous hair was now much thinner and quite grey. His former fine, upright figure, was sparse and bent, his clothes hanging on him limply.

'Lord, Sir,' said Cook. 'I will have to fatten ye up, and put some colour back in dose cheeks, wit some good home cookin' and bakin'. But O, Mr Moore sir, we are all of one mind, it is good to see ye back where dose that care for ye is.' And looking around for approval from the others, she stepped back, flushed with their approbation, and her genuine gladness that the master had returned.

Gradually the household returned to some normality. Michael, though very frail, took back the reins of his farm from Kit, who, gratefully, returned to Blanche in Wicklow, having found it a great strain coming to Blackrock twice a week.

Every day Michael seemed to grow stronger, and he put back some of the flesh he had lost. He was overwhelmed by the concern expressed in the letters he received from the few members of the family who had learned of his illness. Among these, there was one from his aunts-in-law in Wales. They would, they said, like to spend the summer months in Ireland. It had now been some time since their last visit, and they were anxious to see the family. Michael discussed this proposal with his mother-in-law, who had received a similar letter. They decided that the two old ladies should be invited to come at the end of July, and that they should stay with Lady Matilde in Priory Lodge, visiting Priory House as often as they wished.

In June, Henrietta paid a surprise visit, giving only two days' notice of her arrival. She wanted to see for herself that her father was being properly cared for, and was very put out when he refused to return to France with her. As usual, she caused upheaval, and upset everyone and everything, so that even

Grossmutter was glad when she left to return to her beloved Jean Louis.

The Misses Barker-Grey arrived in due course, surrounded by enough luggage to supply a battalion. Eamonn drove Charlotte to Kingstown to meet the mailboat from Holyhead and to look after the baggage. Owen, who was at home, had volunteered to go, but his father had needed him to accompany him on his farm rounds, as he was still not strong enough to do them on his own. The twins, home from school, also clamoured to be allowed to go, for, they said, they were seasoned travellers themselves.

Charlotte was dismayed to see how her great aunts had aged. She ran to hug them together, and separately, as soon as they came down the gangway.

They returned to Priory Lodge, where the rest of the family was waiting for them, and Charlotte was moved when she saw the three old ladies shed tears of happiness at their reunion. They tutted and laa'ed at how the boys had grown, and produced gifts for everyone. Michael enjoyed their visit, and being fussed over by them made him feel quite young again. One day they announced that they were going to give a party in honour of Charlotte's coming of age and receiving her degree. They would arrange everything, and it was to be their treat. Charlotte should have a beautiful gown made for her, and she would have slippers to match.

At first Michael was reluctant to agree. His pride at allowing someone else to pay for a party in his home went against the grain. But he was slowly persuaded that it would be a lovely occasion, and even began to catch the excitement of the others as the plans were made. He looked around his house and saw the shabbiness of time on the yellowed ceilings and weather-worn hall door and other paintwork. He knew he could never afford a general refurbishment, but decided that Eamonn, Seán and the boys could smarten up the worst areas with a coat of white paint.

The lists of guests were made, and Charlotte, after some thought, included Olive's name, deciding that past events should stay firmly there, and that, after all, Olive had been one of her two closest friends, supporting her at a time when she sorely needed it. Of course, she discussed all her plans with Constance, who was as excited as she was about the party.

The invitations were printed. 'For, after all, we must do things properly,' Olwyn said, as usual echoed by Bronwyn, who insisted they be gilt-edged and raised copper plate.

They went in convoy to the local dressmaker, who, Charlotte insisted, was very good indeed, even though her aunts wanted her to go to the best shops in Dublin, or even to send to London for a dress. But Charlotte got her way, saying that she saw no point in spending so much unnecessary money when Mrs Flaherty was the best there was, having trained and worked in an haute-mode establishment in her youth. She chose a stunning pattern from a magazine. Smokey grey chiffon over a silver lame underdress, embroidered with crystal and iridescent beading, like drops of rain running down the skirt, which stopped at different lengths, in points, just above her ankles. The local shoemaker covered a pair of pumps in matching fabric, to set off the ensemble, and Mrs Flaherty embroidered a headband with the same beading, which twinkled and shone amongst her abundant curls, as the light caught it.

The day before the party, the women raided the gardens and woods for flowers to fill the house, and the men arranged lanterns between the trees that edged the lawn, where a three-piece band was to play and where a wooden floor was laid for dancing.

As they went to bed, exhausted but satisfied, each said their own little prayer for good weather, and no rain. As the day dawned, their prayers were answered. The sun shone with that special light that comes to the east coast of Ireland in the late summer and no clouds appeared in a clear sky. Cook, putting the finishing touches to days of preparation, was unapproachable, and Nanny directed the spreading of huge embroidered white cloths, which she unfolded from a swaddling of black tissue paper, onto the buffet tables. Ita rubbed the few pieces of silver that Michael had not sold, to a final burnished polish, and flicked any speck of dust that her gimlet eye detected. The boys were set to see that all the shoes to be worn were polished, and that all the ice would be ready for drinks, and that the wine was chilling in ice buckets. Eamonn supervised the setting up of a table in the hall, from which to dispense these liquid refreshments, and Amy saw to it that everyone's clothes were ready and waiting.

The three ladies, and Gerda, thought it would be politic to stay away from the house until evening, and gave lunch at Priory Lodge to Willie Fitzgerald and to Blanche and Kit Moore, who had come from Wicklow.

At long last, everything and everybody was ready. Darragh looked particularly smart in his uniform. They all gathered in the drawingroom ten minutes before the appointed time for the guests to arrive. Grossmutter, as usual, commandeered the most comfortable chair, where she would sit for the evening, expecting everyone to come and pay homage to her, as if she were royalty. Even the twins had to acknowledge that she had the bearing and demeanour for the part.

Michael and Lotte had insisted that Olwyn and Bronwyn stand with them to receive the guests, as co-hostesses. The twins had been instructed to help Ita take cloaks and to put them into the study. Charlotte could not keep still, and wandered about the room touching the flowers in their vases, and rearranging photographs and ornaments. The boys fingered their stiff collars, mumbling about being trussed up like turkeys for Lotte's beano.

At long last the first motor car was heard crunching the gravel. The two ladies, along with Michael and Lotte, made their way into the hall to greet their guests. After that, people arrived in a steady stream, and soon young voices could be heard on the lawn, whilst older guests found quieter surroundings in the house.

Michael checked from time to time to see if Lotte was enjoying her party, and each time he looked at his beautiful daughter, his heart swelled with love and pride. He sought out the two aunts, bent to kiss them, squeeze their hands, and express his gratitude for their thoughtfulness. Then, feeling very tired, he went to his bedroom to rest for a while. For the first time in many years, he spoke to and wept for his Jessica.

Lotte felt the night was like a fairytale, or some fabulous scene from a movie picture. She danced every dance, ragtime, Charleston, bunnyhug, and all the other dances that were in fashion, and thought each of her partners more wonderful than the last. When Olive arrived, there was a slight hesitancy between both girls before Charlotte stepped forward and hugged her friend in her usual warm way. Constance, standing nearby, also hugged her two friends, and they stood for a moment, as so many times in the past, arms around each other's waists. They introduced Olive to as many young people as they could, and spying David Minns, Charlotte asked him to especially look after Olive and see that she had a good time. She thought David looked handsome and very bronzed, and when he claimed his dance, felt a thrill go through her as he took her in his arms for a foxtrot.

Eamonn struck a gong to announce that supper was being served. When everyone had eaten their fill, Michael, who had made a supreme effort to come down, asked that everyone charge their glasses and join him in drinking a toast to the success and happiness of his beloved daughter, Charlotte Jane.

Then Cook and Nanny produced a surprise birthday cake, with twenty-one candles, which Lotte had to blow out. The twins led the singing of 'Happy Birthday' and 'She's a Jolly Good Fellow'.

Darragh Ryan claimed the first dance with Charlotte after supper, and everyone made their way back to the dance floor. Lotte again danced every dance, twirling in the arms of one young man after another, some making her feel as though her feet were hardly touching the ground, and others making them feel like lead. But the music, the warm, star-filled night, and snatched sips of wine, made her head spin with lightness and fun, and she was delighted that the glimpses she caught of her two dearest friends showed that they too were having a good time.

When David Minns again claimed her, she was pleased to acquiesce when he suggested they take a short stroll, instead of dancing. They brought each other up to date with their happenings since Christmas. Charlotte wished him luck in his new home, and with his practice, and he wished her well in her new career of social worker. They were so involved in their conversation that they did not realise how far they had walked, until they saw the gazebo in front of them.

'Let us sit inside for a while, I have something to give to you,' said David. Looking at him shyly, she followed him as he led her by the hand inside. Once seated, he produced his gift, and gave it to her. She excitedly undid the wrapping and opened the velvet case. He heard her little squeal of pleasure as she took out the trinket. O David, how beautiful, and how extravagant! I shall feel so elegant taking my cards out of this lovely holder. You are generous and a sweetie.' The hours of hunting were well repaid as he saw her shining eyes look at him with warmth and gaiety.

'It is not nearly as lovely as you are, darling.' He saw her blush at his extravagant compliment, and unable to stop himself he put his arms around her, and in his kiss she felt the ardour this man had for her, and responded with equal measure.

She suddenly broke away, and looking at him, delightful in her confusion, mumbled something like 'Have to get back to my guests . . . I'll be missed', and ran back along the path ahead of David, to rejoin the others.

He felt she avoided him for the rest of the evening, and, mentally kicking himself for startling her, he chatted with Kit and Blanche, while he followed her with his eyes, once again thinking how like moonbeams she was, darting and throwing light here and there as she weaved her way through her guests.

Dawn was breaking as the last of the young people left. David thanked Charlotte for inviting him and for a memorable evening, and said he would be in touch with her again soon.

The next day he dropped a 'Thank You' note to her. He asked her to come to tea to see his house the following day, and if this was not convenient to telephone him. If it was, he would expect to see her at three-thirty.

Chapter Twenty-Seven

The next afternoon Charlotte felt a frisson of anticipation as she went up the steps to David's house. At first she had not intended accepting his invitation, aware that she felt a dangerous attraction to him and sensing that David would not be satisfied with just a casual flirtation. She also knew that any permanent alliance would be impossible. But, in the end, curiosity got the better of her. Without saying where she was going, she put on her best suit and hat, made sure her gloves were clean, and ran to catch the next tram car to town.

The door was opened by a trim maid in uniform, who showed her up to the first-floor drawingroom, where she found David and his sister waiting for her.

David rose to greet Charlotte. 'Do you remember my sister Hilda? I think you met once.'

'Of course I do,' said Charlotte, shaking hands with the shy girl, who had also risen to meet her brother's guest.

When the formalities had been taken care of, Charlotte looked around her. She took in the cool colours of the paintwork and wallpaper, the fresh curtains, toning carpet and furniture, and turning to her host with genuine enthusiasm, she said, 'I think it is a most elegant and lovely room.' David was delighted at her praise, and walked to the bell pull to signal that tea should be brought in.

After tea, Hilda excused herself. 'I have to be at a piano lesson shortly. I was very sorry to have missed your wonderful party, but my parents considered me far too young to attend, though I appreciated being asked.'

'I quite understand. I am so pleased David has given me the opportunity to meet you again today.'

When Hilda had left, David asked Charlotte if she would like to see the rest of the house, and when she nodded, he gave her what he laughingly called 'The Royal Tour'.

'Well David,' she said when she had seen everything, 'I certainly think you have made a good and wise choice. This is a home of which you can be proud. I am sure that your uncle is right, and that it will become a valuable property. I really must go now, as I must not be late home to dinner. Kit, Blanche and Olive are still with us, and I feel I ought to give a helping hand. Thank you so much.' She held her hand out to him. He promptly took it in both of his, and looking into her eyes, which made her heart flutter, he said, 'You must know I care for you, and, if it is only in friendship, I have to see you very soon again.'

She stammered an excuse about being very busy, tearing her gaze away and looking down. She suggested that if he would telephone in a week or so, perhaps they could meet again for tea.

'No Charlotte, it is no use trying to put me off. It won't work. I suspect that you do not find me quite repulsive, and if that is so, when I call for you tomorrow evening after I have made my house calls, I hope you will come for a drive with me in my motor car.'

She pulled her hand free and made her way out of the house, her thoughts in chaos. Of course he was right, she did feel something for him. What, she did not know yet. But she knew that when he called for her the next evening, she would be ready.

After that, with the exception of the Jewish high holy days, the Christian festivals, and certain family occasions, David and Charlotte spent a great deal of their non-working hours together. David's birthday, then Christmas and New Year, came and went. In the cold dark days of January and February they would sit in front of a roaring fire in David's study, reading, talking, playing chess and draughts and laughing a lot. They discussed literature and music, and found that they had similar tastes, and Charlotte absolutely adored the Jewish food that David's mother sent in each week, and said that she thought it was 'scrummy'.

March came with its cheerful daffodils and crocuses. They ventured out of doors for long walks in the Phoenix Park, or to the woods in Mount Merrion, and even occasionally, at the latter end of the month, along the strand at Sandymount.

David knew that the day was coming when the relationship would not be sufficient in its present form and that soon they would have to talk about their future.

Charlotte also felt a great sense of well-being. Michael seemed, if not any better, to be holding his own. She had found that she could work part time as a social worker with the almoner in the Royal City of Dublin Hospital, in Baggot Street, and still have time to be with Michael, before flying to meet David in the evenings and at weekends. She knew that the situation could not remain static. But whenever such thoughts crossed her mind, she would push them aside, thinking . . . soon . . . no need to think about it yet.

Matters drifted on over the summer. The boys returned home for Easter, and then the summer holidays. Owen Moore spent most of his time with his father, learning about the farm and its workings, only catching up with his friends when his brother Darragh or the twins were around to keep Michael Moore company in his stead.

Darragh Ryan was a constant visitor to the house. He played chess while at the same time keeping his eye on Michael as a patient. If the day was warm, Michael was persuaded to go out for a walk, or even to go as far as Priory Lodge to lunch. But on the cold or blustery days, he often spent the entire time in his bed. Charlotte was afraid at these times that he may have hidden some alcohol in his room. But Eamonn assured her that such was not the case.

At the end of the holidays Owen Moore announced that he would not be returning to university, explaining that he loved Priory House and the farm, and wished to be a farmer and to be there full time. Michael tried to argue with him, but he did not have the energy to hold out against the enthusiasm and vigour of the younger man.

Now that he had a strong pair of shoulders to lean on, Michael withdrew more and more into his own world, rereading old and loved books, or scribbling on some imagined project at his desk.

Charlotte, writing in her diary, realised that it was a year since her first visit to David's house. When they met that evening she reminded him of that occasion. 'Yes, my sweet, a year since your birthday, since I first declared my love for you. Did you think I had forgotten?' He handed her a box containing a tiny gold heart suspended from a chain.

'How lovely, David, you are most thoughtful. I really love it, and shall wear it always.'

'I hope it is the first of many gifts that I will give to you over the years, which brings me to something that we must discuss. You know that we cannot just drift on in this fashion, that I want, and desperately need you, as my wife, and that there are many obstacles to be overcome before that can happen?'

'Yes, David darling, I do know, and I want to be your wife. You know that I would lay down my life for you. But David . . . David . . . what do we do?'

David Minns took her in his arms. 'Lotte. The main thing is that we love each other. We will find a way. But I must be honest with you. I once made a promise to my parents that I would only marry a Jewish girl, and I cannot ever break that promise. I have often thought of asking you to embrace Judaism. But your family, and how they feel, must also be taken into consideration. Besides, the course, if you are accepted, is so difficult that I could not expect you to go through such rigours. It is filled with many obscure and seemingly peculiar rituals. But, my sweet, my love for you is so great that I am going to ask it. Or at least, for you to give it some thought. My conscience, and my concern for you, will not allow me to go on seeing you without a commitment. Yet, to be apart from you is unthinkable.'

She sat still for a moment, listening to his words. Then throwing her arms around his neck she said, 'David, you are my life, nothing but being with you matters. Of course I will undertake anything that is necessary, if in the end it means I will be your wife. Don't you know that?'

'You are the most loving and generous girl in the world, but turning your back on your upbringing, and perhaps being reviled by your family, will be an enormous step. You must think about all it will mean very carefully. Talk to your father, grandmother and your vicar, and maybe even Darragh and Joan Ryan, before we go one step further. I think it will be for the best if we do not see each other for the next week, then our being together will not cloud your judgement.'

When she arrived home, Charlotte, with her usual impulsiveness, went straight to Michael and told him what had passed between David and herself. Michael said, 'My darling daughter, sit here on the side of my bed. This does not come as a total surprise to me. I have known for some months you have been seeing young Minns, and have feared, that with your loving nature, you might perhaps have been carried away. He is a worthy man, and I do not have any doubts that he will love and honour you all your days. But, my darling daughter, the Jewish faith is alien to us. We have very little experience of their ways, for even Hannah von Zeit did not practise her faith, and there are, unfortunately, many sections of our society in which they are not acceptable. Have you considered all this? No, do not interrupt me. I know you must listen to the dictates of your heart. I only remember the happiness of my life with your adored mother, and would not change one moment if, knowing everything, I had it all to do again. But Charlotte, marriage under the most ideal circumstances is not easy, and for it to work, both people must compromise to some degree, there must be give and take on both sides, but if you have really thought everything through, and are aware of all the pitfalls, and the Minns family are also happy, you will have my blessing. I would also like to talk to David, and I think you should tell your grandmother first thing in the morning. Now dear girl, I am very tired. Kiss me goodnight.'

Charlotte, holding back the tears in her eyes, thanked her father, kissed him and left his room.

Next morning, her heart thumping with trepidation, she took the path to Priory Lodge, passed the gazebo, which held so many memories, and cornered Grossmutter in her morningroom. She made her announcement in a defiant voice, and her stance dared Lady Matilde to disapprove.

'Pray, are you telling me, or are you asking me what I sink, you minx?' said Matilde, with a beetling frown on her face. 'Sit down and start at the beginning. Don't leave out anything, do you understand?'

Charlotte felt like a little girl who had been commanded to confess some misbehaviour, and trying to regain her adult status, nevertheless complied with her grossmutter's order, and told the story, both from her own point of view, and that of her beloved, ending with, 'Isn't it a marvellous coincidence that both our grandfathers were named David?', as if this was the final bond of approbation for their union.

When she had finished, Matilde looked at the flaxen-haired beauty, and saw the softness of love for her young man in her eyes, but felt it her duty to her dead daughter to probe matters further.

'And do you honestly believe zat zis will be a proof of love to your David? To change your religion, to turn your back on your own traditions? What right has he to ask such a sing anyway? Promise or no promise, I do not consider such behaviour so honourable.'

Charlotte grew most indignant at this slur on David and retorted, 'Uncle Otto married Aunt Hannah, and she is good and wonderful and they are happy. Don't you like her? I love her. She was very good to me when I lived in Germany, and to you for that matter. Perhaps you don't consider that marriage honourable either.'

'Zere, Zere, Miss, don't go on so. As for your Uncle Otto, he was not the one who had to change, and of course I love Hannah. But I also remember how difficult and heartbreaking it was for her to be ostracised by her Jewish family, and I wonder if it is to be zat way for you. Would you have ze special character zat is needed to take such a course?'

'My father has given me his blessing, so it will not be necessary for me to turn my back on him. But if I had to, I would. I would regret it if you turned against me, but I would learn to live without your love. So, it is entirely up to you, Grossmutter.'

The old lady chuckled. 'Well, if your mind is made up, you do not need to live wizout my love. I add my blessings to your father's, and I will watch over you always. Now, kiss me and go, for I am sure you have many sings to tell your David.'

Charlotte embraced Lady Barker-Grey with much enthusiasm and gratitude, and fled back to the main house to telephone David. The telephone rang and he heard her joyful news, but he knew that only half the battle had been won. He now had to win over, first his own parents, and then his grandparents, to accepting a non-Jewish girl as his wife. David's mind whirled and his heart burst with happiness that his wildest dream was about to become a reality. Then he plummeted into despair as he feared that Charlotte might change her mind, or that her family and friends would persuade her that she was committing a folly in marrying a Jew. That to become one would make her an outcast and pariah to her own society. At the very bottom of his imaginings, he could even hear them bringing up all the old ignorant and superstitious stories about Jews. He berated himself for these fantasies, and for having so little faith in Charlotte, and so little respect for the intelligence of her family.

The problem was, which way to go about it. Rack his brains as he would, he discarded every plan. He held innumerable imaginary conversations with different people, and each petered out as he, also in imagination, found that the men as well as the women were sobbing and pleading with him not to do this thing.

An only son to betray his father, and the grandfather of blessed memory, after whom he was named, and who had brought them to a safe haven in this country.

At last, when he felt as though he would go mad, he decided that he would speak to his cousin, Harold Minns, and see if someone of his own generation could help him to solve his predicament. Harold had married a Jewish girl from within the Dublin community, Queenie Lazarus, and they lived in a house on the Rathgar Road. Michael immediately contacted Harold, saying that he needed to speak to him urgently, and was invited to dine the following evening.

After dinner, and the mind-numbing domestic chatter of Queenie, he and Harold excused themselves and retired to the drawingroom, where David poured his heart out to his cousin.

'It comes as very little surprise, David. Everyone has known you have been seeing this girl. But, quite honestly, we have all hoped it would die a natural death, like all infatuations. But I see we were wrong, and that you are really deeply in love with her. You know, without my telling you, how serious this is. I would not be in your shoes for the world. Can't you find a nice girl like my Queenie, and in time forget this Christian girl? No! Well, I don't know. Yes I do. You must go and see Rabbi Chanaan, he will tell you what you must do. If this girl is really serious about becoming Jewish, he will have all the information you will both need. Tell me David, does she have a ***nidan***, a dowry?'

'What the hell does that have to do with anything? I don't know what she has, and it makes no difference.'

'All right, all right! I only asked. You never know what might help. No, I would not like to be in your shoes.'

'I did not expect you, of all people, to take that attitude Harold. Is that how lawyers think? But I do thank you for your advice. I think it is a very good idea to see the rabbi. I don't know why I did not think of it myself. I am so confused. Please say goodnight and thank you to Queenie for me, and I would appreciate it if this conversation stays between you and me for the present.'

Chapter Twenty-Eight

Having considered the best approach to the rabbi in the shortest possible time, David decided to attend morning prayers in the synagogue, where he knew the rabbi would be in attendance. After the blessings of the phylacteries and the remainder of the service, the men dispersed to their various places of business. David waited for the rabbi, who greeted him.

'Dr Minns. What a pleasure to see you. You have become a stranger to us these days,' he said, in his idiosyncratic, low-pitched voice, which his congregants always felt was loaded with extra meaning.

'I know, Rabbi, I will really have to make more of an effort to attend services in the future.'

'Good, good. Were you waiting for me?'

'Yes, Rabbi. I have a problem on which I need your advice.'

'Well now, I have some time on hand at present. Come along home with me, and we will have breakfast together.'

David drove them to the rabbi's home on the South Circular Road, not too far from his grandmother's house.

When they were settled in the rabbi's study, having eaten a substantial breakfast, the rabbi asked after David's parents and sisters.

'They are in Bray. As you know the family has spent the summer there for many years. Grandmother likes to take the hot saltwater baths, then sit on the promenade and gossip with her friends. They will be back in Dublin for the High Holy Days.'

'Now my boy, what can I do for you?'

David told Rabbi Chanaan the whole story. The circumstances of his original meeting with Charlotte, the friendship formed with Kit, of turning away from his deeply felt feelings for Charlotte, of his renouncing of her and going away, and then the unexpected meeting which had led to the present situation. His face reflected the torments he had gone through, the happiness and upset of the present. The rabbi, a clever and astute man, saw that this was not a situation he could lightly dismiss with a few well-chosen platitudes.

'David. I have known your family now for three generations and I have never known one, man, woman or child, to do a dishonourable act, and I do not expect that you will either. I hope I am a modern man and can accept Gentiles as people who have their own way of worshipping, as we have ours. I am forced by my position of authority and spiritual leadership to ask you if you have fully thought the situation through. Have you thought what you must ask this girl to go through? That she must deny her own origins, her own teachings, to embrace ours? And, I must warn you, it is not enough to do so for love of you, she must do it because of love of Jewishness. Our ways are not easy, even for those born to them, how much more difficult they are for an outsider. I know you have said she has lived as a child with her Jewish great aunt. But you know that, in the eyes of orthodox Jewish opinion, that woman is no longer Jewish. As Jews, we do not proselytise, and, therefore, to join us the conversion is made very difficult, and only the strongest will fulfil all that is required of them. My dear young man, I know that what I am saying is harsh. But these are the realities. One, she must come and convince me that her wish to be Jewish is not that of expediency. Two, if she does, she will have to study our ways, she will have to learn to speak and read Hebrew, in order to make blessings, and recite our prayers. Three, she will have to live in a strictly orthodox home, and learn about *kashrut*, observe the preparations for the Sabbath and festivals, learn all the laws that are inculcated into our women from birth, to fulfil the destiny of a Jewish wife and mother. All this, and more, will take two to four years. In all that time you will never be alone together, there will always be a third party present. Can you explain this to her, and can you go through with it? Because, you know that you will also have to play your part. You will not be able to practise your profession on the Sabbath and holy days, unless in an extreme emergency in order to save a life. Her application will have to be approved of by the Beth Din, the Jewish court, in London. David, I do not want any answer now. Go! Think about what I have said. Do not speak yet to the girl, or your parents. In two or three days, come and see me again, and we will talk some more.'

Every moment that David could spare from his work, he thought over what had been said to him. He pictured Charlotte sitting across the room, divided from him by some unknown third person. Looking at her, longing to take her in his arms, and unable. What agony! And then he realised that this was a thoroughly selfish attitude. Lotte would have to learn all the rituals he had seen his mother, sisters and grandmothers performing, and which he had taken for granted. If she could do all that, then he could be celibate, for the rewards would be tenfold sweeter.

His head swam with a myriad of thoughts. He knew that for Charlotte the most difficult part would be to leave her secure and loving home, to dwell with strangers. He hoped that the strength of their love would carry them through, and that even in crowds they would be alone, in their own cocoon.

The following day, David went again to see Rabbi Chanaan, and told him that he had spent the last two days searching his heart and conscience, and that he felt that he could now say, honestly, that he was prepared to put the whole picture to Charlotte, confident that she would have the necessary attitude.

'Well then, David. You must tell your parents. The girl must inform her family and you must bring Miss Moore to see me as soon as possible.'

'How do I tell my father, Rabbi? How? I know he will be heartbroken. I know also that he likes Charlotte. Who wouldn't? But how do I get him to accept that this is where my heart and happiness lie and that, with or without his blessing, I will marry my love?'

'Have faith in your father's love. You have faith in Charlotte's. But tell your mother first. Women are better than men at accepting the inevitable, they are more pragmatic. And let me know when to expect you and how matters fare.'

David spoke to Charlotte that evening, and painted the picture for her just as the rabbi had painted it for him. 'I don't want to frighten you,' he said, 'but you must be very sure what you are letting yourself in for before making the most important decision of your life, a life that will be utterly changed by these events.'

'My darling David, I am not afraid. I have had many changes in my life already. I know that I can adapt. I love you so much, that whatever you belong to must be right, to have made you the fine person you are. And I have already read in college many things that draw me to Judaism, and its ways. In any religion or philosophy, there are ideas and practices that are less appealing than others, but they are acceptable as part of the total good. Don't worry, my love, we will get through the years, and the time spent will only make the end more worthwhile.'

He kissed her and held her tenderly in gratitude for the miracle that had brought her to him. He went to Blackrock with her to thank Michael and Grossmutter for their trust and understanding. He told them that he was now going to his own family, and hoped that they would react in the same loving way that they had.

The next day, David Minns telephoned both his parents and arranged to see them together that evening. All day, the anxiety of the meeting haunted him and, most unusually, he found his concentration wandering during his work. With an effort, he pulled himself together, and somehow or another, the day passed.

Armed with his love for Charlotte, he faced his parents, told them that he had, for several years, tried to suppress this love but now he could no longer do so, and that Charlotte had not only consented to be his wife, but to convert to Judaism.

When he had finished, he drew back slightly, as if waiting for an onslaught. Fanny slowly rose to her feet from the armchair, and crossing the room, she skirted the desk where her husband sat, and half closed the heavy velvet curtains before returning to her chair. The room, which normally glowed with colour from the paintings on the walls, and the book bindings on the shelves, was plunged into gloom. Neither Fanny nor Joseph moved. Out of the shadow came a despairing sob, and a chanting of the 'Prayer for the Dead' in the cracked, emotional voice of David's father. Fanny staggered to her feet and switched on the light. She saw her son recoil in horror, as if he had been physically hit, and her husband swaying back and forth, his face ghostly grey, as he continued his keening, the tears running down his face and spittle dribbling from his mouth.

'For God's sake, Joseph, stop this madness! Talk to David. This is our son, named after your father, Dovid Minsky, of blessed memory. Joseph! Joseph! Listen to me!' And she too burst into tears, covering her face with her hands.

'Look, you ***mamzer***, bastard, what you have done,' said Joseph, also now on his feet and approaching David. 'Get out! Go to your *shiksa*. You have just broken my heart!'

By now, David was equally angry. 'That's it exactly. Your heart. What do you care for my mother's heart, or my heart? All you think about is yourself, your pride. Try, for once, to think of someone else!' And David looked with anger and pleading into Joseph's face.

'You talk about thinking of others . . . hypocrite! Why don't you think about what this is doing to your family, your mother, grandparents, sisters? Yes! Your sister, Hilda. Who will want to marry the sister of a turncoat? I know. No one! Even if the rabbi will convert her, will that change the facts? Think of others... think even of this girl you say you love . . . think what an outcast she will be. Think of your children! What will they be? They will be *mamzerim*, children that cannot be recognised. They can never be my grandchildren. Hypocrite! Telling others they only think of themselves. I hate what you are doing to this family. Go!' And he turned and walked, an old man, back to his desk, spent and heartbroken.

Fanny poured some white liquid from a bottle on a side table, and handed it to Joseph. 'Take a little schnapps, my dear, and let us try and talk.'

'Talk, talk. What good will talk do? Our son is going to marry a Gentile girl, and expects our blessing? No! Fanny, no! I cannot. We must stand firm against this. For me, this line of the family name ends here.'

Fanny went to David and drew him from the room. 'Leave it for now David. Give him time. I don't promise anything, but give him time. You know I also do not agree with what you are doing, but, my darling son, I love you and do not want to lose you. Bring Charlotte to see me one day when Father is out, and we will speak together. How did her family take the news?'

'They understood, Mother. They were kind and loving. Lady Matilde Barker-Grey is such a stickler and a tartar, we expected a strong reaction of disapproval from her, but no, they were pretty wonderful. As you know, there is already a Jewish aunt whom they all adore. So they really do understand.'

'I will try, David, to understand, and I know your grandmother Sarah will try. We won't tell your grandparents and uncles in Bradford until we get everything straight here. But for now, you will have to contain your soul in patience.'

For the first time since their new relationship, David dreaded meeting Charlotte. He did not know, in the face of her family's understanding, how he was to tell her of his father's reaction. Even he did not quite understand the vehemence of Joseph spurning an only son, and, for a split second, his resolution faltered. But as soon as he saw her welcoming smile as he met her at the gazebo, he was once again under her spell, and all his doubts evaporated.

At first when he told her, she was horrified, and burst into tears. 'Why does he hate me?' she cried. 'Does he not know I would not wilfully hurt anyone. That all we want is to love one another, and to live our lives in happiness. I don't believe in curses or bad omens, but I can't live in the shadow of such bitterness.' She sobbed and sobbed until she had cried herself out, and lay on the cushions, eyes closed, unable to speak, whilst David stood looking out of the window, despair in every line of his body.

'David,' Charlotte whispered. 'Let us elope! When we are married, there will be nothing he can do. He will have to accept the situation.'

David sat beside Charlotte, and raising her and taking her in his arms, he gently told her that this would be impossible. 'If we did such a thing, it would be dishonourable for us and both our families. Those who have faith in us would lose it, and eventually we would lose faith and respect for each other. Besides, it would alter nothing. Jewish fathers do not accept so easily. We would be as dead to my father. Our children would be as if they did not exist, and my mother and sisters would be forbidden to have anything to do with us. No, my darling. That, as much as I would love it, is not the answer. We must, as my mother says, have patience. Wait until the shock has worn away a little, and hope that he will meet you again, and I am confident that you will win him over.'

With that they had to be content for the present. They decided to say nothing to the Moores. It would be time enough if matters had to change.

Constance Wall was working at the same hospital as Charlotte, and they met frequently. Charlotte sought out her friend the next lunchtime, and, as they sat together, Constance heard the full story of the love between David and Charlotte, and the seeming impasse they had arrived at with regard to Joseph Minns.

'What on earth am I to do, Cons? I don't want to separate David from his family, and break their hearts. But nor do I want to lose him. I would die, Cons, if I had to give him up, simply die.' And it was with the utmost difficulty she held back the tears which threatened to flow.

'I have seen Jewish people go to their synagogue from our front windows, Lotte, and whilst some of the men look most unusual, with their beards, wide-brimmed black hats and long frock coats, they look kindly and interesting, and the children, with their great dark solemn eyes, are beautifully behaved, walking quietly with their families, not running or shouting. Sometimes I have even heard their songs, when it has been warm, and the windows have been open, and the sound has filled my soul. Surely such people could not be as cruel as you say.'

'Apparently they can, Cons. They are so entrenched in their beliefs that there seems to be little room for compassion.'

'And yet, Lotte, they are known for their good deeds and charity. You love your David, and after all, he is one of them.'

'Oh, I know, I know, that is why I am so confused. I just don't know what to do. Tell me, Constance! Advise me.'

'Why don't you wait until you have been to see Mrs Minns? Maybe she will have some answers for you.'

Charlotte went to her meeting with Fanny, filled with trepidation, and was equally filled with thankfulness by the older woman's gentleness and understanding. Fanny explained in detail, in a way that made Charlotte realise all the common sense, beauty and tradition that were involved in the many facets that she would have to learn over the coming months and years.

Fanny also accompanied Charlotte to see Sarah. David had broken the news to his grandmother, and Charlotte was impressed by that lady's dignity and warmth, and felt that here was a worthy counterpart to her own dear Grossmutter.

Gradually she met the rest of the family, even travelling to Cork to visit with David's uncles and their families. They were all enchanted by the lovely girl, and each promised to help her in every way to reach Joseph, though each was filled with fear that the same thing would happen in their own families. But they were modern, and knew that times were changing, and that they would have to change along with them, and learn to accept the unacceptable. Each secretly prayed however that this was one situation they would never have to face.

Some weeks later David telephoned Charlotte to say that the rabbi wished to see them. Hearts beating, they presented themselves to him at the appointed time.

'Well, my dear young people. The Beth Din, the Jewish religious and legal court in London, has promised to look at Miss Moore's conversion with favour. But, until such time as there is an official acceptance, nothing should be taken for granted. This alone could take several months to obtain. She will, of course, have to undertake a long, complicated study course, lasting perhaps two or more years, spending part of the time living with an orthodox and observant family. But I am sure, if you truly love one another, time will pass and, God willing, in time you will be united under the marriage canopy.

Charlotte and David looked at each other, smiles of joy and happiness lighting their faces. Then David became grim. 'You know, Rabbi, my father, no matter what is said to him, refuses to recognise Charlotte. We do not know what else we can do. Can you help, talk to him? We do not want to alienate him, and through him my family. We need his love and his blessings.'

'I don't promise anything, but let me try,' said Rabbi Chanaan.

It took many hours of talking by Rabbi Chanaan and other members of the Jewish clergy, as well as pressure from Fanny, Sarah and, surprisingly, Theodore Zucker, who came especially from Bradford, to persuade Joseph to the point where he said he would meet with the girl, but not until after her conversion, and even then, he would not promise any more. With this, everyone had to be satisfied.

Sarah found pious women who were willing to begin Charlotte's instruction. She found her days filled with tutoring in the many aspects of Jewishness she had to master. Every day culinary arts, household koshering, studying the Hebrew language, laws and rituals. She found she loved most of what she was taught, and David's encouragement helped her through the rest.

David insisted that they spend as much time in Blackrock as before. He found that Lady Barker-Grey was not nearly as formidable as he had previously thought, and he grew very fond of her. He bought Charlotte a sapphire and diamond ring to mark their betrothal, and she gave him a gold pen with which to write, as she said, 'marvellous prescriptions and important medical papers'.

Soon they fell into the habit of dining together once a week in Baggot Street, with Hilda present to chaperone them. Charlotte usually would prepare one of the meals she had learned during her cookery class. Sometimes they would be delicious, and at other times it took all David's pride in her achievements to make him swallow some failure, glaring at Hilda, daring her to make any remark.

Afterwards, they would go to the study, where Charlotte would work on some piece of embroidery, or play cards with Hilda, while David worked at his desk, only breaking for tea before David took each of them home.

One evening Hilda, feeling very unwell, was attended to by David, and then taken home to Rathmines. The maid left the tea tray, as usual, and said good night to Charlotte. Soon David returned and assured Lotte that his sister was now tucked up in bed, and would be much better in the morning. Lotte offered David another piece of the cake she had made that day. He took it, not wishing to offend her, but laughingly said, 'Darling, I feel I am being fattened before being sacrificed. The buttons on my waistcoat are having great difficulty fastening.' Charlotte laughed and dropped to her knees in front of him, and began to tickle him as she said, 'All the more to love, my dear!' Soon they were helpless with giggling as David tickled her in turn.

Then they were still. Lotte met his ardent gaze; she felt her own desire mount as they moved closer towards each other. She felt his hot lips meet her own, and as she responded, pressing her body to his, he slowly undid the buttons at the back of her blouse.

'Darling, what about the servants?' she said, but she made no move to stop him as the garment slipped off her shoulders. He covered their smoothness with hungry kisses which gathered momentum as they reached her now exposed breasts. His mouth closed on her nipple, and she felt the hot rush of passion course through her, as, her legs unable to support her any longer, she slipped to the floor, and felt David's weight on top of her.

Clasping him, she whispered, 'Make me yours David . . . O darling, I want you so!'

'Are you sure, Lotte? My wonderful, wonderful girl, are you sure?'

'Yes! Yes! I am sure . . . never so sure of anything in my life. . . only don't hurt me . . . as you know, you are the first!'

Charlotte felt disappointed that she was unfulfilled by David's lovemaking, and when he made attempts to arouse her a second time, she forced herself to respond. But this time, with less urgency, they explored each other, and when they reached a climax, Lotte heard their two voices raised in exaltation. When their passion was spent, they lay in contented silence side by side.

They were brought back to reality by the shrill ringing of the telephone bell. David answered it, spoke to someone and, replacing the earpiece, faced Charlotte. 'That was Owen, darling. He thinks we should go to Blackrock at once.'

'What is wrong?'

'He did not say, but I gather someone is not well.'

'O my God! It's Grossmutter!' They dressed quickly and left Baggot Street immediately to go to Blackrock.

When they arrived at Priory House, all the lights were on, which alarmed Charlotte. She sprang from the car and ran up to the front door. Before she could open it with her key, Eamonn was standing in the doorway.

'We heard the car, Miss Charlotte. Come in quickly!'

Charlotte and David ran into the hallway to be greeted by Lady Matilde and Amy. Nanny was on the stairs with the twins, who were sobbing into her apron. Owen was on the telephone, and one look at his ghastly white face told the young couple, more than words could, that some disaster had occurred.

'What is it Grossmutter? Amy, what has happened? Who is with Father, is he in bed?'

Lady Barker-Grey took a deep breath. 'My darling, you must be very brave. Your beloved father has gone to join your mother.'

'What are you saying? He was fine when I went out this morning. There is some mistake . . .' And she ran across the hall to mount the stairs.

Darragh Ryan appeared on the landing at this moment.

'Dr Ryan,' said David. 'What has happened?'

'Michael had a heart attack this evening around nine o'clock. I was called immediately, and we put him to bed. He slipped into a coma and never woke up. The end was very quick, and very peaceful.' He tried to hold in his pent-up emotions, but his voice cracked as he said, 'I am sorry, Lotte. You have lost a loved parent, and I have lost my dearest friend. But he is at peace now, God rest his soul.'

The following days merged one into the other. Henrietta and Jean Louis arrived from France, Darragh, Margaret, Cuthbert and Arthur from England, and Kit and Blanche from Wicklow. Otto and Hannah von Zeit were too old to undertake the journey from Germany, as were the Misses Barker-Grey from Wales. But Rudi von Zeit, and his wife Katerina, did make the voyage to represent the family.

On the day of the funeral the church, and then the house, were filled to capacity with friends and relatives who had known Michael since childhood, and who wished to honour him and pay their last respects to a gentleman.

The letters and cards that poured through the letterbox, including one from Fanny and Sarah Minns, told of the high esteem in which Michael and the family were held, by people from many walks of life. The sentiments expressed did much to assure the family that he would not be forgotten.

Chapter Twenty-Nine

As the weeks passed, it became clear that Nanny was becoming very feeble. Sadly, she said to Lady Matilde, 'There is no more I can do for the family now. The children are grown up, and even the twins do not need me anymore. I would like to spend my remaining days back home in Wales. My niece has a very large house, and many times she has offered me a home there with her. I do not feel I am deserting you, for Amy Philips is now part of the family, and can be relied on to help in every way.'

David, who had been in Blackrock every moment he could spare, and who had been a tower of strength to everyone, felt as upset as the rest of the family when he heard this news, and understood when Charlotte said, 'I feel as though parting from Nanny is another bereavement. She has been with us all our lives, we love her so much, and now we might never see her again.'

Kit, as Michael's executor, oversaw that the provisions in his will were carried out as Michael had wished. Owen had inherited the house and farm, on the understanding that there would always be a home for Charlotte, Darragh and the twins, for as long as any of them should need one. When the estate duties had been paid and all debts discharged, it was discovered that there would be no money to continue employing the servants. Amy, by arrangement with Lady Barker-Grey, would stay and keep house. When they were told, Cook said that they were not to worry, that she would like to retire anyway, and to go back to the family holding in Wexford, where there would be plenty for her to do to make herself useful. Eamonn surprised everyone when he said that he and his wife had always wanted to open a general shop, and that they had enough saved to do so. Owen told them that, apart from the bequests left to them by Michael, there would of course be a small pension for each of them.

Kit was surprised when he opened Michael's strong box, to find that he had kept all of Jessica's jewellery, in spite of being so desperately in need of money. Lady Barker-Grey now divided the pieces between Jessica's and Michael's two daughters, with the exception of some keepsakes for the boys. The heart-shaped diamond pendant, Michael's wedding gift, she gave to Henrietta, and the pearl collar she and her husband had given to Jessica would now belong to Charlotte. Henrietta again showed the unpleasant side of her nature, especially to Charlotte, when, even in their joint sorrow, she expressed her feelings that as the eldest daughter, and the mother of two girls, she should have been given all of her mother's possessions.

Charlotte did not seem to be able to settle down to anything, and she began to lose weight. It was obvious that Nanny could not travel on her own, so Lady Matilde, having discussed the matter with David, felt that it would do Lotte good to get away from Ireland for a while, and, if she were to accompany Nanny, she could spend some time with her great aunts in Neath.

At first Charlotte did not want to go, but when Nanny said 'it will give us a little more time together, cariad', she agreed. David was glad, he had noticed a change in her since that fateful night that had brought such joy and such sorrow.

He hoped that when she had had a change of scene, and had been spoiled and petted by her aunts, she would return as the sunny and fun-loving girl he knew.

As the day of departure drew nearer, Nanny was perpetually wailing. Each time she came in contact with one of the family, they were deluged in a flood of Nanny's memories. With Lady Barker-Grey, she spoke of Jessica's childhood, and Sir David, and the Misses Olwyn and Bronwyn Barker-Grey. With the children, she spoke of their parents, and of their grandparents from

Wicklow, of times before the fire, and of the grand life Henrietta was leading. She expressed a wish to visit the graves of those dearly loved people to bid farewell, and Owen and Lady Matilde took her, and supported her when the memories became too much and she broke down.

Nanny left the family with hugs and kisses, and instructions on how to behave themselves. She gave strict injunctions to Amy and Ita on how they were to conduct the household, and made them promise to look after her family for her. Nanny gathered her handbag and umbrella. They all gave her the gifts they had prepared for her as tokens of their affection, and to remember them by. The old lady was so overcome that it took the joint efforts of Owen and Eamonn to get her into the car, and Charlotte pulled faces at David and threw her eyes up to Heaven, as much as to say, 'What have you all let me in for?', which David understood was her way of coping with the parting.

As the taxi drew up in front of the Misses Barker-Grey's house, the two elderly ladies were standing on the step to greet Charlotte. She jumped from the car and ran to them. With an arm around each, and instructions to the driver to bring in her bags, she went with them into the house.

When all the hellos had been said to their cook and house parlourmaid, whom she remembered well from her last visit, and she had been shown her room, which had been repainted in honour of her visit, and was fresh with starched curtains, and snowy white bed linen and towels, she joined her aunts for tea in the drawingroom. They were impatient for her to bring them up to date on all the family news since her father died. They were also anxious to learn if Nanny had been happy when Charlotte had left her with her niece in Port Talbot. 'Parting from darling Nanny was very sad. I promised that I would write to her often, and that David and I would come and visit her as often as possible. Of course I told her that if ever she would like to return to us, we will be only too happy to have her.'

The planned stay of one week extended to two, then three, as Charlotte saw the pleasure her visit was giving to her aunts. They loved taking her to visit her cousins, and having tea parties for friends who remembered her mother.

Although David wrote every day, saying how much he was missing her, she had a strange reluctance to end her holiday too quickly.

One evening, at dinner with the cousins who now lived in her grandfather's old home, something she ate filled her with nausea. Although this persisted for some days, she did not wish to worry anyone, and continued going out, but each time with greater and greater discomfort.

One morning at breakfast, she caused consternation by suddenly keeling over and passing out. When she came to, her aunts wanted to call the doctor, but she would not hear of it, saying that it was just the pressure of the past couple of months catching up with her. They were not to worry, she would soon be all right. But the sensations did not pass, and she decided to stay in bed. It was the first time that she had had any time to herself, and as she went over all that had happened in the preceding months, a terrifying suspicion came into her mind. Counting up her monthly calendar, she realised that all her symptoms pointed to the possibility that she was pregnant.

Her first instinct was to pack immediately and go home to David. But when she thought about it, and all the ramifications of such news, she faltered, and a terrible dread came over her at the thought of facing, not only Grossmutter and her own family, but David's family, especially his father, as well as all their friends. What kind of girl would they take her to be? Joseph would say that he told everyone so, and that this was a vindication of his attitude. No! She could not face it, nor could she face letting David down. No matter how much he loved her, could he bear this? No! What was she to do? Where could she go?

First thing next day, she went to a doctor in a neighbouring town. He confirmed her worst fears. She must write to David immediately and break their engagement. He must never know of this child. Then she must make some plans to leave Wales, and decide how she was to have the baby.

She thought and thought, until the glimmering of an idea came to her. She wrote to Olive in London and asked her if she might come and stay for a few days. While waiting for her friend's reply, she composed a letter to David. In it she simply said, 'I find that I cannot go through with the conversion. I will always love you, no matter what. Please try not to think too badly of me. I will have left Wales by the time you receive this letter, so there is no point following me. Anyway, my mind is quite made up. I am very sorry to cause you pain, but circumstances seem to work against our union. I hope one day, when you have forgotten me, you will meet someone to whom marriage will not be so complicated, and that you will be very happy. I fervently wish for this. When you do remember me, I hope it will be with some affection, and not with too much bitterness. I do not wish to trust your beautiful ring to the postal service, so I am making arrangements to have it returned to you through safer channels.'

When Olive's letter arrived saying how much she was looking forward to seeing Charlotte, she went to her aunts, and told them that with time to think, she realised that it would be a grave mistake to marry David Minns, and that she had written to him to tell him so. Also, she had written to the family breaking the news to them. 'I am going away, out of reach, for a few months. If there is any post, please send it to the Post Restante in London. I will have it picked up there. Thank you my darlings for your kindness and love to me. I will be in touch with you soon.'

Olive lived in a pretty little house in Chelsea. The rooms were tiny, but they reflected Olive's very good taste, and were filled with bric-à-brac that had come with her from her home in Ireland, as well as some that she had collected herself. As they sat together over a cocktail before dinner, time seemed to slip away. They fell into the close companionship of their schooldays. This made it much easier for Charlotte to unburden herself to her friend who, far from being shocked at the news, was concerned for Charlotte and her well-being.

At first she said that she thought Charlotte should tell David, that it was his child, that he had a right to know, and that the child had a right to know its father. But when she had been made to understand all that that would mean in Jewish terms, she saw that perhaps it was better Lotte's way, but, as Lotte had already pointed out, where was she to live until the baby was born?

'No point going to Henrietta. Your life would be made a misery, telling you how wrong you had been . . . oh gosh no. Definitely not Henrietta! Have you written to Cons? She is a rock of sense, and may have a suggestion. No? You don't want her to know, eh! What about the old aunts? How would your family in Germany receive you? Don't keep shaking your head at everything I suggest. Oh, I'm sorry Lotte, please don't cry, we'll find a way. Let's eat, things are always clearer somehow after food.'

One thing was clear, and that was that Charlotte could only stay with Olive for a short time, in case David came to the Chelsea house. So the first thing was to find somewhere for Lotte to stay temporarily, until some other arrangements could be made.

Olive asked around among her friends, and heard of a very nice respectable ladies' residence in South Kensington, where they ensconced Charlotte the following week, and, as it turned out, not a day too soon, as David did call on Olive, sure that he would find Charlotte there.

'How did he look Ollie? What did he say?'

'He looked very pale, and he asked me to tell you that nothing else matters, only you. That he loves you and wants you back on any terms.'

'Poor David! I know that one day he will thank me for not parting him from his father and his family. I have been thinking hard, and have gone over everyone I can approach, including my aunt Meg, and I have had a thought. Maybe my aunt Blanche can help me. I wouldn't mind confiding in her, as she always has had very forward ideas about women's independence. What do you think?'

'It's certainly worth trying. She is a very nice woman, and I agree, she will understand.'

Charlotte wrote straight away to Blanche, asking her to keep the matter confidential, even from Uncle Kit, and on no account to let David know anything. She received a telegram in reply: MATTER UNDER CONSIDERATION STOP MAKING NECESSARY ENQUIRIES STOP WRITING MORE FULLY STOP LOVE AUNT BLANCHE.

For the first time Charlotte felt a sense of relief that someone in the family was there to help her, and she waited anxiously for Blanche's letter. When it came, it said everything that she needed to hear, and included some practical support, in the shape of a cheque to buy a layette for the baby. Blanche had found out, from a friend of hers, about a woman in Horsham, in Sussex, who helped other girls from good families in similar circumstances.

'Charlotte, if you agree, you will live with the woman until your confinement is due, and then you will go to the local Cottage Hospital for the delivery. Afterwards, you and the baby will return to Mrs Rose Higgins, who will look after both of you for six weeks. The Higgins have a small farm, mainly stock and roots. They have no children of their own, but love babies. The charges will be modest, well within your ability to pay from the sum you mentioned you have in your savings account. I will try and visit you some time in the six weeks after the birth. In the meantime, I will organise sending the remainder of your clothes to Larch Hill Farm, when you, or Olive, give the all clear.'

Charlotte and Olive went to visit Rose and Albert Higgins, and fell in love with the apple-cheeked couple, their shaggy dog, their well scrubbed house and tidy farm. They arranged for Charlotte to move there in time for Christmas. They also arranged that all letters from home would go to Olive's house, to be redirected to her. They would do the same, in reverse, to

Ireland. She enjoined Olive again that, not only must David not know where to find her, but that Constance must not know either, for 'although thoroughly dependable, you know she is incapable of keeping a secret'.

Charlotte soon acquired a sense of security with Rose Higgins, and willingly placed herself into the care of the even-tempered and practical woman. Rose helped her to crochet and knit, and between them they made many beautiful things for the baby, which helped to pass the months of waiting.

Jeanette, like her mother before her, could not wait full term to be born, and arrived three weeks early. She had the warm skin tones of her father, with his blue black hair, and she favoured him in every feature, except for the wonderful eyes of her great grandmother Moore.

On hearing the news, first Olive, and then Blanche, arrived to welcome Charlotte and Jeanette back to the farm. Charlotte told them, 'I have chosen the name Jeanette, because I wanted to call her both Blanche and Olive, and could not choose which, and besides, if you remember, Olive, I always called my dolls and cuddly toys "Jeanette". And now here I am with a real live doll, who has not only Jeanette, but Blanche and Olive also, as her names, and therefore is bound to grow into a splendid woman.'

As Blanche gently asked her what surname she was going to give the child, Lotte's eyes filled with tears.

'Yes, I have been thinking about that one, and I know I cannot call her Minns or Moore, or Barker-Grey. They all seem to be out of the question. I really don't know the answer.'

'I have also been thinking about it, and may I make a suggestion?' said Blanche. 'Neither Willie nor I have any children, or ever seem likely to do so. We would be honoured if you would use the name "Fitzgerald".'

Charlotte looked at her with wide open eyes, unable for the moment to speak, she was so filled with emotion.

'What a generous thought, my dear aunt, the honour would be mine, to give such a distinguished name to my daughter, but are you sure you should not speak to Willie about such an important matter first?'

'I am sure you know Willie can be the soul of discretion, so I have already consulted him, and he is delighted to share his name with Jeanette Blanche Olive.'

'Then "Fitzgerald" it is, and thank you, thank you, and Willie. What a magnificent gift!'

The next matter that had to be decided was what Charlotte was going to do at the end of the next month. Rose Higgins said, 'You can stay here a little longer. I have no booking until the end of the summer, but I advise that the sooner arrangements are made in these circumstances, the easier it is. Will you be putting the mite up for adoption?' She received three such emphatic 'No's', that she recoiled at the fierceness of their response.

Among the bundle of letters Olive had brought to Sussex were several from David which, as previously, she asked Olive to return unopened. There were many from the family in Blackrock, and two that made Charlotte very thoughtful. The first came from Fanny Minns and she read it with tightened lips. In it, Fanny rebuked her for the consternation she had caused in all their lives, and the heartbreak she was putting her darling son through. 'Especially as I, and other members of our family, stood by you in every possible way. I cannot understand the casual way you undertook to convert to Judaism, the time you took, and then wasted, with the rabbi and the good women who were your teachers, if you were not absolutely sure and positive in yourself what it was you wanted. I hope David will, in time, put the whole experience behind him, and find someone who will truly love him, not just satisfy some selfish whim, but deeply and forever. I do not wish you any ill, Charlotte, but hope that you too will eventually find happiness. Only the next time, be really sure before making such a deep commitment.'

The second letter came from her aunts in Wales, saying that they hoped dear Charlotte was quite well, as they had been a little disturbed at the tone of her last letter, and were just the 'teeniest' bit worried about her.

When she read both letters to Blanche – Olive having gone back to London – she railed at the unfairness of Fanny Minns! 'She did not have to go through a birth on her own, with no husband or family near, or have to make the decision on how to bring up and provide for her child. What right does she have to pass judgement?'

'Calm down, my dear girl. Of course she has a right. After all, she knows nothing about the child, or I am sure she would react quite differently. And, if the truth be aired, the decision not to let her, or David, know of Jeanette's existence is entirely yours, and it may, in some eyes, appear that you are being very selfish.'

'O Aunt Blanche, of course you are right, and maybe I am being selfish. But I know that in the long run, it is the right decision for all concerned. Right now, I am really more concerned about where Jeanette and I will go when we leave here, and to this end I have been racking my brains as to what I can do. My options are really very limited. I cannot return to Ireland, any part of it, and I cannot stay in London, work and look after my baby. So, I have decided to go to Wales, see my aunts, throw myself on their mercy, and ask them if they will give us a home. As you know, Aunt Blanche, neither of them ever married. Neither has ever known of the joys and tribulations of having a child grow up in their home. Perhaps, watching Jeanette develop will be a small compensation to them, now, in the twilight of their years. If, on the other hand, they are unable to accept the moral dilemma I am presenting to them, I will have to reconsider my position. But they are old, and I am sure I can make myself useful to them, relieving them of the tedium of mundane tasks that always seem necessary in maintaining a house.

Chapter Thirty

David Minns returned to Baggot Street and to his patients with a heavy heart. How could he go on without Charlotte? What did his work and his house mean to him now that she was not with him to share his life?

He sat at his desk looking at the photograph of her lovely face, smiling and happy. He wondered if she was smiling now. He felt that he certainly would never find anything to smile about again. Dear God, what have I done? It must seem to her that I put my parents wishes above my love for her. She has more generosity of spirit than anyone I have ever known. Her love for me was more than her love for her own family, or herself. Why, oh why did I not see it all more clearly. My poor darling, I did not deserve you. You gave me everything. Love, heart and body. What did I give to you? Unhappiness, self-interest, complacency. O my love, come back, come back, all I want is you. And in an uncontrolled cry from the heart, he called out to God to forgive him for any sins he may have committed, for which he would atone for the rest of his days, but only to send his Charlotte, his life, back to him. His cries were so vehement, that the maid, worried and frightened by the dreadful, hysterical sounds, rang his mother who, coming immediately, went to him and tried to comfort him.

'My son, we will make a new life for you. Time is a great healer. I know you will never forget the girl, but time will dull the pain, and you will feel happy again.'

'Go away, Mother! I feel nothing for you or father or my Jewishness. You all stand for that which is lost to me . . . go away!

Live your own lives and let me live mine. Father can sit Shiva for me, I don't give a damn. Just go . . . go!'

He went about his work like an automaton, visited his patients, attended the hospital, and eventually, joylessly, gained his extra diploma.

David had hired a private detective in London, but after six months of negative reports, ceased to employ him. He kept in constant touch with Blanche and Kit, going to Wicklow whenever time permitted, repeating over and over to them how sincere he was in asking them to help him to find Charlotte, that all that mattered to him was that they would be together. There would be no conversion, no interference from his family, only that which would make her happy. The Moores were kind to him, but unhelpful. Priory Lodge was equally unforthcoming, as were the replies to his letters to Olive.

Somehow he got through the days and weeks. After a year of silence from Charlotte, and in a frame of mind to think more rationally, he accepted, heartbrokenly, that she no longer wanted him. He still cut himself off from his family, in spite of many efforts from Joseph, Sarah, Fanny and the girls, prevailing on him to return to the family and to resume his attendance at the synagogue.

He now found time hanging more heavily, and immersed himself in his work. Since qualifying, he had received literature about medical meetings, covering a wide field of medical topics, from centres all over the world, but so far he had ignored them, too afraid to spend more than a few days away from Ireland and possible news of Charlotte. But, when he finally realised there was not going to be any news, he decided to attend a medical conference in New York.

He was bowled over by New York. He found it exciting, fantastic and overwhelming. The Americans he met were warm and hospitable, inviting him to visit with them any time he found himself in 'their neck of the woods'. There were social events laid on for the delegates, with bright young people to look after the unattached visitors, and in this way he met Millie Blumfeldt, the attractive daughter of one of the hospital administrators. Hungry for congenial female company, he allowed himself to be swept along by her amiable and vivacious personality. He also allowed himself to be enticed by her father to extend his visit, and to spend some time working at the hospital where he administered, before returning to Ireland.

Feeling no great urge to return to Dublin, he wired his locum and asked him to stay on longer. Receiving by return a positive response, he accepted the invitation to stay for a further three months.

American hospital work was very different to that of Irish hospitals. David was absorbed by and interested in everything in which he was permitted to be involved. Millie organised his social life, giving him no opportunity to make plans of his own. Living on Manhattan Island as she did, gave her plenty of opportunity to monopolise him. She drove him all over the state of New York in her little coupé, showing him the different sights, staying with friends and relatives when it became too late to return to the city, which gave them to understand that he was a 'special friend'.

David found her an amusing companion, comfortable to be with. The mild petting they indulged in left him unaroused, but not totally disinterested. Millie tried to find out about his life in Ireland, his family and his friends. She made several coy references to girlfriends and was frustrated at the way he always managed to change the subject.

One evening, some weeks into their friendship, Millie was unusually quiet and downcast, during a shared meal in the hospital canteen. David, unused to lengthy silences in Millie's chatter, politely said, 'You don't seem to be your bright self tonight. Is there something wrong, can I help, Millie?'

'Wrong, David. Wrong? Sure there is something wrong. I have been fool enough to fall in love with you, that's all! In a few weeks you'll be five thousand miles away, back in your own life, your own world, and our time together will be a faded memory. But not for me, David. You've spoilt me for anybody else with your quiet Irish charm. That's what's wrong. Not that I ever meant to tell you. But now I'm glad you know. I also know I am taking a chance of never seeing you again, David. But if I don't, I suddenly realise that the agony of being beside you, but not being with you, every time we meet, will be over, and that, with help, maybe, one far off day, I'll start over again, and that's fine too!'

David was silent for so long that Millie could not bear it, and forgetting where she was, she said loudly, 'For God's sake David, say something . . . or I'll explode!'

David stood, and pulling back her chair, he said, 'I think we should go somewhere else, somewhere where we can talk properly.' She meekly followed him out into the hospital courtyard, her heart beating as if it would choke her. She was afraid he was going to let her down lightly, afraid that she had made a fool of herself. But, at the same time, somehow, not afraid that he would ever let anyone know.

He sat down on a bench, and she sat beside him, not touching him or even looking at him. 'Millie, you are the sweetest girl I have met in a long time. I love being with you. But I would be dishonest if I said I reciprocated your feelings. I am certainly attracted to you, and would be a fool not to know how much you are honouring me, and how lucky I am. However, you must be made aware that I do not love you. But, if my life, name and affection are enough to be going on with, I ask you to be my wife.'

If this was not quite the romantic proposal Millie had dreamed about, what did it matter? He was asking her to marry him, wasn't he, and to share his life.

'Oh yes, David, it will. It'll be enough for now . . . I know you'll come to love me. I'll make you.' And she threw her arms around him and kissed him passionately. David's pretended response was all she had hoped for. But she did not know how his heart was aching, and breaking, because she was not Charlotte.

In spite of David's pleas that the wedding should be kept small, quiet and informal, and that it should be arranged as quickly as possible, as there would be no time, before his impending return to Dublin, to allow his parents, grandparents and family to come to New York, he found himself standing under the *chuppah* marriage canopy, in a swank synagogue on Fifth Avenue, and having to face an enormous, elaborate dinner and reception at the Hotel Pierre afterwards. As the day progressed, he became angrier about what he called the 'circus', at which he was the main attraction, being billed as 'my Irish Yiddish son-in-law, the doctor!', coupled with statements such as 'His people have a store like Macey's, ya know'. He kept imagining how, had Millie been Charlotte, the wedding would have been conducted with decorum and dignity. Millie really did look marvellous and her retinue of bridesmaids were very pretty, but O God, would it never end?

Finally he and Millie were alone, and her love and trust in him roused him to a tenderness and desire that fulfilled her marriage-bed expectations.

Millie felt a natural empathy with the Minns family. Joseph welcomed his Jewish daughter-in-law with an open heart, relieved that David, in accordance with his predictions, had finally brought home a *shane maidela* to run his home in a *balabattishe*, housewifely, way and bear him, Joseph, fine Jewish grandchildren. Fanny also liked the young American and was gratified by the girl's deference in asking for her advice on how things should be done in Dublin.

Millie loved the dignity of her new home, and enjoyed showing it off to her new family and circle of acquaintances by holding musical evenings, and introducing the 5–7pm cocktail party, which, disappointingly, she found did not suit the businessmen of the Dublin Jewish community. Like most Jewish girls of her generation anywhere in the world, she had been taught the skills of good housekeeping, and always made sure that David's comforts were attended to.

David found her a co-operative and innovative companion in bed, and often wished that he could love her in the same way he still loved Charlotte. But as time went by, her coquettish ways irritated him, and he, unfairly, often lost patience with her.

During the summer months following their marriage, the Blumfeldts came to visit with their daughter and son-in-law in Dublin. They more than often hinted that it must somehow be David's family's fault that their daughter was not yet expecting. 'For', as they said, 'nobody in any of our families has had any problem in that direction.'

After her parents had returned home, this became a constant bone of contention between Millie and David. More to keep her quiet than a real desire to have children, David sent her to an eminent gynaecologist to be examined and tested to find out why she had not conceived. The results showed that, due to an accident she had been in as a child, Millie could never conceive. She was distraught with grief, frustration and shame at her barrenness. No matter how many times David assured her that it really did not matter to him, she would not be comforted. She explained to him that now that she knew the truth, she was too ashamed to face people. She lay in bed day after day, neglecting her appearance, her household, and all the other duties she had undertaken.

As the day of their second anniversary came about, she would not accept the present David had bought her, saying, 'That's for a wife who is happy and fulfilled in motherhood.'

'Millie, this situation cannot go on. Look at yourself. You used to be so attractive and smart. Now all you do is lie around, unbathed, your hair lank with grease, totally distasteful. So much so that, as you have seen, I have had to move into another bedroom. Millie, you used to say you loved me. Am I no longer enough for you? You know there is more to a good marriage than children. My dear wife, can't you see this is destroying everything between us? Won't you try and pull yourself together for my sake, so that we may start over again?'

'You don't understand, do you? You just can't understand how a woman feels. What the hell do they teach you in your Irish medical schools? Can't you understand that I don't even feel like a woman anymore? For God's sake, David. What use am I . . . what use am I? If it's sex you're talking about, what do you want? That I should be your whore? Go away, David . . . go away . . . let me be!'

David, filled with an anger he had never imagined he could feel, pulled back the bedclothes, dragged her out of the bed, across the room and down the hall to the bathroom. Still holding her with one hand, he filled the bath, emptying bathsalts into it, tore off her nightclothes, picked her up and put her into the water, and in a voice dark with fury said, 'I'll be waiting downstairs for you to join me for dinner. Get yourself properly dressed and take up your wifely duties again. Do you understand me, Millie?'

Millie made a valiant attempt to comply with David's dictates, going to and having the family back for meals. But it was obvious that she was dreadfully unhappy. Her rounded figure was now scrawny. Her large eyes were enormous and solemn in her shrunken face.

David in turn was filled with pity and irritation and, at times, with guilt, so that in May, when she said she would like to spend the summer with her family in their house in the Catskill Mountains in New York state, to his shame he readily agreed that she should go. He offered to travel with her, but she declined, saying that perhaps when she felt better he would come and stay for a while, and then they could come home together.

In the beginning she wrote every week, letters filled with self-recrimination and apology. She said that she was beginning to put back on a little weight under her mother's watchful eye. Life in the summer community was full and varied, and she was meeting old friends and making new acquaintances. Her parents had taken her to see a friend of theirs, who was an expert in depression caused by trauma, and she was finding it helpful just talking to him. She wanted to hear all the news from Dublin, and always sent her abiding love to David, and said she was missing him.

David was glad she was progressing, but could not, honestly, admit that he missed her a great deal. He soon fell into his old routines, rarely at home except to sleep and see patients.

At first he did not notice that the gap between Millie's letters was growing. It therefore came as a mild shock when one arrived, spelling out the end of their marriage.

Dear David,

I feel that this letter will come as no great surprise to you, but I have filed for divorce.

I feel sure you will not oppose the petition, or deny your permission to obtain a Jewish ritual severance of our marriage. I want you to know I lay no blame for the failure of our marriage on you. You always behaved in an affectionate and dutiful manner toward me. My sessions with my analyst have made it clear that I pushed our relationship along too fast, giving neither of us time to cement even friendship, let alone anything deeper. I have loved you and our life in Dublin and have no regrets about that time, as I hope you will not. Who knows, if we had had children, maybe the bonds they would have created between us would have been enough. But it was not to be.

I heard a long time ago of the deep hurt you suffered in a previous love affair, and only now realise I caught you on the rebound. My hopes for you David are, that you will find someone some day, when everything will come together in the right way for you.

I want you to know also, that I am not too unhappy, and even begin to know some peace again. You will always mean a lot to me, David, and I will always value you, and look forward to a time when it may be possible for us to meet and talk, and to be good friends.

My lawyers will be in touch with you,
Millie

David received a letter from a legal firm in New York, and was surprised to read that Mrs Millicent Minns was making no claims on Dr David Minns for any settlement during the dissolution of their marriage by the courts, in the city of New York, in the State of New York, USA, where the original marriage was contracted. They also went on to say that this was against their advice, as she would at least be entitled to maintenance until such time as she remarried. This would pertain, even under the Irish Separation Act.

David wrote back through his own solicitors and said that he appreciated his wife's generosity, but that if she needed anything, he would be more than willing to make a settlement with her. Also, that he had arranged to have her belongings, including her flatware and other valuables, shipped to her.

He went to the rabbi to arrange the religious divorce, and then sat down to write to Millie.

My dear Millie,

Although I have accepted the inevitability of your decision, I do so with sadness and regret. You blame yourself too much for our marriage not working. It takes two to make a bargain. I also have had time to think, and know that I took all your efforts to make a home and life for us for granted. I did not pull my fair weight in the marriage, using my professional involvement as an excuse not to be with you as much as I might have been. Your integrity of purpose far outshone my own, and had I been able to love you the way you needed to be loved, maybe you would have been able to settle just for me, when you found out about your infertility, and that if you had felt secure enough emotionally, in time we might have adopted children. I know such speculations are empty now, but I want you to realise that I did, and do, respect you and admire your qualities. Who knows what life holds for us, and if it is fate that our paths will cross again, I for one will be joyful of it.

Look after yourself and be happy,
Affectionately,
David

Word soon went around the Jewish community that the young Doctor Minns was divorced, and therefore again eligible. But as before, he turned down all invitations, determined never again to allow himself to be caught in such an undesirable situation.

He made a social life outside the community, and satisfied his sexual needs in short, casual relationships. He laid plans for the time when he would be totally free from his marriage, and on the very day he received news of his Decree Nisi, he wrote to another private detective agency, instructing them to search for Charlotte.

Chapter Thirty-One

In the third decade of the twentieth century, although still lonely for David, Charlotte Moore found that life held a great deal of contentment. Her aunts, the Misses Bronwyn and Olwyn Barker-Grey, after their initial shock reaction to Charlotte's story, and having failed to persuade her to return to David, found that they had liked the idea of Charlotte and Jeanette coming to live with them. It was a decision that they never regretted in the following years. They supported the story that Charlotte had made an unwise marriage; the honour of their family and their loyalty to their brother's memory, as well as their fondness for Charlotte, was uppermost in their minds. They had been most unhappy at the wan and haunted look Charlotte had worn when she had first come to enlist their help, and were gratified to see it gradually disappear. Their joy at the progress of the baby, especially when she smiled at them, was everything that Charlotte had hoped for.

Charlotte's social life was not very active. She made one visit to London to see Olive, and another to Dublin, with Jeanette, to see Grossmutter and the boys. They had accepted the story of Charlotte's 'brief marriage', although Grossmutter was very angry. 'Fancy, young miss, you did not see fit to acquaint us zat you intended to marry. We would have made enquiries about ze young man, and saved you ze heartache of a broken marriage. Are you divorcing? We have never had such a sing in ze family. Still, the child is lovely, so, some good has come of ze episode.' But looking at her granddaughter in a knowing way, she said, 'I gather zat your husband is also very dark, like David Minns. It seems, young lady, zat zis is ze type you admire. Of course, in compliance wiz your wishes, none of us ever say to anyone where you are living now.'

Charlotte's other social activities in Neath mainly consisted of church functions and dinner parties, when an extra lady was needed to make up numbers. Her Barker-Grey relatives included her whenever possible, but as they suspected the circumstances of Jeanette's birth, notwithstanding the story that Charlotte had made an impulsive and disastrous marriage on the rebound, they only included her when they felt they must honour family obligation.

On receiving one such invitation for a Friday night, Charlotte said, 'If it is as dull as all the other occasions, I would prefer to stay at home and listen to music on the gramophone, or read a good book.' However, she was persuaded to go.

'Perhaps there will be some nice young people this time, and you will meet someone.'

'You always say that, and so far I have met a retired vicar, who had been widowed, an old schoolmaster of cousin Jasper's, and the teenage brothers of Iris and Caroline's friends. No, Cousin Miranda is not too imaginative in matching her dinner guests. All right... All right, I'll go, but I know I will not enjoy myself.'

When she arrived at the Barker-Grey house, she was, as usual, greeted by Miranda, a pale wispy woman with a will of iron, which she used to rule her husband and two plump and jolly daughters. 'My dear Charlotte, we have a very special guest this evening. He is the son of one of Jasper's business acquaintances from Germany, who has come to observe our mining skills. He will be in the valleys for three months, and will spend his free time with us. He seems a very bright young man, with beautiful manners. I want you to be very nice to him and engage him in conversation at dinner, and besides, you speak such perfect German.'

Her heart sank as she was introduced to Dieter Schulz, and he clicked his heels and bowed. He was very tall, very blond and very thin. His pale, watery blue eyes were fringed by colourless lashes, and when he smiled, his thin red lips stretched across his angular face in a way that made Charlotte shudder. At the table she noticed that he had extremely beautiful hands, long-fingered and sensitive, and she was not really surprised to find out that he played the violin very well.

The evening passed much more pleasantly than she had anticipated. Lotte found that behind his rather forbidding exterior, Dieter had a lively and witty mind. As she was leaving, he said how much he had enjoyed meeting her, and would like to see her again. She invited him to lunch the following week to meet her aunts.

In three months of meeting frequently, Charlotte forgot Dieter's appearance, and she looked forward to seeing him whenever he was free. The first time he kissed her, she drew back. But when she saw the bewildered and hurt look on his face, she allowed him a quick peck. He was the first man she had had any physical contact with since the day she had said goodbye to David, on Kingstown Pier. On subsequent occasions, when he kissed her, she responded to Dieter more than she knew was proper.

They found they had much in common. The time they spent together went by very quickly. Now there was only one more week left of Dieter's stay, and it was with mutual sadness and regret that they realised the time for Dieter to return to Germany had arrived.

They arranged that Charlotte should bring Jeanette to the boat to say farewell, on the following Sunday morning. Although it was already April, it was an unusually cold day, and Charlotte and Jeanette wrapped up very warmly, as did the two old ladies, who left the house at the same time to attend the service at the small local church where they had worshipped all their lives.

Dieter was waiting for them at the dockside, armed with a large doll for Jeanette, flowers and chocolates for Charlotte, and two bottles of eau-de-Cologne, from his mother's home town, for the Misses Barker-Grey. As they stood making small talk, they noticed an agitated buzz among the people on the quayside, and enquired as to its cause. 'There has been a great explosion in a small church in one of the nearby towns. We are waiting now to hear where it is!'

Her heart sinking with trepidation, Charlotte telephoned to her aunts' house. Glynis, her aunts' maid, answered. 'It is ower church, Miss Lotte, and look you, there is no news of the two misses. Indeed to goodness, I don't know what we should do next. We did not have any way to let you know. O Miss, we are so worried.'

'Stay in the house and have my aunts' beds warm for them when they return. They will be in shock, and will need a hot sweet drink.'

Her face, white as a ghost, told Dieter quicker than words that some catastrophe had occurred. When he heard what she had to tell him, he quickly summoned a taxi cab and bundled all three of them inside.

As her mind started working again, Charlotte remembered that Dieter would by now have missed his sailing. Lapsing into German, he assured her, 'I can catch another boat next week, it is far more important for me to be with you at this time.' She put her hand on his in gratitude, being relieved to have someone to lean on, to be at her side until she could contact her family in Ireland, and have their support, if the worst were to happen.

They took Jeanette straight home, then went directly to the scene of the accident. They were greeted by a sight that was more usual at the mines of the area than at a church. People were standing in groups, dust covered and shocked, waiting for news of those who had not been as fortunate as themselves in escaping the blast. Others gathered around various prone forms, covered, in respect, with anything to hand, and grieving for the dead that had already been found.

Charlotte tumbled from the taxi, her mind returning to the last occasion she had made a horribly similar journey, the night

Jeanette was conceived. She recalled the terrible memories of that night, and prayed, 'Please, O please God, let my aunts be safe. Please, O please, dear God.'

She looked for, and found, the minister, dishevelled, bewildered, his own arm in a sling. 'No, my dear, I have no news of your aunts. What a dreadful thing on the Lord's Day, and in his House. My wife is also missing. As you know, she sits near your aunts. The doctor and his family have not been found. I warned the elders that we should have electricity, that with gas this would inevitably happen. But would they listen? No! Now look. I am sorry I cannot help you, I must go.'

The army of rescuers worked through the afternoon, bringing out bodies of men, women and children. Ambulances came and went with a chilling regularity, their bells rending the air with ominous sounds of despair. Women from neighbouring churches and chapels supplied endless cups of tea and plates of sandwiches for those who did not yet know the fate of loved ones, and who sat on piles of rubble, or on the grassy verges of the churchyard, waiting . . . just waiting.

Charlotte was grateful that Dieter was with her. He made her sit whilst he ran back and forth, seeking news of the ladies. At last he came towards her, his grime-encrusted face gaunt and grave. 'Dear Charlotte,' he said, 'I have to tell you that your aunts' bodies have been found. They are being brought out now.'

She jumped to her feet to go to them, but Dieter restrained her. 'I am afraid, *liebchen*, that they are not a pleasant sight, and I am sure they would not want you to look at them in this way, but to remember them as they were in life.'

'O God, Dieter. Why are all the people I love taken from me? Life is too cruel . . . too cruel. I cannot bear it', and she broke down and wept heartbrokenly in his dusty, but protective arms.

Later that evening she telephoned Blackrock and spoke to Amy. 'Go to Grossmutter, Amy. Try to tell her gently. She did love my aunts very much in her own way. If the boys are there, I will speak with them.'

'Hello Charlotte, Owen here. What a rotten thing to have happened. How are you, old thing? Darragh, the twins and I will leave straight away to be with you for the funeral. Also, I will let Henrietta and Jean Louis know what has happened. Grossmutter is a bit frail, so we may not tell her the news for the moment. We'll see. Leave it to us, you have enough to contend with. See you soon.'

Dieter insisted on staying in the local inn, but he came each day to help Charlotte and Jasper Barker-Grey with the funeral arrangements. He ran all sorts of errands and kept Jeanette occupied. Olive came from London, breaking her journey to tell Nanny the sad news. Henrietta could not make the journey, as she was expecting her third child very soon and had been advised not to travel.

The funeral came and went, as did those who had come to attend it. Charlotte would have been completely lost without Dieter's supportive presence.

The wills of the Misses Barker-Grey were read immediately after the family returned from the interment. With the exception of some small bequests to Cook and Glynis, the housemaid, and some trinkets to Henrietta, and small sums of money to the boys, the bulk of their estate, comprising the house, contents and the income from their shares in the mine, was left to Charlotte, for her use during her lifetime. The house to dispose of as she chose. The income, hers for life, to continue for as long as the mines produced, and was then to be paid to Jeanette, and any other issue which Charlotte might have.

Dieter finally said that he must return home, his father needed him. 'Charlotte, you know how much I admire you, and how much affection I have for you. Perhaps now is not the right time to speak of such matters, but my heart is yours if you will take it. One day, perhaps soon, you will agree to be my wife. First you will come and visit, and get to know my family, as I know yours, and the fine pure line you come from. Until that day, I will live for your letter to say that you and Jeanette are coming to the Fatherland.'

Chapter Thirty-Two

In the late spring of 1935, after continuous correspondence and deep soul-searching, Charlotte and Jeanette set sail from Lowestoft in Suffolk, for Braemerhaven. Charlotte had opted for the shorter sea route, instead of sailing from Swansea, as she did not know if her child would cope with a five-day journey by sea. At least on the train across England, there were many sights to keep Jeanette interested, and then the sailing from Norfolk would pass more quickly.

Charlotte went to say goodbye to Nanny, who was now very frail and almost immobile. She left Port Talbot feeling despondent and sad, sensing that the old woman's state of health was deteriorating very rapidly. A whole generation is passing away from me, she thought. Thank God Grossmutter is still in good health for her age, although the deaths of first Uncle Otto and then Aunt Hannah have made her feel her own mortality. Amy wrote to tell her that Gerda often found Lady Matilde looking at old photographs and rereading old letters through a magnifying glass.

Charlotte had written to Lady Barker-Grey telling her of her plans. The reply she had received was less than enthusiastic.

My dearest granddaughter,

I am enclosing some letters of introduction to connections of our family in Bremen. I want you to contact them to find out about this family, 'Schulz'. Not a very imposing name! I will be writing to them myself with my instructions to guard you from further mistakes.

Look after yourself and your sweet little one. Take care. These are troubled times in the land of my birth. Thank God, you will not be too far away from Hamburg. I wish my dear brother and his dear wife were still alive. I would feel more contented. I am enclosing your cousins' addresses in Hamburg in case you have lost them. Gerda is writing this for me as my eyes are not too good anymore.

I love you very much, mein kind,

Grossmutter

Charlotte made arrangements about her household with Cook and Glynis. Armed with the addresses and letters of credit, drawn on Charlotte's legacy, the travellers left by train from Cardiff. They were seen off by Jasper and Miranda Barker-Grey, who filled both their arms with magazines, books, chocolates and a big doll for Jeanette.

As the train pulled away, Charlotte stood at the window. Her cousins waved and called to her to enjoy herself, to remember them to Dieter, and to write and tell them all her news.

Soon the train was speeding through the countryside. It seemed no time at all until they were changing trains at Leicester. A porter trundled their luggage from the platform of arrival to the platform of departure. Jeanette clutched her doll, held her mother's hand and skipped along at Charlotte's side, chatting incessantly.

The next leg of the journey went quickly. Lunch in the dining car was eaten, accompanied by giggles from Jeanette, as the swaying of the train made it difficult for the little girl to manage her food. 'Mummy, my spoon keeps missing my mouth, and my milk is slurping out of my glass. Isn't this all great fun?'

They returned to their carriage where Jeanette slept for the remainder of the journey, and as the sun was setting, their port of embarkation was reached. Mother and daughter quickly made their way to the boat, which would sail later. They had been given a cabin near the stairway, and after a light supper, settled down for the night.

They arrived at Braemerhaven and disembarked as the first light of day broke. As they stood on the quayside looking for Dieter, they saw an army car pull onto the quay and an officer in uniform step out. Charlotte was startled as the man approached, for she saw it was Dieter, grinning from ear to ear. He stood in front of her, and in true Prussian manner, saluted and clicked his heels. In his almost faultless and clipped English, he said, 'Major Dieter Schulz at your service, Frau Moore.' He took off his hat and laughed at her expression. 'You are surprised . . . hein? I have wanted so much to tell you, but I have kept my news to surprise you, *liebling*. Are you impressed? I am one of the youngest majors, at twenty-eight, in the whole German army.' He seemed so proud of himself, that Charlotte bit back the things she would have liked to say, until a more suitable time.

'Come. My driver will collect your luggage. We will go to the car. My mother and father wait impatiently to meet both of you.' And he scooped Jeanette up into his arms and kissed her, as he made his way to the waiting vehicle, Charlotte trailing behind.

Lotte's host and hostess were waiting for them in the morningroom, where there was a table laden with breakfast foods. Frau Olga Schulz was a large, raw-boned woman with a sallow complexion and mousy brown hair. Her most notable feature was her piercing, deep blue eyes which, as Charlotte later learned, became almost black when she was angry. It was from his mother that Dieter inherited his beautiful hands and love of and ability to play the violin. Wilheim Schulz was a tall man, whose blond hair had gone prematurely white. He too had unusual eyes, steely grey, but they were not nearly as mesmeric as those of his wife.

When they had eaten and the conventional pleasantries had been exchanged, Olga took Charlotte and Jeanette up to their room, where their luggage had already been placed. Charlotte gave a gasp of delight at the prettiness of the room, with its billowing white curtains and embroidered pelmet and bedspread, looking crisp and inviting. She loved the colour scheme of deep blue and white, with touches of pink and green in the wash-stand set, towels and dressing table appointments.

'I am so glad you like this room. It is a copy of my grandmother's room in Dresden, where she lived as a young girl. There is hot water in the jug if you wish to freshen up. When you have unpacked I will show you the rest of the house and gardens, and we will have a chat, hein?'

Charlotte unpacked, changed, and put Jeanette into bed for a sleep, as the child was exhausted from all her new and different experiences. She made her own way down the rather dark staircase, and found the morningroom again, where the three members of the Schulz family were waiting for her. Dieter came towards her as she appeared in the doorway. He put an arm around her shoulders, and drew her further into the room.

'I cannot express how *wunderbar* it is to have you here, Lotte. I have imagined it so often, and now it is true. Isn't she everything I said, Mummie?' And not waiting for a reply he went on, 'I regret, Lotte, I must leave you until this evening. It will give you all a chance to get to know each other a little. Until dinner . . . *auf Wiedersehen!*'

As she saw him disappear through the door, Charlotte felt very alone, and for some reason she could not quite fathom, a little frightened. However, as she was conducted through the large house, which was full of contrasts and contradictions, she relaxed somewhat. She was shown through the airy bedrooms and dark sombre reception rooms, to an attic filled with memorabilia of Dieter's childhood, which she had to examine in detail, and about which she listened to countless stories. She was taken to the functional kitchen, with its gleaming utensils and shining floor. There, one of the maids came to tell her that the little girl was awake and looking for her mummy. Charlotte, her head whirling, was glad of an opportunity to leave her tour at that point.

At dinner and afterwards, Charlotte was regaled with stories of Dieter from birth, and presented with albums of photos of the Schulz family. Those gone, those living abroad, and the ones she would meet over the coming weeks. After a while, it became harder and harder to make interested 'mews' and 'ohhs' as one face blurred into another, until Dieter, at last seeing her distress, with an amused smile took the latest album from her, closed it and firmly said to his mother, 'Lotte will have the rest of her life to learn all the world-shattering details of our family.'

Gradually Charlotte and Jeanette settled down and became used to hearing only German spoken. Jeanette soon seemed to understand what was said to her and even to say one or two words in response. She was perfectly happy playing in the large well-kept garden with the two Alsatians and three dachshunds. The housemaid kept her well supplied with milk and lemonade and small biscuits.

Charlotte was content to leave her daughter to be looked after by 'Kis', as Jeanette called the maid, when she went out with either Dieter or Olga to shop or meet friends. On the whole, she found them very friendly, and interested in her life in Ireland and Wales. They were invited to luncheons, dinners and dances. It came as a surprise to Charlotte to learn that Dieter was something of a local hero and the tennis champion of his club. There was to be an important inter-city tournament the following weekend, at which he was expected to carry off the men's trophy, and until then, all other social activities were suspended.

The Tennis Day, as it was called, was warm and fine, with a light breeze. Dieter left the house early. The rest of the family, including two house guests from Berlin, were to follow at a more leisurely pace. The ladies wore silk dresses and pretty hats in the latest mode. Some of the older ladies carried parasols, which added to the picturesque pageantry of the day. Although not all playing, men wore white shirts and white flannel trousers, and club blazers. Charlotte was amused at how many of the men still wore monocles, and how many sported tiny brush moustaches, in the style of the German Chancellor, Herr Adolph Hitler. Most of the conversation in the sports grounds was of the Berlin Olympics the following year.

Dieter had won his two early matches very comfortably, in straight sets. When he joined the family, they sat down to a delicious lunch. Many of his acquaintances came to wish him good luck in his final matches, single and double, later in the day.

Two elderly ladies approached Frau Schulz and introduced themselves. Lotte heard her give a little cry of pleasure as they did so, and turning to her said, 'Lotte, *liebchen*, these two charming ladies are the relatives you spoke about.' Turning back to them, she said, 'Please do join our table.' They seemed a little reluctant to do so, but eventually were persuaded.

Looking at them, Lottie could just detect a resemblance to Grossmutter. But she thought it was more of bearing and expression, than feature. 'You must be cousins Beatrice and Camille von Zeit. My grandmother, Matilde, has given me letters of introduction to you, which I had hoped to have the pleasure of presenting next week. I am so delighted to make your acquaintance. This is my daughter, Jeanette. Say, how do you do, to cousins Beatrice and Camille, Nettie.'

The child obediently and solemnly shook hands with each lady. 'We remember your grandmother quite well, Charlotte,' said Beatrice, 'and have heard from her of your arrival. We were quite small last time we saw her, like Jeanette, and she was quite grown up. We used to spend part of our vacation with her family in the mountains, and Matilde was always so stately and perfect in every way, we were quite in awe of her!'

Charlotte laughed. 'She has not changed, but we children, that is my sister, brothers and I, long ago found that she was not nearly as fierce as she pretended. Only if you really displeased her you had to beware. Otherwise she is very loving and very kind and thoughtful. I spent the years of the war with her in the mountain schloss of which you speak, and I found her so comforting to me.' Turning to the others, she explained that her mother had just died at that time, and she had been visiting Germany with her grossmutter when war broke out, and they could not return to Ireland.

After some more pleasantries, the two Fräuleins von Zeit excused themselves, saying that they must return to their friends at their table. They made arrangements for Charlotte and Jeanette to come to tea the following week, and insisted that Mr and Mrs Schulz and Dieter must come along too.

When the ladies had left, Herr Kestler, one of the Berlin guests, remarked that the name 'von Zeit' was not unfamiliar to him, and that he seemed to recollect there was something that he should remember about the family, but which escaped him at the moment, but he was sure that he would remember what it was soon.

After lunch, which Dieter had barely eaten, saying that he did not want to be slowed down and handicapped by a full stomach, the rest of the party returned to their seats on the terrace, beside the court, to watch him play against the champion from Frankfurt. At the outset, it was apparent that it was not going to be an easy match for either player. Charlotte felt excited every time Dieter won a point and was filled with admiration at his agile athleticism and the firmness of purpose with which he chased each point, his chin set with a stubbornness and fierce intensity that spoke of his character in all pursuits.

After two hours of hard-fought sets, Dieter just managed to win. He came off the court to the thunderous applause and 'bravos' of his fellow club members. Charlotte was thrilled when he made his way directly to her, and in front of everybody, kissed her hand.

Later that night, lying in bed, going over the day, she thought, I have made the right decision to marry Dieter, and she fell asleep thinking of all the happiness and security in the years ahead.

On Monday of the following week, as Charlotte was supervising Jeanette's bath and putting the little girl to bed, she heard the front door slam, Dieter run up the stairs, and knock on his parents' door. After a few minutes she heard their voices raised in heated discussion, although she could not hear what was being said. Then she heard the three of them going downstairs, and wondered what had happened to cause such an upset.

When Jeanette had settled, Charlotte went to her bathroom. She was just about to go back to her room to dress for dinner, when there was a knock on the door. Opening it, she found the maid there with a message, 'Would she join the family immediately in the drawingroom.' She thanked the girl, quickly brushed her hair, dressed and went down. As she entered the room she saw three hostile faces glaring at her, and felt alarmed and very vulnerable. 'Is there something wrong Dieter?'

'Yes, there is something wrong. Why did you not tell me? Putting me in such an untenable position in front of our friends, not to mention my superiors, pretending to be such a pure family. I will never live this down and can only thank my good fortune I found out in time!'

By now, Charlotte was terribly afraid. She had never seen anyone in such a temper. Dieter's face was almost purple with rage, and his voice ranted in uncontrolled fury. 'Found out what? I don't know what you are talking about.'

'Jew lover!' Frau Schulz spat at her, her eyes black with fury. 'You did not see fit to tell us that half your family are Jews!'

'Yes, I have some Jewish relations, but what does it matter? They are good people.'

' "What does it matter?" she says,' interjected Herr Schulz, 'What does it matter? I'll tell you what it matters. The Jews nearly ruined Germany. They stole businesses and land and positions from good Aryan people, and turned them into profit for themselves. They tried to rule Germany through their newspapers and philosophers, and leave us with nothing, to be their slaves. That's what it matters! But we will show them. We will show the world that Germany is not to be trifled with, not to be made fools of, not to be tricked into being under the thumb of the Jew. Thank God, Herr Kestler investigated and found out about your Jew family. He felt that the von Zeits were people that needed scrutinisation. Some of those Jews' sly cunning ways have rubbed off onto you, Charlotte, but their plans to embroil our family will not be fulfilled.'

'Of course you realise I cannot marry you now, Charlotte . . . nor would I wish to . . . to be connected, even through marriage, with Jews . . . unthinkable!'

Charlotte felt the blood drain from her face, and through a haze of disbelief and horror, heard herself say, 'I will leave at once. I will pack our belongings and dress Jeanette. We will trouble you no further, except to ask you to be so good as to call a taxi cab for me.' She stumbled out of the room before they could see what a desperate state of shock, fear and horror she felt.

The next couple of hours were the beginning of a nightmare. She found herself handed into a taxi by Dieter. 'If only you had been honest with me, Charlotte, this would not have happened. I thought we could have been happy. I trusted you, and this is all the reward I get. I would advise you to leave Germany immediately. The Third Reich does not like its officers being made to look fools.' He slammed the taxi door, underlining the finality of the end of their relationship.

Charlotte had made a quick decision to go straight to her two von Zeit cousins, whom she had so recently met, secure in the knowledge that they would not turn a member of their family away. But, so as not to put them in any difficulties with the authorities, as the two elderly ladies would be singularly unprotected, she would go, first thing in the morning, to the family in Hamburg.

When they arrived in Hamburg at the home of Ava, née von Zeit, and Hyman Urbach, Charlotte told them the whole story, and how good the two women in Bremen had been, asking no questions; 'They just took Jeanette and myself in, comforted us, and made all the arrangements for us to come to you.'

'What you have told us comes really as no surprise,' said Hyman Urbach. We Jews are beginning to feel very afraid for our safety. Already, some of our acquaintances have disappeared, while others are leaving the country in case they too are taken away.'

'My dear family,' said Lotte. 'From what I can gather, I think those who are leaving are wise. I urge you to do the same. Ava, you and Hyman, and you dear Renata and Marcus, and Ernst and Judith, take your children. Take them to somewhere safe.'

'It is not so easy to leave at a moment's notice,' said Marcus Rotenburg. 'There is a business to dispose of, and the house and contents. If we suddenly take money from the bank, questions will be asked! No, Lotte, we know what you are saying is right, but what I am saying is, it is not so easy.'

'Can't Uncle Rudi and Aunt Katerina see to things for us?' asked Ernst Urbach. 'They are not Jewish, and have no children to worry about.'

'My brother is not so well, and not so young anymore,' said Ava. 'And come to think of it, neither are Hyman nor myself. I don't think we will be in any danger. We are too old. No, we will stay. You all go, and we will dispose of everything and send you whatever monies we realise on your assets.'

'No Mama, Papa, we will not go without you,' said Renata Rotenburg. 'Either we all go, or we all stay!'

'I think Charlotte knows what she is talking about, and I vote that, if she will, Charlotte will take the children on ahead and we will follow in a few months. We have money in London for now, and we can send more immediately,' said Marcus.

'How can we expect Charlotte to take four children, travel with them and look after them by herself. Besides, not that I don't trust you Charlotte, but I don't know if I can let my little angels go so far without me,' said Judith, wringing her hands, and finally breaking into tears.

Ava put her arms around her daughter-in-law, Judith, to comfort her. 'I know it won't be easy, my dear, but we must do what is best for our little ones. It will only be for a short time, and besides, maybe it will all blow over, and then everyone will be together again. You know for now it is best, and you will have to stay with Ernst and help him in the weeks to come.' Suddenly she said to Charlotte, 'We are taking so much for granted with this talk. Maybe you feel you cannot undertake such a task. Maybe it will be too big a burden to place on your shoulders, hein?'

'No, no. I am quite prepared to take the children. It will only be for a short while, and it will be such fun for Nettie to have companionship. If it can be arranged, I will willingly take Otto and Hans and the twins, Hannah and Irwin, back with me.'

They discussed the most expedient way for them to travel, and how to obtain travel permits for the children. Hymen pointed out that some form of temporary guardianship of the children, properly authorised and witnessed, must be given to Charlotte, along with letters of credit.

Listening to all that was being said, Charlotte began to wonder what she had let herself in for. She saw the anguish the young parents were going through at the impending parting with their children, and tried to imagine how she would feel if it was herself and Nettie, and thanked the Almighty that she could do this blessed deed. That even out of her own bitter experience, some good was to come.

'By the way,' Lotte interjected, 'please don't worry about *kashrut* and the children's Jewish education. I was going to marry a Jewish man at one time, and went through a term of instruction to be converted to Judaism. I just want to assure you that I will carry on with Jewish traditions until you come.'

For a moment there was total silence, and everyone looked at her. Then as if in one voice, they thanked her for her consideration and thoughtfulness, that the mere fact that she had felt she must put their minds at rest on that score reassured them that she would look after their babies as if they were her own.

By now, it was well after midnight, and they were all exhausted. The Rotenburgs and the younger Urbachs went home, and the others went to bed. Charlotte had so many things tumbling through her mind that she thought sleep would be impossible, but nature took over, and soon she fell into a deep slumber that renewed and refreshed her for what lay ahead.

They were all in agreement that there was no time to lose, and that everything should be done with great expedience. So it was that two days later, Charlotte and the five children were being driven to the Dutch border by Ernst Urbach. Hyman Urbach had called in many favours, and paid large sums of money, to expedite the travel papers for his grandchildren, but it was still felt that the nearer to a border they were put on a train, the safer would be their passage out of Germany. They had all been looking over their shoulders, sure that Charlotte had been followed, and that their houses were being watched by the 'Black Shirt' Special Police.

Charlotte, Ernst and the children left Hamburg early in the morning and travelled on secondary roads, reaching the border in the afternoon. Making their way to the station, Ernst booked sleepers on the train to Rotterdam, where they would take passage to London. He found them a carriage to themselves.

Ernst bought the children sweets and picture books, and hugged each one, warning them to behave themselves, and to obey Charlotte. Then, on a lighter note, he wished them a happy holiday, and reminded them that he and the other parents would see them in Wales soon. Having settled the children into their seats, he took Charlotte, who was still standing on the platform, into his arms, and thanked her yet again for the *mitzvah* she was doing. He told her that she was not to worry about those she was leaving behind, she would see them very soon. And he almost ran so that he could get away before he broke down in front of the little ones.

The whistle blew for the train to depart, and Charlotte was about to climb into the carriage when she felt her arm being grabbed. She was filled with terror. Her heart thumping, she turned, fully expecting to see a uniformed officer. Instead, her eyes met those of a woman, even more terrified than she, who babbled something about *zwei kinder,* and thrusting a parcel into her hands, pushed two small girls ahead of Charlotte into the train, and ran before Lotte could speak to her. The train started,

Lotte jumped aboard and fell into a corner seat. When she had caught her breath, she looked and saw two pale and scared girls of about eight or nine staring at her out of large, solemn dark eyes.

'Sit children, sit. You others move up and make room. Now, what are your names?'

'Zena and Marta Kroteshine, Frau,' said the older girl in a tiny and strained voice. 'We have travelled from Berlin with Frau Gruber, who has been looking after us since Mama and Papa were taken away. She said you will look after us now, and take us to our aunt and uncle in London, England.'

Charlotte looked at the children, speechless, not knowing what to say. In the old-fashioned way of children who have had to grow up too quickly, Zena said, 'There is a letter from Frau Gruber for you on the outside of the parcel, which will explain everything.'

Charlotte opened the soiled piece of paper, which had been slipped under the string of the package, and read: My name is Freda Gruber. I am a member of an organisation that is helping Jewish people under threat from the authorities, to leave Germany. I have been watching you since you arrived at the station, and overhearing some of your conversation, recognised that you too are prepared to undertake such missions of mercy. The little girls I have entrusted to you will, I know, be safe in your care. There is further information about them, and money to take care of them, in the package. Please get them to their relatives, Mr and Mrs James Brown, 5 Hyacinth Lawn, Golders Green, London. No more time . . . God will bless you.

When Lotte opened the parcel there was a shoe box, and in the box were the children's birth certificates, travel permits, their parents' marriage certificate, and bundles of Swiss francs. There was also a letter stating that Professor Abraham Kroteshine was a lecturer in philosophy at the university, and he and his wife were arrested and sent to a concentration camp for allegedly teaching seditious propaganda against the new German Order. As both parents were fully Jewish, it was deemed wise to get their two daughters to England, to relatives who had left Germany some time ago. Both parents were upright and honourable people, and their children should think of them with pride, and hope that one day they will be reunited with them.

Charlotte was very moved by what she had read, and looking at the troubled faces of the two girls, did her best to comfort them.

The journey through Holland, and across the sea to England, was unreal for Charlotte, and when later she was asked about it, she could remember no details.

She had wired Olive before embarking, and when she saw her friend at the station as the train pulled into London, she felt relief at having got all the children safely this far, without any mishaps. She thanked God she was home, in a free land, a freedom she would never again take for granted.

Chapter Thirty-Three

They all piled into two taxis and went back to Olive's cosy house. She had prepared a scrumptious lunch for them, to which everyone did full justice. Afterwards she insisted that the children should have a rest, before Charlotte telephoned the Browns. When the children had fallen asleep, Charlotte told Olive the whole story.

'How putrid for you, Lotte. You really do have the most rotten luck with men.'

'What is wrong with me Ollie? I don't seem to be able to form lasting relationships. Yes, I know what you are going to say, but I thought that I really, deeply, loved David, and yet, I was able to leave him. You know, now that I am safely back here, I only feel relief that, even the Dieter I knew before all the awfulness, is out of my life. There seems to be something lacking in me. O God, am I to be alone always?' She put her head on her arms and cried, deep, dry, racking sobs, that spoke volumes about the depths of hopelessness within her.

Later the Browns, or, as they explained, originally Mannie and Esther Braun, arrived to collect their two nieces. They said that they had had no news of their family in Germany for some time, and had been very worried. Now that they had learned the fate of some of their relations, they would continue waiting to hear about the others, even though they were no longer quite so hopeful of seeing them again. They thanked Charlotte profusely for what she had done, and assured her that she would be forever remembered by them. Charlotte gave them the precious box with the papers and money. She said that she was thankful that she had been able to help, and wished them good tidings of their dear ones.

Soon they were gone. Charlotte and Olive saw to supper for the other children, put them to bed, and settled down to discuss Lotte's plans for the immediate future.

The following day, Lotte returned to Wales with the five children. Thomas, the chauffeur gardener, met them, as instructed on the telephone by Olive.

As she walked into the familiar house, holding a twin by each hand, the others running ahead of her, she felt so safe. The smells of Cook's good baking wafted through the hall, mingling with the scent of the flowers Thomas had gathered from the garden, and which Glynis had arranged in bowls all over the house to welcome her. The two faithful women came, exclaiming, 'You poor things Lord, you must be weary! Oh, the lovely little ones. Come, and Cookie will give you some lovely biscuits and milk.'

The children followed Jeanette and the unlikely Pied Piper.

Charlotte was glad to be alone for a few minutes. To flop into a favourite armchair. To remember how this house had once before been a haven for her in a time of trouble.

As the weeks went by, the children settled in, and Charlotte was very amused that the English they learned came out with a Welsh lilt. She contacted the Jewish community in Swansea and arranged for the children to take part in the synagogue services. She also arranged for kosher meat to be delivered to her house. She drove Cook mad with all the culinary changes that were required in order to keep the promise she had made with regard to *kashrut* to her family in Hamburg. She was very busy and happy, and felt very involved and needed, looking after her five children.

Her Barker-Grey cousins were filled with disgust and alarm when they heard of her experiences. They felt very responsible for having introduced her to Dieter Schulz. At the same time they also voiced their opinion that, 'Perhaps it is not the wisest thing for you to have undertaken such a responsibility, looking after four extra children, Jewish or otherwise.'

'Thank you for your concern, but I assure you that I can manage beautifully. My real concern is that I have not heard from any of my German cousins. I write week after week without receiving any reply. I have also written to the Misses von Zeit in Bremen, but when I received their answer, they said they too had tried to learn some news of the whereabouts of their cousins, that when they had telephoned Hamburg there had still been no answer from any of the family there.

She spoke to senior members of the Jewish community. They made enquiries, but the only information they could find was that neighbours thought the family had gone away, possibly left the country.

Lotte found it increasingly difficult to find ways of allaying the children's fears and answering their questions about when their parents would arrive in Wales. She invented excuse after excuse, but knew that they only believed her because they needed to.

1935 ended, and 1936 was ushered in by the excitement of the preparations for the Berlin Olympics. Olive had recently, out of the blue, become engaged to a man who was the trainer of the British rowing team, and he was requested to make enquiries on Charlotte's behalf about the von Zeit family, when he went to Germany. He too could find no information about the families in Hamburg. By now, Charlotte was at her wit's end to know what to do.

It was as if life was dealing one blow after another when she was hastily summoned to Dublin as Grossmutter was dying. She never forgave herself for arriving too late to say once more 'I love you, Grossmutter'. She stayed for the funeral, but returned to the children immediately after. She learned later that Grossmutter had left Priory Lodge to Darragh, and that her personal possessions were to be divided equally between her five grandchildren. Blanche wrote to tell Charlotte that, in face of this bequest, Kit was in the process of transferring the title of

Glenavon to the twins, so that there would be a continuity in Wicklow of the Moore name.

Olive and her fiancé had set the date for their marriage, but Charlotte could not feel the joy that participating in Olive's wedding deserved. As both Mr and Mrs Bailey had died some years previously, Olive decided that there was no need to go back to Ireland for the ceremony. 'Besides, Lotts, at our age we have decided on a simple wedding at Caxton Hall, with you and Cons to be my witness, and Dick's only brother to be his, and of course my brothers will be here. Afterwards we will have lunch in a nearby restaurant, and then all go home.'

Chapter Thirty-Four

Storm clouds were gathering force in Europe. In London, Sir Oswald Moseley showed brutal and open contempt for Jews.

Charlotte managed her household in Neath as best she could, given the circumstances. Constance came to stay for a few days after Olive's wedding. She had, years ago, been told Lotte's secret, and although she did not approve of the deception, she had stood by her friend.

One day Glynis came to tell Charlotte that a gentleman with a foreign accent had called, and was asking to see Charlotte Moore. Feeling faint from the hard, loud pounding of her heart, afraid of what she might hear, she made her way into the hall. The light was behind the man, and for a few seconds she could not see his face. 'You asked to see me. Do you have news of my family? Won't you come in?'

As he came further into the hall, she saw him in full light, and let out a scream. 'Ernst, Ernst, is it really you?' She went to him, and holding him by the arms as if to make sure he was not a hallucination, continued, 'Come in, come into the drawingroom, sit down. Where have you come from? Where are the others? Oh, I must call the children', and she made to do so.

'Stop, please stop,' said Ernst. 'First I must tell you everything that has happened.'

For the first time, she saw the grave expression on his face, and how much he had aged in the year since she had last seen him.

He sat silent, his head bent, his hands hanging between his knees. Then, with a supreme effort, he raised his head, and in a voice lacking any vitality, spoke in German. 'I left you at the train because I did not want the children to see me weep. I stood at the entrance until I saw the train safely pull away and cross the border. The emotions of the event had drained me of all energy, and I did not feel capable at that moment of driving back to Hamburg. I went to a nearby café to drink coffee, and to collect my wits. While I was quiet and by myself, I tried to make some plans for the rest of us to follow you as quickly as possible. I sat thus for about an hour. No plan I thought of seemed feasible. I realised that everywhere, banks, offices, utilities, there were people who for their own gain, and to ingratiate themselves with the new regime, would betray erstwhile friends and colleagues. Slowly the realisation came that, in my present state of mind, I would solve nothing. Also, that the family would be sitting waiting at my parents' house for confirmation of your safety.

'I went to a telephone and asked the operator to connect me with my mother's number,' he went on. 'It rang and rang, but nobody answered. At first I thought the operator had dialled the wrong number, and asked her to try again. Still there was no answer. Then, I thought that perhaps they had gone either to my house, or to my sister's home. I tried both those numbers. The same thing . . . no answer. I decided at that point, it would be best to get on the road again.

'As I drove, the thought that was constantly in my mind was, where my family might be. Only one possibility seemed likely. For some reason they had gone to Uncle Rudi and Aunt Katerina von Zeit's. Stopping at the first telephone available, I tried their number, and was again met by a blanket of silence. Frightened at I knew not what, I then put a call through to my mother's neighbour. Here I did get a reply. Identifying myself, I asked her if she knew anything of my family's whereabouts. When she was sure who I was, she became hysterical. She shouted to me to go away, leave the country! "Your family has been arrested by the Special Branch, and taken to God knows where. They came storming into the street, in their black cars, many of them, menacing in their swift movements, surrounding the house. It all happened so fast. I was on my own in my house, there was nothing I could do. I am still shaking from the shock. There is nothing more I can tell you', and she put down the receiver.

'I felt as though I had been physically struck, and stood for several minutes, unnerved by what I had just been told. In my heart I knew that what had been said was true, but I telephoned our head office. Maybe my father had gone there, and he would know what had happened. I spoke to the general manager of the hotel and asked him if my father was there. "No," he replied, "I can confirm those reservations have all been officially relocated." "What do you mean?" I asked. "Where is my wife, my family?" "They too have been relocated, Sir," he said.

'Suddenly I realised he was not alone, and his cryptic phrases were his way of relaying information to me. "Do you know where they are?" I pressed on. "No Sir, we have no confirmation of that address." "Can you find out?" "I am retiring from business, Sir, and can be of no further use to you, but may I suggest...", and suddenly the line went dead.

'By now I was stunned by all the dreadful things I had been told. I did not know which way to go. If I went back to Hamburg, to any of the houses, or to the hotel, I was sure they would be carefully watched, and I would be quickly picked up. Yet I needed money to move anywhere. I did not have very much with me, and I knew that all lines of credit would by now have been cut off. Also, I needed money to set investigations in motion, to find out what had happened to everyone, and who, exactly, had been caught in the net, and why!

'I hung onto the thought that at least the children were safe, and I think that saved my sanity. I also thanked God that at least I was free to help the others, although the thought was mixed with a fear of the future, and guilt that I was not with my darling wife, to comfort and support her.

'Think . . . think, I kept saying to myself. But no plan would form. I did have the presence of mind to remove the "yellow star" from my clothing, which all Jews have to wear by decree, so that I would not draw unfavourable attention to myself. My instinct told me to keep on the move. I once again got into the car, but this time headed south. It had started to rain and the windscreen blades made a repetitive word, which eventually beat into my brain, and started my thought process. Safety . . . safety . . . safety.

'What if I made my way to one of our smaller hotels. The one in Strasbourg! I knew it intimately. We had spent many holidays there at Eastertime as children. There was a warren of cellars in which I could hide indefinitely. The manager was a distant relative of my Aryan aunt, Katerina, and devoted to my father. I knew I could trust him, that he would help me!

'I drove until tiredness and hunger made me stop. I had just entered Münster, a sizeable town, where I would not be too conspicuous. Though close to physical and nervous exhaustion, my brain was now crystal clear and sharp. I looked at my coat and saw that there was a mark where I had removed the badge of my race. I needed to buy a raincoat. I went to the nearest large store, wearing only my shirt and braces, and rolled up my sleeves to look like a worker. I bought a cheap, mass-produced mackintosh, a cardigan and a chauffeur's cap, and went with my purchases back to my refuge in the car. I wrapped my own coat, jacket and hat in the brown paper, and on my way to a café for some food, dropped the parcel into a litter bin. When I had eaten, I wondered where I would spend the night. I was too weary to drive much further, but was afraid to go to even the meanest hotel, in case my photograph had been circulated. I decided to drive into a side street, where other cars were parked, and sleep for a few hours there.

'I woke after those all too short hours and started to lay plans for my journey. I counted my money and found that if I was careful, I would just about have enough for petrol. I had made up my mind to take the chance of keeping my car instead of using the more dangerous trains, always fearful of detection. I bought a razor and a comb, some simple food to take me through the day, and set off on the backroads I had marked on the map that I always kept in the car. It took me nine days to reach Strasbourg. I won't go into the details of that nightmarish journey. I lived through it, the continuous looking over my shoulder, afraid that, every time someone glanced my way, they were going to report me. How I crossed over the border is a story for another day, and of the proffered, and unexpected, help I received from a thief, who thought, like him, I was running from the police, because I was also a criminal. I gave him my car in payment for his help, and continued on foot.

'Raymond Heugen, the hotel manager, had already heard what had happened in Hamburg. It was his custom to keep in touch by telephone with my father every week, something that I had totally forgotten. When he had been unable to speak with Father, he had made several other calls and he had pieced most of the story together. He had found out that the arrest followed the apprehension of the man who had forged the papers for the children, and who had not destroyed the evidence. The authorities swooped relentlessly, like birds of prey, as soon as any legitimate excuse could be found to condemn prominent Jews. They had taken both my parents, my wife, my sister and her husband, my aunt and uncle, and my wife's parents. Where they had been taken, or for how long they would be held, no one knew. Such dark fears grabbed my heart. My poor Judith, my darling wife, who would jump with fright if a floorboard creaked. What had become of her? What depths of misery was she going through? The not knowing was the hardest part.

'Raymond Heugen effected an introduction for me to the president of the small Jewish community of Strasbourg. He listened to my story. "My God, not another," he murmured. "Every day we are hearing these stories. We have been to the office concerned at the League of Nations. Even they do not seem to be able to find out anything. Jews are leaving Germany in their thousands. Still, for some it is not soon enough. I ask you to leave the situation with me for the present, and as soon as I have any news I will let you know immediately." With this, I had to be content for the moment.

'I could not even contact you, Charlotte, I did not have any addresses with me, and I could not remember any of your families' names. The days were long and empty. I helped in the hotel to keep myself busy, but it was not enough. At night, sleepless, I tossed for hours, my mind imagining all sorts of untold horrors.

'Waiting is soul destroying. I could not eat, and soon I became ill. I am told that for days I was delirious with fever, and that the doctor was fearful for my life. But little by little, I recovered. It took many months to regain my strength. Finally, the president of the community was allowed to see me. He brought another with him, a Palestinian Jew, who represented the Jewish Agency. What they told me made me retch, filling my mouth with bile at the foul deeds they recounted.

'All my dear ones, along with other families, had been kept in a prison in Hamburg. They had been questioned relentlessly, questions to which they had no answers. My Uncle Rudi had had a heart attack, and died. I guess he was the lucky one. The others were beaten, the women raped, and eventually, those who were still alive were sent to a concentration camp until it was decided what should be done with them.'

Charlotte sat unquestioning at the edge of her seat as he continued his story.

'Soon my father and Marcus Rotenburg were sent for trial for treason, convicted, and shot, as examples to other Jews. The women were still alive as far as the Jewish agent could find out. My mother, mother-in-law and aunt, were all very ill. He knew nothing of Judith or Renata, my darling wife and sister. Judith depended on me so much. She is not the stuff that heroines are made of, she cannot stand pain, and feels so much for others. I can't imagine the mental tortures she is going through, never mind the physical ones. When I see, in my mind, her being used by some great German oaf, I feel as though, if I had him, or anyone else involved, near me, I would squeeze their life away with my bare hands. How can such men live and breathe, instituting and carrying out such acts? Animals are kinder to creatures at their mercy. Your poet Oscar Wilde said that some men when they kill do it slowly, while others are kinder and kill swiftly, with a sharp knife. I no longer understand these people, amongst whom my family has lived for generations. They have great minds, with art and music that is amongst the finest. They are so advanced in science, engineering and medicine, and have no fear of experimentation. Yet they are a cruel people – ambitious, brutal, ruthless in obtaining their goals. They have produced the Huns, the Goths, the Visigoths and the Vandals! Because of their discipline and orderliness, everything is done with a thoroughness that is terrifying in its philosophy and expediency. Oh, my poor Judith, Renata and Mother.'

Ernst sat, drained, obviously unable to utter one more word. Charlotte also sat, paralysed by what she had heard, unable to move to help this poor man, whose hands hung down between his knees, his head bent, sorrow and dejection in every line of his body. Eventually she heard the children's voices and knew that somehow they would both have to put on a brave face. She filled two glasses with brandy from a tray on the table in the corner and, giving one to Ernst, told him to drink it down quickly, and that she would then show him to the bathroom to refresh himself, whilst she told the children of his arrival.

When he came back downstairs, and returned to the drawingroom, he was nearly knocked down as his daughter and son rushed into his arms and smothered him with kisses. 'Papa! Papa! We have waited so long for you . . . where is Mummie?' The boys also ran to him, and with anxious faces, wanted to know where their mummie and papa were.

'*Kinder, kinder*, wait, I will tell you.' Looking over their heads at Charlotte, he launched into an obviously well rehearsed story. 'Your mama and papa, and Hannah and Irwin's mama, have had to wait for a while, because Grossmutter and Grossvater are not very well, and they stayed to look after them. They sent me to tell you why they have been delayed, and to stay with you until they can come. They have sent presents to you. I will get them from my luggage soon. Now let me look at you. Have you been good for cousin Charlotte? You have all become so tall,' he said with a smile, 'I will have to treat you in a more grown-up way. Come and hug me, *kinder*, all of you. You too, Jeanette. You all look well. I love you so much.' He gathered them to him, finding it almost impossible to hide his emotions.

And that was how Charlotte left them, as she went to organise a room for Ernst.

Chapter Thirty-Five

In the weeks after his arrival, Ernst seemed to have lost all his energy, and even the small amount he expended playing with the children left him inert. But gradually, the clean Welsh air and the nourishing meals that Cook prepared for him, restored him, and his vitality returned. He reinitiated his search for his missing wife and sister. This entailed his travelling backwards and forwards from Neath to London. Sometimes he was away for two and three days at a time, sometimes for longer. When Charlotte remarked that she was worried in case all this travelling would undermine his health again, he explained that the travelling was inevitable, as sometimes he had to wait for hours in offices, for reports to come in from investigators on the Continent, who were making enquiries with regard to the family, and at other times he would have to wait to interview people who had already been rescued, in case they had heard of, or met with, any of his family.

Charlotte had written to Dublin, and to Ria in France, to tell them of all that had befallen their relations. In her typical fashion, Henrietta wrote back to say that she was very sorry to hear the tragic news, but that she had heard of many other families that had fled Germany before such things happened to them, and that the von Zeits should have had the foresight to do likewise. If ever an opportunity for her to visit Wales should occur, she would come and meet Ernst and the children then. Charlotte was so ashamed of Ria's attitude that she never showed the letter to Ernst.

The Moore twins, Lawrence and James, still in college in England, both visited Neath to meet Ernst. The children were delighted to have someone nearer their own age to take them on rambles and to play with them. When Laurie and Jim had gone back to college, the children kept asking, 'When will they come back again?'

Ernst had been in London several days when Charlotte received a phone call from him, asking her to meet him there, as, at last, he had some news. He would say nothing more on the telephone, so she hastily put some things into an overnight bag, made some arrangements for the children, phoned Olive, and caught the next train to London. She had booked a sleeper, and arrived in London early the following morning.

Charlotte went straight to Olive's new house and telephoned Ernst from there, arranging for him to come immediately to see her. As soon as she saw Ernst, she knew that the news was bad. He told her that one of the investigators had found the camp that the women had been taken to. Of the older women, nothing was known, but this did not necessarily mean that they had died, only that their identities had been lost. But of Judith and Renata there was more definite news. Judith was known to have died. How she had met her end, or when, nobody was sure, only that one night she was not there for roll call. 'I cannot even sit Shiva for her, but I have been to a synagogue and arranged to have prayers said for the repose of her dear soul. As to Renata, she is alive, and is one of a number of women sent to clean an officer's home, and to help his wife with the cleaning. So as long as she is useful to them, she will be safe! I will need a lot of money if she is to be rescued, so I am selling the Strasbourg Hotel and liquidating all our other holdings, in France and England. This brings me to my next point. While I was in France I met, as I have told you, people from the Jewish Agency. They are convinced there is going to be an immense war in Europe, a total conflagration between the allied and the axis powers. They say that what is happening to Jews in Germany now is as nothing compared to what is going to happen, and they are advising as many as possible to leave Europe at once. Palestine is still open, even if only within the allowed quota. It is the natural homeland for the Jewish people, and there is much work to do there. I have decided to take the four children and start a new life. I'll be there, ready for her, when my sister Renata will be free to join us. I have been arranging passports and visas for us. We will leave almost immediately.'

Ernst leaned forward in his chair and took Charlotte's hands in his own. He looked from his own heartbroken eyes into her deeply troubled ones. 'I have also made provisional arrangements, if you and Jeanette would like to join us. One family, making a fresh start together. I know you have few ties here now, and I also have guessed that Jeanette is part Jewish, so you will be bringing her to a people to whom she, in part, belongs. Don't give me your answer now, think about it.'

'No matter what I decide, Ernst, I want you to know how much I appreciate your asking me to join you, and my answer will not be one of either impulse or scantily considered thought.'

Later, when Ernst had gone, Lotte and Olive sat, as they had so many times over the years, talking through the situation. They discussed all the pros and cons for Lotte and her daughter to make the move to the Middle East. The clock showed that many hours had passed when Charlotte, rising to her feet, stood looking down into her friend's face, and said in a voice that brooked no argument, 'You know, Olive, I have finally made up my mind not to go. I have, one way or another, all my life, either been taken away, or I have run away, from sad and difficult situations. To Germany when Mother died, to Wales when Father died, to you when I was pregnant. I ran back to Wales from Dieter, and now I am tempted to run again. I must stop running sometime. So no! I will not go to Palestine, Olive. I am going to go back to Ireland. I am going to tell David about Jeanette. I know he will never forgive me! But they both have a right, which I have denied them for too long, to know each other. Thank you, Olive, my dearest friend, for always being such a tower of strength to me.

But, from now on, I must stand on my own two feet. I will let you know, Ollie, exactly what further plans I decide upon, and also what happens as a result of my decisions.'

They hugged and Olive whispered, 'Good luck, my dear friend.'

Charlotte left early in the morning. She made a plan of action on the train to Neath. 'First, I will somehow have to explain everything to Jeanette. Then I will have to tell Ernst that, for now, we will not be joining him and the children on their journey to Palestine. Next I will make bookings for Nettie and myself, for our passage to Dublin, and straightaway let Amy know when to expect us, and of course I must let Constance know of our plans. I must also write to Blanche and make an appointment to see the rabbi. And then, I must take my courage in both hands, and arrange to meet with David.'

Chapter Thirty-Six

David stood as Charlotte was shown into his consulting room, his last appointment of the day. How beautiful she still is, he thought. His heart beat a little faster as he advanced towards her, hand held out.

'You look well, Charlotte. You don't seem to have changed at all.'

'Thank you, David. I see the years have also treated you kindly. How are you?'

'Well, thank you. Please take a seat.'

He went behind his desk as Charlotte, seated, looked around, remembering the room so well. He sat down.

'Now, how can I help you. Is it a medical matter?'

'David, I have finally come to my senses. It took a very long time, but for what it's worth, I'm so very sorry for the dreadful wrong I have done to you.' And she handed him a photograph which she took from an envelope. David looked at the likeness of Jeanette, and then looked enquiringly at Charlotte.

'That is Jeanette, our daughter, conceived in this room on the night my father died.'

She saw David's lips whiten in shock and anger. His gaze met hers. There was a terrible silence which Charlotte felt unable to break. It seemed to go on and on.

'And where is the child now?'

'I left her with Amy, at home, whilst I came here.'

'Does she know about me?'

'Yes. She is a very intelligent child, and I was able to explain most of our relationship to her.'

'Would you do me the same courtesy, and explain your extraordinary behaviour to me?'

Charlotte had not expected this contained manner from David. She had been prepared to be raved at, condemned out of hand, even dismissed. But the coldness and restraint of the man put her at an even greater disadvantage, and all her carefully rehearsed phrases left her.

'You see, David, it was the shock of Father's death, happening at the moment when we had fulfilled our love, when we were so happy. Then our home in Blackrock was breaking up, Nanny going back to Wales, the servants having to leave. My thinking was confused when I found that I was pregnant. I felt that I could not face your family, or shame you. I ran David, I ran. I wouldn't listen to Olive or Blanche when they advised me to come back. I was afraid you wouldn't want me any more. I'm sorry David, I was wrong.'

The last words came in such low tones, that, if it were not for the perfect silence in the room, they would have been lost.

'I see, Charlotte. You had so little faith in my love for you, you ran from me, without giving me the chance to confirm how much I loved you. No thought as to how I might feel, as opposed to how I might react. Is that it? And what name did you give our daughter? I know it was not Moore, because I searched for years for you under that name.'

'Blanche and Willy gave the gift of Fitzgerald to us.'

'I see. And where have you been living?'

'In Wales. With my great aunts.'

'And what do you expect from me now, Charlotte, ten years later?'

'Nothing, David, I expect nothing. I only want you to know your child, and for her to know you.'

'I am glad you expect nothing. For after this news, I feel I have nothing to give! My car is outside. Take me to the child.'

On the way to Blackrock, David asked her if she had any plans. She told him the story of Dieter and of her German family, of the journey with the children, the months with no news, and finally of Ernst turning up, and of everything he had learned. She told of his decision to go with the four children to Palestine, and his offer to include herself and Jeanette, if she wished.

'I have an appointment with the rabbi tomorrow to discuss continuing with my conversion. Not because of you, David, or your father, but because I want it for myself, and for my daughter. One day, I want both of us to have the right to go to Palestine, and to join the others there.'

The meeting between David and Jeanette did not go as well as Charlotte had hoped. The little girl was shy, and hid, first behind her mother, and then behind Amy. David was gentle and patient with her, slowly drawing her out.

'Your mummy has told you who I am, and why we are meeting only now. I also have lots more things to tell you. You have a grandma and a grandpa, and two aunts and uncles and lots of cousins.'

'I already have lots of cousins, thank you. They are Irwin, Hannah, Otto and Hans. And we all live together, and we play lots of games together.'

'I'm sure they are very nice. But I would like you to know of these others as well. What would you like to call me? Most children in Ireland call their fathers "Daddy". Will you try that?'

'If you wish.'

'David,' said Charlotte softly, 'I think that may be enough for now.'

'You are right, Charlotte. She is very beautiful and everything I would wish for in a daughter. I am now going to tell my parents what has happened. I feel sure they, or at least my mother, will wish to meet Jeanette. Shall we say two-thirty tomorrow at my house?'

'I am meeting Rabbi Chanaan at three o'clock tomorrow. I will leave Jeanette and Amy at your house on my way. In any case, it may be better if I'm not there. Easier.'

'Very well then. Until tomorrow.'

He formally shook hands with Jeanette, Amy and Charlotte, and took his leave.

David went to Rathmines to his parents' home. Joseph and Fanny were sitting in the study, as they always did when they were alone together.

'How lovely to see you, David,' said Fanny, when David came into the room. 'You look a little strained. You're working too hard!'

'Hard work never killed anyone,' mumbled Joseph. 'So noo? What brings you to us so late in the evening?'

'Mother, Father,' said David, sitting between the two chairs on which his parents sat. 'Today I have had the most startling news of my life, news that has left me in a state of amazement and elation. A ghost from my past has appeared. Not to haunt me, but to present me with all the joy I have missed. I don't want you to interrupt me, Father, until you have heard me out. And even then, speak gently. Charlotte Moore has been to see me.'

He saw the scowl on his father's face, and the anxiety on his mother's.

'This is going to be a shock to you. She told me I have a daughter. I have seen the child, and there is no possible doubt but that she is mine, a Minns. So like grandma Sarah. I have not come to ask your advice, for I do not need it. I have come to tell you, because I feel that you have a right to know.'

Again David paused. He saw the look of scepticism on Joseph's face, and the tears in Fanny's eyes. Each grasped the arms of their chairs tightly.

'Years ago, Father, you drove my love, my Lotte, away with your cruelty and bigotry. She was too ashamed and frightened to come and face us when she found that she was pregnant. And so I was deprived of my wife and my child, and you of a daughter and a granddaughter. I nearly ruined another woman's life, and I am grateful that Millie has now met someone else. Mother, Father, if you wish to meet Jeanette, you may do so, at my house tomorrow, at two-thirty. Charlotte will not be there. She will be with Rabbi Chanaan, arranging with him for her and Jeanette's conversion. Not for me, or for you, but because of her love for her Jewish family in Germany, who have suffered and died because they were Jewish, and also because she loves our ways. So now it is up to you. But if you do come, come with love. For this time nothing will make me lose Charlotte again, unless Charlotte herself says no, that she does not want me, but I fervently pray she will.'

As arranged, Jeanette and Amy were deposited at Baggot Street at two-thirty the next day, and Charlotte continued on to the South Circular Road for her own appointment. She renewed her acquaintance with Rabbi and Mrs Chanaan, and over the next two hours discussed the various aspects of what she and Jeanette must learn, and the examinations that they must take, in order to become fully recognised members of the Jewish faith. At long last she rose to leave, her head whirling with all the information, in her hands the papers and books she had been given to study.

When they got back to Blackrock, Jeanette was full of chat about her new daddy and grandparents, and would not leave the beautifully dressed doll that David had given to her out of her sight.

'If you will agree, Mummy, my new daddy is going to call for me tomorrow again, and I am going to be taken to Grandma and Grandpa's house to see where Daddy grew up, and to see his bedroom and all his books which Grandma has kept.'

Charlotte looked at Amy.

'She was very comfortable with them,' said Amy. 'They were gentle and kind with her, and even that awful Mr Minns had tears in his eyes when he saw her, and he hugged her when she said goodbye.'

'O Amy, I am frightened I might lose her to them, they have so much to offer her.'

'I don't think that you should worry, Charlotte. I feel that Doctor David will protect you.'

David spoke to Charlotte by telephone, asking her permission to see Jeanette for some part of each day. He promised to collect her in person, and likewise to bring her home. Charlotte felt that, having created the situation, she was not in a position to put boundaries on David's access to Jeanette. But she felt, after her last meeting with him, that as far as she was concerned he had made it perfectly plain that he had no wish to renew any relationship with her. Accordingly, she made sure that either she was out, or invisible within the house, when he called. She often saw him from a window, or heard him as he spoke with Amy or, when he was in, Owen, and her heart would flutter as she heard the well remembered voice. Gradually, as the weeks passed, she admitted the truth that she had for so long suppressed. She loved David. The realisation of this hurt more than any of the other events that had befallen her . . . she had thrown away her happiness. At night she cried for her broken heart, and broken dreams. She knew that she had lost her happiness through her own stupid stubbornness in not listening, all those years ago, to the good advice given to her to return to David.

It took David several visits to realise that Charlotte was avoiding him. But he decided not to force her to see him, thinking that if he did so, he might frighten her away. Eventually, after several weeks, he could not bear being so close and yet not seeing her, and he made up his mind to make contact with her. So, early one morning, when he knew she would still be at home, he telephoned and asked to speak to her. To his delight she came to the phone.

'Good morning, David,' she said, 'I believe you wish to speak to me.'

'Yes, Charlotte. Don't you think it is time we met and discussed Jeanette's future?'

Charlotte's heart sank. Was David going to try and take Jeanette away from her?

'I don't know what you mean, David. In what way can we discuss Nettie's future? I have already told you that we will both be converted, and then we will be going to join my cousins in Palestine. I fail to see what else there is to discuss.'

'Please Charlotte. Won't you see me? We do need to talk, you know,' he said very gently.

Charlotte paused. She did not know, because of her feelings for him, if she could bear to see David, and for him to treat her in a disdainful and cold manner.

'What would it avail, David?'

'Please Charlotte. Please allow me to see you.'

'Very well! If you insist. I will be here when you come for Nettie this afternoon.'

When he arrived at Priory House, David was shown into Michael's old study to wait for Charlotte. It was the first time in many years that he had been in the room. Memories came flooding back. He recalled visiting Kit when he had come back to Priory House from hospital, after the fire that had destroyed his home, his parents, and almost destroyed himself. He remembered the hours helping Kit to regain his health and hope. He also recalled conversations he had had with Michael, in which he had learned to admire and honour his integrity and, in contrast, the hours he had spent watching him crumble, being helpless to come to his aid. Then there was time spent with Charlotte, looking through the books which lined the walls. The laughter and happiness of those times! He remembered Lady Matilde coming into the room, on some pretext or other, when he and Charlotte were alone. She had never lost her cool elegance, rather it had been themselves, though thoroughly innocent then, who had felt at an embarrassed disadvantage. He walked behind the desk and saw the ink marks the boys had made whilst poring over some holiday task they had been set.

The door opened and Charlotte stood in the entrance. David was startled to recognise the same lost look on her face as he had noticed the first time he had seen her at Harcourt Street Station.

'Lotte, my dear,' he said, and with an instinctive action he walked towards her. 'You look so troubled. What is it? Can I help?'

'O David, I'm such a fool. I lost you, and now I am going to lose Jeanette.'

'You silly girl. Not only will you never lose Jeanette, but don't you know you never lost me. I love you. I have always loved you. Can you learn to love me again?'

Charlotte's heart sang. Her eyes shining with tears of happiness, she held out her arms to David.